Leonardo Padura was born in Havana in 1955 and lives in Cuba. He has published a number of novels, short-story collections and literary essays. International fame came with the *Havana Quartet*, all featuring Inspector Mario Conde, of which *Havana Blue* is the third to be available in English. The *Quartet* has won a number of literary prizes including the Spanish Premio Hammett. It has sold widely in Spain, France, Italy and Germany.

Other Bitter Lemon books featuring
Inspector Mario Conde

Havana Black
Havana Red

HAVANA BLUE

Leonardo Padura

Translated from the Spanish
by Peter Bush

BITTER LEMON PRESS
LONDON

BITTER LEMON PRESS

First published in the United Kingdom in 2006 by
Bitter Lemon Press, 37 Arundel Gardens, London W11 2LW

www.bitterlemonpress.com

First published in Spanish as *Pasado Perfecto* by
Tusquets Editores, S.A., Barcelona, 2000

Bitter Lemon Press gratefully acknowledges the financial assistance
of the Arts Council of England

A CIP record for this book is available from the British Library

ISBN 978-1-904738-22-0

Typeset by RefineCatch Limited, Broad Street, Bungay, Suffolk
Printed and bound by
TJ International Ltd, Padstow, Cornwall

For Lucía, with love and squalor

Author's Note

The events narrated in this novel are not real, although they could have been, as reality itself has shown.

Any resemblance to real people and events is then merely that plus cussedness on the part of reality.

Consequently, nobody should feel alluded to in the novel. Equally, nobody should feel excluded if they do see some pertinent reference or other.

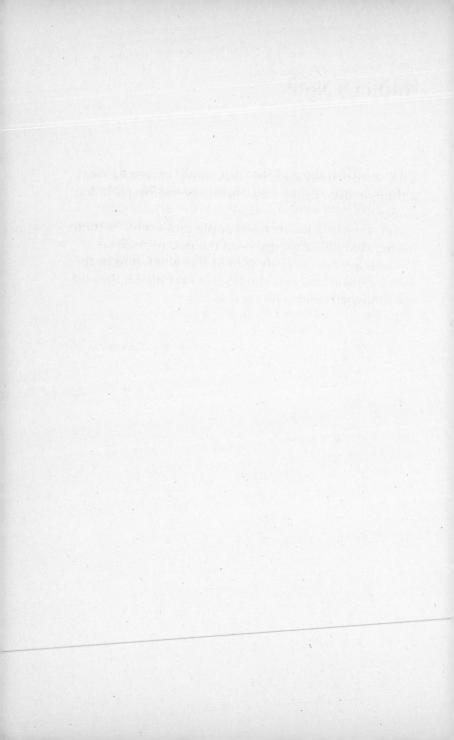

WINTER 1989

He whirled about. "Shut up, you!" he cried. We didn't say anything, said the mountains. We didn't say anything, said the sky. We didn't say anything, said the wreckage. "All right, then," he said, swaying. "See that you don't." Everything was normal.

Ray Bradbury, *Perchance To Dream*

possessing only
between heaven and earth
my memory, this time . . .

Eliseo Diego, *Testament*

I don't have to think to know the most difficult step would be opening my eyes. If the morning sun, glinting brightly on the windowpanes, bathing the whole room in glorious light, struck them and sparked off the vital act of raising my eyelids, the slippery dough settling in my skull would be set to start a painful dance at the least movement of my body. To sleep, perchance to dream, he told himself, revisiting a phrase that had buzzed in his brain five hours earlier, when he had fallen on his bed and breathed in the deep dark aroma of solitude. In distant shadows he saw himself as a guilty penitent, kneeling before the pan, unloading wave after wave of apparently endless bitter amber vomit. But the telephone persisted, its machine-gun *ring-ring*s drilling his eardrums and lashing a brain tortured by its exquisitely cyclical, clinical brutality. He dared to. Slightly raised his eyelids, which he then shut immediately: the pain entered via his pupils and he simply felt like dying, although grimly aware such a desire would go unfulfilled. He felt very weak, with no strength to lift his arms, support his forehead and exorcize the explosion each malign *ring-ring* made imminent, until he finally decided to confront the pain, raised an arm, opened a hand and grabbed the receiver, slipping it from its cradle in order to regain the state of grace that is silence.

That victory made him want to laugh, but he couldn't. He tried to persuade himself he was awake,

1

but he wasn't at all convinced. His arm dangled down one side of the bed like a severed branch, and he knew the dynamite lodged in his brain was fizzing furiously, threatening to explode at any moment. He was afraid, an all too familiar fear, although one he always quickly forgot. He also tried to complain, but his tongue had dissolved down the back of his mouth by the time the telephone mounted its second offensive. Go away, fuck you! All right, all right, he groaned, forcing his hand to grip the receiver, and lurching like a rusty crane, his arm lifted it to his ear and lodged it there.

First there was silence: oh, blessed silence. Then came the voice, a thick resonant voice he found awesome.

"Hey, hey, you hearing me?" it seemed to say. "Mario, hello, Mario, can you hear me?" And he hadn't the courage to say no, no, he couldn't or didn't want to hear or, simply, that it was a wrong number.

"Yes, Chief," he finally whispered, but only after he'd taken a breath, filled his lungs with air, set his arms to work around his head, his hands spread, pressing down on his temples trying to curb the dizzy merry-go-round unleashed in his brain.

"Hey, what's up with you? What the hell *is* up with you?" retorted not a voice but an unholy bellow.

He took one more deep breath and tried to spit. Then felt his tongue had swollen or no longer belonged to him.

"Nothing really, Chief, a spot of migraine. Or high blood pressure, I'm . . ."

"Hey, Mario, don't try that line again. I'm the one with the high blood pressure, and don't keep calling me Chief. What's up?"

"What I said, Chief, a spot of headache."

"So you've woken up after the party, I suppose? Well, get this: your holidays are over."

Not even daring to contemplate such a thing, he opened his eyes. As he'd imagined, the sunlight was flooding in through the big windows, and everything around him was bright and warm. Perhaps the cold had retreated outside and it might be a beautiful morning, but he felt like crying or something of that nature.

"No, Boss, hell, don't do that to me. It's *my* weekend. That's what you said. You forgotten?"

"It *was* your weekend, my boy, it was. No one press-ganged you into the police."

"But, Boss, why does it have to be me? You've got loads of people," he protested as he tried to sit up. The errant weight of his brain crashed against his fore-head, and he had to close his eyes again. The nausea in his gut surged up; his bladder felt about to burst. He gritted his teeth and groped after the cigarettes on his bedside table.

"Hey, Mario, I don't intend putting it to a vote. Do you know why it's your turn? Because that's what I damn well want. So shake a leg: get out of bed."

"You're not joking, are you?"

"Mario, that's enough . . . I'm already at work, get me?" the voice warned, and Mario understood he was really at work. "Listen: on Thursday they informed us that a chief executive in the Ministry for Industry had disappeared, you hearing me?"

"I want to. I swear I do."

"Well, want on and don't swear in vain. His wife made a statement at nine that night, but the guy's still not put in an appearance: we've alerted the whole country. I reckon it stinks. You know that chief execu-tives at vice-ministerial rank don't go missing like that in Cuba," continued the Boss, making sure his voice communicated his concern. Finally seated on the edge of his bed, the other man tried to relieve the tension.

"And he's not in my trouser pocket. Cross my heart."

"Mario, Mario, you can cut the backchat right away," and he switched to another tone now. "The case is down to us, and I want you here in an hour. If you've got high blood pressure, give yourself a fix, then get here quick!"

He found the packet of cigarettes on the floor. It was the first pleasant thing to happen that morning. The packet was grimy and had been trampled on, but he gazed at it optimistically. Slid off the edge of the mattress and sat on the floor. Put two fingers in the packet, and the saddest of cigarettes seemed like a reward for his titanic effort.

"Got any matches, Boss?" he asked down the telephone.

"Why you asking, Mario?"

"Nothing really. What's your smoke of the day?"

"You'll never guess," and his voice sounded pleasantly viscous. "A Davidoff, a New Year's Eve present from my son-in-law."

He could imagine the rest: the Boss gazing at his cigar's ultra-smooth skin, exhaling a slender thread of smoke and trying to sustain the half-inch of ash that made it the perfect smoke. Just as well, he thought.

"Keep one for me, right?"

"Hey, you don't smoke cigars. Buy some Populares on the street corner and get your body here."

"Yes, I've got you . . . Hey, what's the man's name?"

"Wait a minute . . . Here it is. Rafael Morín Rodríguez, head of the Wholesale Import and Export Division within the Ministry for Industry."

"Hold on there," begged Mario as he watched his cigarette wilt. It was shaking between his fingers, although the cause was possibly not alcoholic. "I don't think I heard you properly, Rafael what did you say?"

"Rafael Morín Rodríguez. Did it register this time? Well, now you've got fifty-five minutes to get to headquarters," said the Boss before he slammed the phone down.

The belch crept up on him like his nausea: a taste of steaming fermented alcohol hit Detective Lieutenant Mario Conde's mouth. He saw his shirt on the ground next to his underpants. Kneeled slowly down and crawled over till he reached a sleeve. Smiled. Found matches in the pocket and finally lit the cigarette that had gone moist between his lips. The smoke invaded his body, and after the redeeming recovery of the mangled cigarette, it became the second pleasant sensation of a day that had begun with machine-gun blasts, the Boss's voice and a name he'd almost forgotten. Rafael Morín Rodríguez, he pondered. He leaned on his bed, pulled himself up and *en route* his eyes stared at the morning energy of Rufino on his bookcase, his fighting fish racing round the endless circle of his goldfish bowl. "What happened, Rufo?" he whispered as he contemplated the spectacle of his latest shipwreck. He wondered whether he should pick up his underpants, hang up his shirt, iron his old blue jeans or turn out his jacket sleeves. Later. He trod all over his trousers when he walked towards the bathroom after recalling he'd been close to pissing himself for ages. Standing in front of the bowl he contemplated the spurt creating fresh beer foam at the bottom of the pan, though it was nothing of the sort, since it stank, and the rotten stench from his offload reached even his benumbed nose. He watched the last drops of relief splash on the glaze, and his arms and legs felt weak like a broken puppet's longing for a quiet corner. To sleep, perchance to dream, if only.

He opened his medicine chest and looked for the packet of painkillers. It had been beyond him to swallow one the night before, an unpardonable error he now regretted. He placed three pills on the palm of his hand and filled a glass with water. Tossed the pills down a throat sore from retching and drank. Shut the chest and in the mirror confronted the image of a face that seemed both distantly familiar and unmistakeable: the devil, he muttered, and leaned his hands on the washbasin. Rafael Morín Rodríguez, he thought, while remembering that in order to think he needed a large cup of coffee and a cigarette that he didn't have and resolved to expiate all known sins under the caustic coldness of a shower.

"What a fucking disaster," he muttered as he sat on his bed and smeared his forehead with the warm refreshing Chinese pomade that always brought him back to life.

With a nostalgia he found increasingly irritating, the Count surveyed the main street in his barrio, overflowing rubbish containers, wrappings from late-night last-minute pizzas blowing in the wind, the wasteland where he'd learned to play baseball transformed into a repository for junk generated by the repair shop on the corner. Where do you learn to play baseball now? He greeted the beautiful warm morning he'd anticipated, and wasn't it a pleasure to stroll still savouring the taste of coffee? But then he saw the dead dog, its head crushed by a car, putrefying by the kerb and thought how he always saw the worst, even on a morning like this. He lamented the luckless destiny of those animals cut painfully down by a slice of injustice he

6

couldn't attempt to remedy. It had been too long since he'd owned a dog, since Robin suffered that miserably drawn-out old age, and he'd stuck to his pledge never again to become infatuated with an animal, until he plumped for the silent companionship of a fighting fish, which he insisted on calling Rufino, after his Granddad, a breeder of fighting cocks: plain characterless fish that could be replaced on death by similar beasts, also dubbed Rufino and confined to the same bowl where they could proudly parade the fuzzy blue fins of a fighting fish. He'd have preferred his women to succeed each other as easily as those fish without a history, but women and dogs were totally unlike fish, even the fighting kind: moreover, he couldn't rehearse in respect of women the hands-off pledges he'd sworn in relation to dogs. At the end of the day, he predicted, he'd join a society for the protection of street animals and men who were out of luck with women.

He put on his dark glasses and headed towards the bus-stop thinking that the barrio must look like he did, a landscape after an almost devastating battle, and he felt some innermost memory stirring. The evident reality of the main street clashed too sharply with the saccharine image of his memory of that street, an image the truth of which he'd come to doubt, or had he inherited it from the nostalgic tales his grandfather told him or simply invented it in order to pacify the past? You can't spend your whole fucking life thinking, he muttered, while registering that the mild morning heat was helping the painkillers in their mission to restore weight, stability and primary functions to whatever he carried in his head, as he promised never again to repeat such alcoholic excess. His eyes were still smarting from sleep when he bought a packet of cigarettes and felt the smoke complementing the taste of coffee; once again he was a being in a fit state to think, perchance to remember. He regretted saying he wanted to die and to demonstrate his regret ran to catch an unimaginable almost empty bus that made him suspect that the New Year was off to an absurd start and that the absurd wasn't always so benign as to appear in the form of an empty bus at such a time in the morning.

It was twenty past one but everybody was there; sure, nobody was missing. They'd divided into groups, and there were some two hundred students, and you could recognize them from their appearance: beneath the *majagua* trees, against the wrought-iron fence, were the people from Varona, long-time owners of that privileged spot with the best shade. For them, high school was about crossing the street that separated them from their lower school and no more than that: they talked loudly, laughed and listened to a very loud Elton John on a Meridian transistor radio that picked up to perfection the WQAM Miami wavelength, and by their side they had the tastiest lookers of the afternoon. That much was beyond dispute.

The cocky contingent from the backwoods of Párraga was fighting the September sun in the middle of the Red Square, and I bet they were as nervous as anything. Their bravado made them wary; they were the type who wore heavy-duty underpants just in case; men are men and all else is pansy shit, they'd say, as they scrutinized everything and wiped a handkerchief over their mouths, said little and flaunted their polka dot scarves, a front crew with side tails and manliness. Their gals really weren't at all bad, would make good dancers and more, and they chatted quietly, as if they were rather scared to see so many people for the first time in their life. The Santos Suárez crowd was another matter, seemed more elegant, blonder, more studious, altogether cleaner and better ironed, I reckon: they looked as if they were in the revolutionary vanguard and had powerful mums and dads. The Lawton lot were almost like the bunch from Párraga: most were brawny and eyed everything suspiciously, also wiped handkerchiefs over their mouths, and right away I thought those toughs would be fighting each other.

Those of us from the barrio were the most difficult to pin down: their haircuts and swagger made Loquillo, Potaje, el Ñánara and gang look to be from Párraga; their clothes perhaps made El Pello, Mandrake, Ernestico and Andrés seem from Santos Suárez; others looked to be from Varona because they smoked and talked so self-confidently; and I seemed a right idiot next to Rabbit and Andrés, my eyes trying to take everything in, searching the crowd of strangers for the girl who would be mine: I wanted her to be olive-skinned, long-haired, with great legs, a looker but no slut, nor someone too ladylike to wash my clothes on school trips to the country or else too ladylike, so that I always had to worry about getting laid and so on, after all I wasn't looking for a wife; all the better if she was from La Víbora or Santos Suárez, those people threw terrific parties, and I wasn't going to go back to Párraga or Lawton and wasn't impressed by what the barrio had on offer, they weren't lookers, let alone hookers, and went to parties with their mothers. My girl had to fall in my set: there were more females than males on the register, almost double, I did a quick count and came up with 1.8 per male, a whole one and another headless or titless, remarked Rabbit, perhaps that slant-eyed creature, but she's from Varona and they already have their dudes; and then the bell rang, and on 1 September 1972 the high school gates opened in La Víbora, where I would experience so much.

We were all almost enthusiastic about entering the cage, ah the first day at school; as if there weren't enough space, some ran – mostly girls, naturally – towards the playground where wooden posts carried numbers to indicate where each group should line up. I was in number five, and only Rabbit joined me from our barrio, and he'd been with me since fifth grade. The playground filled up. I'd never seen so many people at the same school, I really hadn't, and I started to look at the women in our group, to start pre-selecting a likely candidate. Reviewing them made me forget the sun, which was fucking burning it down, and then we sang the national anthem, and the head-master climbed on the platform that was beneath the arch in the shade and began to speak into the micro-phone. First he threatened us: females, skirts below the knee and the right hem, that was why you were given the paper about buying the uniform when you enrolled; males, hair cut above the ears, no sideburns or moustaches; females, blouse inside the skirt, with a collar, no frippery, that was why . . .; males, standard trousers, no drainpipes or flares, this is a school not a fashion parade; females, stockings pulled up, not rolled down round the ankles – although that really suited them, even the skinny ones; males, first spot of indiscipline, even if it's nothing serious, straight before the Military Committee, because this is a school and not the Torrens Reformatory; females and males: no smoking in the lavatories at break or any time; and yet again females and males . . . and the sun started to roast me alive. He went on talking in the shade, and the second thing he did was to introduce the president of the SF.

He climbed on the platform and displayed a dazzling smile. Colgate, Skinny must have thought, but I didn't yet know the skinny lad behind me in the line. To get to be student president he must have been in twelfth or thirteenth grade, I later found out he was in thirteenth, and he was tall, almost fair-haired, with very light-coloured eyes – a faded ingenuous blue – and seemed freshly washed, combed, shaved, perfumed and out of bed and, despite his distance from us and the heat, he oozed self-confidence, when, by way of starting his speech, he introduced himself as Rafael Morín Rodríguez, president of the Student Federation of the René O. Reiné High School and a member of the Municipal Youth Committee. I remember him, the sun that gave me such a bad head and the rest, and thinking that that guy was a born leader: he talked and talked.

The lift doors opened slowly like the curtain in a flea-pit, and only then did Lieutenant Mario Conde realize he wasn't viewing that scene through dark glasses. His headache had almost gone, but the familiar image of Rafael Morín stirred recollections he'd thought lost in the dankest corners of his memory. The Count liked remembering, he had a shit-hot memory, Skinny used to say, but he'd have preferred another reason to remember. He walked along the corridor, feeling like sleep, not work, and when he came to the Boss's office he fixed his pistol, which was about to drop from his belt.

Maruchi, the woman in charge of the Boss's office, had deserted the reception area, and he reckoned she must be on her mid-morning break. He tapped on the glass door, opened it and saw Major Antonio Rangel behind his desk. He was listening carefully to something someone was telling him on the telephone, while stress made him shift his cigar from one side of his mouth to the other. His eyes pointed the Count to the file open on his desk. The lieutenant shut the door and sat opposite his chief, waiting for the conversation to end. The major raised his eyebrows, uttered a laconic "agreed, agreed, yes, this afternoon" and hung up.

He then anxiously examined the battered end of his Davidoff. He had hurt the cigar; cigars are jealous, he used to say, and the taste would certainly no longer be the same. Smoking and looking younger were his two favourite occupations, and he devoted himself to both like a conscientious craftsman. He would proudly announce he was fifty-eight years old, while his face smiled an unwrinkled smile, and he stroked his fakir's stomach, wore his belt tight, the grey in his sideburns seemingly a youthful caprice, and spent his free late afternoons between swimming pool and squash court, where he also took his cigars for company. And the Count felt deeply envious: he knew that at sixty – if I ever made it – he'd be disagreeably old and arthritic; hence he envied the major's exuberance, he didn't even cough on his cigars and into the bargain knew all the tricks to being a good chief who could switch from the very pleasant to the very demanding just like that. The voice is mirror to the soul, the Count always thought when decoding the shades of tone and gravity with which the major layered his conversations. But he now had a damaged Davidoff on his hands and an account to settle with a subordinate, and he switched to one of his worst varieties of tone of voice.

12

"I don't want to discuss what happened this morning, but I won't stand for it again. Before I met you I didn't have high blood pressure, and you're not going to see me off with a heart attack. That's not why I swim so many lengths and sweat like a pig on the squash court. I'm your superior and you're a policeman, write that on your bedroom wall so you don't forget it even when you're asleep. And the next time I'll kick your balls in, right? And look at the time, five past ten, what more need I say?"

The Count looked down. A couple of good jokes came to mind, but he knew this wasn't the moment. In fact, it never was with the Boss, but even so he chanced his luck too often.

"You said your son-in-law gave you that Davidoff as a present, didn't you?"

"Yes, a box of twenty-five on New Year's Eve. But don't change the subject, I know you only too well," and he scrutinized yet again his cigar's smoky demise, as if he understood nothing. "I've ruined this fellow . . . Well, I just spoke to the minister for industry. He's very worried about this business. I felt he was really shaken. He says Rafael Morín held an important post in one of the management divisions in his ministry and that he worked with lots of foreign businessmen, and he wants to avoid any possible scandal." He paused to suck on his cigar. "This is all we have for the moment," he added as he pushed the file towards his subordinate.

The Count picked up the file but didn't open it. He sensed it could be a replica of Pandora's dreadful box and preferred not to be the one to release the demons from the past.

"Why did you decide on me in particular for this case?" he then asked.

13

The Boss sucked on his cigar again. He seemed optimistic his cigar would make a surprise recovery: a pale, even healthy ash was forming, and he puffed gently, just enough so each drag didn't fan the flame or sear the cigar's sensitive entrails.

"I'm not going to say, as I did some time ago, because you're the best or because you're fucking lucky and things always turn right for you. Don't imagine that for one minute, never again, OK? How'd do you feel if I say I chose you because I just felt like it or because I prefer having you around here and not at your place dreaming of novels you'll never write or because this is a shit case anyone could solve? Select the option you prefer and put a tick by it."

"I'll stick with the one you don't want to mention."

"That's your problem. All right? Look, there's an officer in every province responsible for searching out Morín. Here's a copy of the statement, the orders that went out yesterday and the list of people who can work with you. I've allotted you Manolo again ... These are the man's details, a photo and a short biography written by his wife."

"Where it says he's squeaky clean."

"I know you don't like the squeaky clean of this world but too bloody bad. It does appear he is an immaculate trustworthy comrade and nobody has the slightest idea where he's holed up or what's happened to him, though I fear the worst ... Hey, you interested?" he thundered, suddenly changing his tone of voice.

"He's left the country?"

"Very unlikely. Besides, there were only two attempts yesterday, and both failed. The north wind is a bastard."

"Hospitals?"

"Nothing, naturally, Mario."

"Hotels?"

The Boss shook his head and leaned his elbows on his desk. Perhaps he was getting bored.

"Political asylum in bars, brothels or clandestine hostelries?"

He finally smiled, his lip barely flinching above his cigar.

"Piss off, Mario, but remember what I said: the next time I'll do you proper, on charges for disrespect and whatever."

Lieutenant Mario Conde stood up. Picked up the file in his left hand, straightened his pistol and gave a half-hearted military salute. He had just started to swing round when Major Rangel rehearsed another of his changes of voice and tone, seeking a rare balance that denoted both persuasiveness and curiosity: "Mario, let me first ask you two questions." And rested his head on his hands. "My boy, tell me once and for all: why did you join the force?"

The Count looked the Boss in the eye as if he'd not understood something. He knew the latter found his mix of indifference and efficiency disconcerting and liked to relish that minimal superiority.

"I don't know, Chief. I've spent the last twelve years trying to find out, and I still don't know why. And what's your other question?"

The major stood up and walked round his desk. Smoothed the top to his uniform, a jacket with stripes and epaulettes that looked fresh from the dry cleaner's. He reviewed the lieutenant's trousers, shirt and face.

"Since you *are* a policeman, why not start dressing like one, hey? And why not shave properly? Look at yourself, you look sick."

"You've asked three questions, Major. You want three answers?"

The Boss smiled and shook his head.

"No, I want you to find Morín. I'm really not interested in why you joined the force and even less in why you don't ditch those faded trousers. I want this sorted quickly. I don't like ministers pressurizing me," he added, mechanically returned his military salute, went back to his desk and watched Lieutenant Mario Conde depart.

SUBJECT: MISSING PERSON
Informant: Tamara Valdemira Méndez
Private address: Santa Catalina,1187, Santos Suárez, Havana City
ID Card: 56071000623
Occupation: Dentist
Case Outline: At 21.35 hours on Thursday 1 January 1989 the informant presented herself in this station to report the disappearance of citizen Rafael Morín Rodríguez, the informant's husband and resident at the above address, ID 52112300565, and following physical features white skin, light brown hair, blue eyes, approximately five foot nine inches tall. The informant explained that, it being the early hours of 1 January and after being at a party where she and her friends and work colleagues had seen in the New Year, the informant returned home accompanied by the said Rafael Morín Rodríguez and that after checking that their mutual son was asleep in his bedroom with the informant's mother, they went to their bedroom and got into bed, and that the following morning, when the informant woke up, citizen Rafael Morín had already left the house, but that initially she was not particularly worried because he often went out without saying where he was going. Around midday,

16

the informant, by now rather concerned, telephoned a few friends and work colleagues as well as the enterprise where Rafael Morín Rodríguez works, without eliciting any information as to his whereabouts. And by this stage she was really worried, since citizen Rafael Morín hadn't used the car that was his property (Lada 2107, number-plate HA11934), or the company car, which was in the garage. By the late afternoon, and accompanied by citizen René Maciques Alba, work-colleague of the Missing Person, they phoned several hospitals to no avail and then visited others they'd been unable to communicate with via phone, with equally negative outcomes. At 21.00 hours, the informant and citizen René Maciques Alba presented themselves in this station with a view to making this statement on the disappearance of citizen Rafael Morín Rodríguez.

Duty Officer: Sgt. Lincoln Capote.

Report Number: 16–0101–89

Station Chief: First Lieut. Jorge Samper.

Annexe 1: Photograph of the Missing Man

Annexe 2: The Missing Man's personal and work details.

Initiate investigation. Raise to priority level 1, Provincial Headquarters Havana C.

He visualized Tamara making her statement and looked back at the photo of the man who'd disappeared. It was like a talisman stirring up distant days and hidden melancholies he'd often tried to forget. It must be recent, the card was shiny, but he could be twenty and would still be the same. You sure? Sure: he seemed impervious to the sorrows of this life and urbane even on his passport photos, always untouched by sweat, acne or fat or the dark threat of stubble,

17

always that air of a perfect pristine angel. Yet now he'd gone missing, was almost a spit-ordinary police case, one more job he'd have preferred to pass on. "What the hell is up, mother?" he wondered and abandoned his desk with no desire to read the report on the personal and work details of squeaky clean Rafael Morín. From the window in his little cubby hole he enjoyed a vista that seemed quite impressionistic, comprising the street lined by ancient laurel trees, a diffuse green smudge in the sunlight yet able to refresh his sore eyes, an unimportant world whose every secret and change he noted: a new sparrows' nest, a branch beginning to wither, a variation in foliage highlighted by the darkness of that diffuse, perpetual green. Behind the trees, a church with high wrought-iron grilles and smooth walls, a few glimpses of other buildings and the very distant sea that could only be perceived as a light or distant smell. The street was empty and hot and his head was fuzzy and empty; he thought how he'd like to sit beneath those laurels, to be sixteen again, to have a dog to stroke and a girlfriend to wait for; then, seated there as ingenuously as possible, he'd play at feeling very happy, as he had almost forgotten you could be happy, and perhaps he'd even succeed in reshaping his past, that would then be his future, and logically calculate what life was going to be like. He was delighted by the idea of such a calculation because he'd try to make it different: there couldn't be a repeat of the long chain of errors and coincidences that had shaped his existence; there must be some way to change it or at least break out and try another formula, in reality another life. His stomach seemed to have settled, and now he wanted a clear head to get into a case that had emerged from his past to plague the sweet void he'd dreamed of for the weekend. He pressed the red intercom button and asked for Sergeant Manuel Palacios. Perhaps he could be like Manolo, he thought, and then thought how lucky it was people like Manolo existed, able to cheer up routine days at work just by their optimistic presence. Manolo was a good friend, acceptably discreet and quietly ambitious, and the Count preferred him to all the sergeants and assistant detectives at headquarters.

He saw the shadow loom against the glass in his door, and Sergeant Manuel Palacios walked in without knocking.

"I didn't think you'd got here yet . . ." he said and sat down in one of the chairs opposite the Count's desk. "This is no life, my friend. Fuck, you look really half-asleep."

"You can't imagine how plastered I got last night. Terrible . . ." – and he felt himself shudder simply at the memory. "It was old Josefina's birthday, and we started on beer that I'd got hold of, then we downed a red wine, half-shitty Rumanian plonk that goes down well nevertheless, and Skinny and I finished up tangling with a quart of vintage rum he was supposedly giving to his mother as a present. I almost died when the Boss rang."

"Maruchi says he was livid with you because you hung up on him," smiled Manolo as he settled down in the chair. He was only just twenty-five and clearly threatened by scoliosis: no seat felt right for his scrawny buttocks, and he couldn't stand still for very long. He had long arms, a lean body and loped like an invertebrate; of all the Count's acquaintances he was the only one able to bite his elbow and lick his nose. He seemed to float along, and on sighting him one might think he was weak, even fragile and certainly much younger than he tried to appear.

19

"Fact is the Boss is stressed out. He also gets calls from his superiors."

"This is a big deal, right? Otherwise he personally wouldn't have phoned me."

"More like heavy duty. Take this with you," he said, placing the items back in the file. "Read this, and we'll leave in half an hour. Give me time to think how we should tackle it."

"You still into thinking, Count?" asked the sergeant as he made a lithe exit from the office.

The Count looked back at the street and smiled. He *was* still thinking, and thought was now a time bomb. He went over to the telephone, dialled, and the metallic ring reminded him of his drastic awakening that morning.

"Hello," said someone.

"Jose, it's me."

"Hey, what state did you wake up in, my boy?" the woman asked, and he felt she at least was cheerful.

"Best forgotten, but it was a good birthday party, wasn't it? How's the beast?"

"Still not up."

"Some people are so lucky."

"Hey, what's up? Where you calling from?"

He sighed and looked back out at the street before replying. The sun in the blue sky was still beating down. It was a made-to-measure Saturday, two days before he'd closed a currency fraud case in which the endless questioning had exhausted him, and he'd intended to sleep in every morning till Monday. And then that man went missing.

"From my incubator, Jose," he complained, referring to his tiny office. "They got me up early. There's no justice for the just, my dear, I swear there ain't."

"So you won't be coming for lunch?"

20

"I don't think so. But what's that I can smell down the telephone?"

The woman smiled. She's always laughing, great.

"Your loss, my boy."

"Something special?"

"No, nothing special but really delicious. Get this: I cooked the *malangas* you bought in a sauce and added plenty of garlic and bitter orange; some pork fillets left over from yesterday, imagine they're almost marinated and there's two apiece; the black beans are getting nice and squashy, like you lot like them, they're getting real tasty, and now I'll add a spot of the Argentine olive oil I bought in the corner store; I've lowered the flame under the rice, and have added more garlic, as advised by that Nicaraguan pal of yours. And salad: lettuce, tomato and radishes. Oh, well, and coconut jam with grated cheese . . . You died on me, Condesito?"

"Just my fucking luck, Jose," he replied, feeling his battered gut realigning. He was mad about big meals, would die for a menu like that and knew Josefina was preparing the meal especially for him and for Skinny and that he'd have to miss it. "Hey, I don't want to talk to you no more. Put Skinny on the line, wake him up, get him up, the skunky drunk . . ."

"Tell me the company you keep . . ." Josefina laughed and put the telephone down. He'd known her for twenty years and never seen her look defeated or resigned even in the worst of times. The Count admired and loved her, sometimes much more tangibly than his own mother, with whom he'd never identified or trusted as he'd trusted the mother of Skinny Carlos who was no longer skinny.

"Go on, say something," said Skinny, and his voice sounded thick and sticky, as horrible as his must have sounded when the Boss woke him up.

"I'm going to get rid of your hangover," announced Mario with a smile.

"Fuck, that would be handy, because I feel wiped out. Hey, you brute, never another one like last night, I swear on your mother."

"Got a headache?"

"It's the only thing that's not aching," replied Skinny. He never got a headache, and Mario knew that: he could drink any amount of alcohol at any time, mix sweet wine, rum and beer and drop down drunk, but his head never ached.

"Well, I just wanted to say ... I got a call this morning."

"From work?"

"I got a call this morning from work," the Count continued, "to put me on an urgent case. Someone's disappeared."

"You're kidding, what? Baby Jane gone missing again?"

"Joke on, my friend, this will kill you. The man who disappeared is none other than a chief executive with a rank of deputy minister and is a friend of yours. By the name of Rafael Morín Rodríguez." A long silence. Right between the eyes, he thought. He didn't even say "fucking hell". "Skinny?"

"Fucking hell. What's happened?"

"What I said, he's disappeared, gone off the map, AWOL, nobody knows where he is. Tamara made a statement on the night of the first, and the prick's still missing."

"And nobody's got a clue?" Expectation grew with each question, and the Count imagined the look on his friend's face, and as Skinny's cries of shock crescendoed he managed to tell him what he knew about the Rafael Morín case. "And what you goin' to do now?" asked Skinny after taking in the information.

"Follow routine. I've not had no brainwaves as yet. Question people, the usual, who knows?"

"Hey, and is it Rafael's fault you're not coming for lunch?"

"Well, while we're on that subject, tell Jose to keep mine back and not to give it to the first hungry bastard passing through. I'll be around yours as soon as I'm finished."

"Keep me informed, right?"

"Will do. As you can imagine, I'll soon be seeing Tamara. Do I give her your regards?"

"And congratulations, because the New Year's begun with new life. Hey, you wild animal, tell me if the twin's as juicy as ever. I'll be expecting you tonight."

"Hey, hey," rapped the Count. "When the haze lifts, put your mind to this mess and we'll talk later."

"What do you think I'm going to do? What else will I have to think about? We'll talk later."

"Enjoy, my brother."

"I'll pass on the message to my old dear, brother," said Skinny and hung up, and Mario thought life is shit.

Skinny Carlos is skinny no more, weighs over two hundred pounds, reeks of the sour smell of the obese, and fate had it in for him. When I first met him he was so skinny he looked as if he would snap in two at any moment. He sat down in front of me, next to Rabbit, not knowing that we'd occupy those three desks next to the window for the duration at high school. He had the sharpest of knives to sharpen pencil-points, and I said: "Skinny, old pal, lend me the blade you got there" and from then on I called him Skinny, although I could never have imagined he would be my best friend and that one day he'd no longer be skinny.

Tamara sat two rows in front of Rabbit, and nobody knew why they'd put her twin sister in another group, given they came from the same school, were the same age and shared the same surnames and prettiest of faces. But we felt happy enough because Aymara and Tamara were so alike we'd probably never have told one from the other. When Skinny and I fell in love with Tamara we almost stopped being friends, but along came Rafael to put us straight: she was to be neither Skinny's nor mine. Rafael declared his love to Tamara, and they were an item within two months of the start of term, the kind that stick together like limpets at break and chat for twenty minutes, holding hands, looking deep into each other's eyes and so far from the madding crowd that they'd snog shamelessly. I could have killed them.

But Skinny and I are still friends, are still in love with her and shared our frustration by wishing all manner of evil upon Rafael: from a broken leg upwards. And when we felt really down, we'd imagine we'd become the boyfriends of Tamara and Aymara – it didn't matter then who got who, although we both always loved Tamara, for some reason or other, as they were both very beautiful – and we'd marry and live in houses as alike as the twin sisters: everything identical, one next to the other. And as we got flustered, we'd sometimes get the wrong house and sister, and Aymara's husband would be with Tamara and vice versa, and thus we consoled ourselves and had a great time, and we'd have boy twins, born on the same day – four at a time – and the doctors, who were also flustered and so on, would get the mothers and children mixed up and say: two to that bed and two to the other and as they grew up together they sucked on the teat of whichever mother was nearby and then always got the wrong house. We spent hours talking about such shit, until the kids grew up and married a quadruplet of girls who were equally identical and it was a big fucking hoot, until Josefina got home from work and turned down the radio, I don't see how you can stand that racket all day, she'd protest, hell, you'll go deaf, but she'd make us milk-shakes – sometimes mango, sometimes strawberry, if not chocolate.

Skinny was still skinny the last time we played at marrying the twins. We were in the third year at high school. He was Dulcita's boyfriend and Cuqui had already fallen out with me when Tamara announced to the class that she and Rafael were getting married and that they were inviting us all to the party at her place – and although they had fantastic parties there, we swore we wouldn't go. That night we had our first memorable binge: at the time a quart of rum could be too much for us, and Josefina had to wash us down, give us a spoonful of belladonna to cope with our sickness and sore heads and even wrap a bag of ice round our balls.

Sergeant Manuel Palacios put the car in reverse, stepped on the accelerator, and the tyres screeched painfully as the car swung backwards in order to leave the parking lot. He seemed less fragile when, from the driver's seat, he looked towards the entrance to headquarters and saw the deadpan expression on Lieutenant Mario Conde's face; perhaps he'd not impressed him with a manoeuvre that was wilder than anything Gene Hackman does in *French Connection*. Although he was so young and people said in a few years he'd be the best detective at headquarters, Sergeant Manuel Palacios displayed rampant immaturity when he got his hands on a woman or a driving wheel. The Count's phobia at what was for him an overly complex activity, your hands steering, your eyes following what was in front and behind, simultaneously accelerating, changing gear or using the footbrake, allowed Manolo to be the perpetual driver whenever the Boss insisted on assigning them to the same case. The Count had always thought such vehicular cohabitation – he saved on a driver – was the reason the major coupled them so often. At headquarters some reckoned the Count was the best detective on the payroll and that Sergeant Palacios would soon overtake him, but few grasped the affinity that had sprung up between the dreadfully penny-pinching lieutenant and an almost emaciated, baby-faced sergeant who must certainly have cheated his way into the Police Academy. Only the Boss realized they might hit it off. In the end that was what happened.

The Count walked over to the car: cigarette between lips, jacket unbuttoned, bags under eyes hidden behind dark glasses. He seemed preoccupied as he opened the car door and climbed into the passenger seat.

"Good, finally, off to the wife's house?" asked Manolo, raring to go.

The Count stayed silent for a few minutes. He put his glasses into his jacket pocket. Extracted the photo of Rafael Morín from the file and placed it on his lap.

"What do you read in that face?" he asked.

"That face? You're the one into psychology, why don't *you* tell me?"

"In the meantime, what's your take on all this?"

"I'm not sure yet, Conde, it makes no sense. I mean,"

he checked himself and looked at the lieutenant, "it's real fucking odd."

"You tell me," replied the Count, egging him on.

"Well, for the moment there's no sign of an accident and no evidence he's fled the country, at least according to the latest reports I've just read, although I'd not bet on it. I don't think he's been kidnapped. That wouldn't make any sense either."

"Forget about any sense and go on."

"Well, a kidnapping doesn't make any sense because I can't see what anyone could ask him for, and I don't figure he's run off with a woman or anything of that sort, because he'd know there'd be one hell of a fuss and he doesn't seem that kind of guy. He'd lose his position, right? I've got one solution with two possible angles: he's been killed by accident or because people wanted to steal something, or because he was mistaken for somebody else, or else was killed because he was involved in some fucking scam. And the only other possibility is quite ridiculous: he's hiding for some reason, but if that's the case, I can't understand why he didn't think up something to delay his wife filing a statement. A trip to the provinces or whatever . . . But the guy stinks like a dead dog on the highway. In the meantime we've no choice but to look everywhere: his home, work, barrio, anywhere, to find something to explain all this."

"Fuck the bastard," exclaimed the Count, staring at the road opening up before him. "Let's go to his place. Off you go to Santa Catalina via Rancho Boyeros."

Manolo drove them on. The streets were still deserted under the bright sun that beat down and invited thoughts of an early afternoon break. A few dirty clouds lurked high on the horizon. The Count tried to think of Josefina's lunch, of tonight's baseball game, of the damage he was self-inflicting by smoking so many cigs a day. He wanted to see off the mixture of melancholy and excitement overcoming him as the car approached Tamara's house.

"Hey, Conde, you still on holiday? What do you reckon?" asked Manolo as they sped past the National Theatre.

"I think more or less the same as you, that's why I said nothing. I'm sure he's not hiding or going to attempt an illegal exit," he replied and took another look at the photo.

"Why do you think so? Because of his position?"

"Yes, right. Just imagine him travelling abroad ten times a year . . . But particularly because I've known him for twenty years."

Manolo missed a gear, and the car almost stalled on him. He accelerated and managed to judder along. He smiled, nodded and looked at his colleague.

"Don't tell me he's a friend of yours."

"I didn't say that. I said I knew him."

"Twenty years back?"

"Seventeen, to be precise. I first heard him speechifying in 1972 at high school in La Víbora. He was president of my student federation."

"And what else?"

"You know, Manolo, I don't want to prejudice you. The fact is he always made me feel sick to my back teeth, but that's irrelevant now. He should just put in a quick reappearance so I can go to bed."

"You really think it's not relevant?"

"Get a move on, catch the green light," he countered, pointing to the traffic light onto Boyeros and the El Cerro highway.

The Count lit another cigarette, coughed a couple of times and put Rafael Morín's photo back in his file.

28

The memory of Tamara telling them of her forthcoming marriage to Rafael had resurrected itself violently and unexpectedly. He could now see the three white stripes on her tunic, her stockings rolled down round her ankles and hair cut in a symmetrical oval. After they'd left high school they'd seen each other barely four or five times, and each time the mere sight of her and her female sensual allure made his skin tingle. They were progressing along the Santa Catalina highway, but the Count wasn't looking at the houses where some of his old school friends lived or the well-trimmed gardens or tranquillity in that eternally tranquil barrio where he'd partied so often with Skinny and Rabbit. He was thinking of another party, Tamara and Aymaras' fifteenth birthday party, almost at the start of the second year at high school, on the second of November, his memory recalled to the day, and the big impression made on him by the house where the girls lived. The garden was like a well kept English park: there was room for tables under the trees, on the lawn and next to the fountain where an old statue of an angel, rescued from some collapsing colonial establishment, pissed on lilies in full bloom. There was even a space where the Gnomes could play, the best, most famous, most expensive of the combos in La Víbora, and more than a hundred couples danced; there were bouquets for every girl and trays of meat croquettes, meat pies and fried cheese balls that were unimaginable in those years of perpetual queues. The twins' parents, ambassadors in London at the time and previously in Brussels and Prague and later Madrid, knew how to throw a party. And Skinny, Rabbit, Andrés and himself were sure they'd never been to a better one. A bottle of rum to each table! "It's like a party in another country," pronounced Rabbit, and they all agreed. Then he thought how even the great, great Gatsby would have enjoyed that gala do. In conquistador mode, Rafael Morín spent the whole night dancing with Tamara, and the Count could still remember the twins' white lace dresses flying though the air to the inevitable "Blue Danube": a white dress that for him was black and backstitched entirely in grey.

"Park there," he ordered the sergeant when they crossed Mayía Rodríguez, and he threw his cigarette end on the road. There on the opposite pavement, right on the corner, stood the two-storey house where the twins had lived, a spectacular house splendid with large swathes of dark glass and red brick and a wall around a professionally manicured garden at the right height not to hide the line of concrete sculptures that denoted the shaping hand of a Wifredo Lam.

"This is it," exclaimed Manolo. "Whenever I drove by here I'd stare at that house and think how I'd like to have lived in a house like that. I even started to think there'd never be problems with the police in such a place and that I'd never get to see the inside."

"Well, it's no house for policemen."

"It was given to him, I suppose."

"No, not this time. It belonged to his wife's parents."

"What can life be like in this kind of house, Conde?"

"Different . . . Hey, Manolo, wait a minute. There's an idea I want to work on: the party on the thirty-first. Rafael Morín disappeared after going to that party. Something may have happened there that impacts on all this business, because I'm not into coincidences. I want to ask you a favour."

Manolo smiled and struck the steering wheel with both hands.

"The Count asking me for a favour? Of a personal or

work nature? Go ahead, I'll be pleased to do anything for you."

"Hey, shut that trap and let me interview Tamara. I've known her for some time, and I think I can handle her better like that. That's the favour: not much to ask, is it? You can tell me later of any thoughts that may come to you. OK?"

"OK, Conde, it's not a problem," the sergeant replied, preparing to make a sacrifice in order to be present at what he guessed would be a settling of accounts with the past. As he locked the car Manolo saw the Count cross the road and disappear between the box-hedges and the head of a terrified concrete horse that seemed more Picasso than Lam. At any rate, that house continued to be far beyond the reach of any policeman.

Her eyes were two classic almonds, polished and slightly moist. Just the minimum to suggest they really were two eyes that might even shed tears. A lock of her artificially curled hair twisted down over her forehead, almost engulfing her thick, very high eyebrows. Her mouth attempted to smile, in fact did so, and her dazzlingly white teeth, like a healthy animal's, deserved the reward of a broad smile. She didn't look thirty-three, he thought as he stood in front of his former schoolmate. Nobody would believe she'd given birth, could still perform ballet pirouettes, although she was now clearly more in control of her profound beauty: rounded, exuberant and provocative, and at the peak of her bodily charms. She could still get into her school tunic and tight-clinging blouse, he thought as he tightened the pistol in his belt and introduced Sergeant Manuel Palacios, whose eyes were bulging out of their sockets. The Count wanted to leave as soon as he sat down on the sofa next to Tamara and she pointed Manolo to an armchair.

She was wearing a gaudy yellow loose-fitting dress, and he noted she was not at all unnerved: even wrapped in that garish colour she was the most beautiful woman he'd ever known, and now he didn't want to leave but to stretch an arm out when she stood up.

"Well, life *is* full of surprises, isn't it?" she remarked. "Wait a minute while I get you some coffee."

She walked towards the passage, and he observed the movement of her buttocks under the fine yellow material. He followed the faint outline of her knickers on her thighs and exchanged glances with an almost panting Manolo. He recalled how that memorable bum had led to lots of tears when her ballet teacher inevitably advised her to revisit her artistic ambitions: those earth-shaking hips, fleshy buttocks and rounded thighs weren't a sylph's or a swan's, but rather an egg-laying goose's, and she'd suggested an immediate transfer to a sweaty, liquor-laden rumba beat.

"A sad fate, right?" he commented, and Manolo shrugged his shoulders and prepared to investigate that inexplicable sadness when she came back and forced him to look at her.

"Mima's just made it, it's still hot," she assured them, offering a cup first to Manolo and then to himself. "Incredible, the Count in person. By now you must be a major or captain? Right, Mario?"

"Lieutenant, and sometimes I wonder how," he replied, tasting the coffee but not daring to add: It's good coffee, bloody hell, especially for friends; it really was the best coffee he'd tasted in years.

"Who would have thought you'd ever join the police?"

"Nobody, I reckon."

"This guy was a right character," she told Manolo and looked back at him. "You were never named as an exemplary pupil because you wouldn't join in the right activities and always bunked off the last classes to go and listen to episodes of *Guaytabó*. I still remember that."

"But I got good marks."

She couldn't repress a smile. The flow of memories between them jumped over the bad moments, erased by time, and only touched down on happy days, memorable events or incidents that had improved with hindsight. She even looked more beautiful: that can't be true.

"You don't write these days, Mario?"

"No, not anymore. But one day," he responded uneasily. "And what's become of your sister?"

"Aymara's in Milan. She went for five years with her husband, who's a representative for Cuban Export. Her new husband, you know?"

"No, I didn't know, but good for her."

"Tell me, Mario, whatever happened to Rabbit? I've never seen him since."

"Nothing much, you know he finished teacher-training but managed to get out of education. He's at the Institute for History still thinking about what would have happened if they hadn't killed Maceo or the English had stayed in Havana and other historical tragedies he likes to invent."

"And how's Carlos these days?"

She said Carlos, and he wanted to disappear down her cleavage. Skinny Carlos used to reckon Tamara and Aymara had big dark nipples, look at their lips, he'd say, they're like a black's and, according to his theory, nipples and lips were directly related in colour and size. They'd often tried to test out his theory in the

33

case of Tamara by waiting for her to bend down to pick up a pencil and by watching her in PE classes, although she was always one to wear bras. But not today?

"He's fine," he lied. "And what about yourself?"

She took the cup from his hands and put it on the glass table, next to an artistic wedding shot in which the smiling Tamara and Rafael, in their wedding outfits, happily embraced and looked at each other in an oval mirror. He was thinking she ought to say fine, but she didn't dare: her husband had disappeared, might be dead and she was distressed but the fact was she looked great, when she finally declared: "I'm very worried, Mario. I've got this feeling, I'm not sure . . ."

"What feeling?"

She shook her head, and that lock of hair danced irreverently over her forehead. She was nervous, rubbed her hand, and her usually tranquil eyes seemed stressed.

"Something's amiss," she said, looking into the silent house. "This is all too strange; something must be going on, right? Hey, Mario, you can smoke if you like," and she got him a pristine ashtray from the shelf under the glass coffee table. Murano, a purple-blue glass flecked with silver. He lit his cigarette and thought what a sin it would be to sully that ashtray.

"Don't you smoke?" she asked Manolo, and the sergeant smiled.

"No, thank you."

"It's incredible, Tamara," said the Count smiling. "I've not been inside this house for fifteen years, and it hasn't changed a bit. Do you remember when I broke that flower vase? I think it was bone china, wasn't it?"

"A Sargadelos." She leaned back on the sofa and tried to tame the lock of hair riding her forehead.

Memories will be the death of you as well, my dear, thought the Count, and he wanted to feel the way he felt when their whole group gathered to study in the library of that house straight out of the films. There were always cold drinks, often sweets, air conditioning and dreams they shared between the bookshelves: Skinny, Rabbit, Cuqui, Dulcita, the Count, would all have a house like that one day, when we are doctors, engineers, historians, economists, writers, all those things they were going to be and didn't all become. He couldn't stand any more memories and said: "I've read the statement you gave at the station. Tell me more."

"I don't know, it was like this," she started after thinking for a moment and crossing her legs, then her arms; she was still so elastic, he noted. "We got back from the party, I went to bed first and was half asleep when I heard him get in, and I asked him if he was OK. He'd drunk a lot at the party. When I got up, there was no sign of Rafael. I didn't really start to get worried till the afternoon, because he'd sometimes go out and not say where he was going, but he had no work on that day."

"Where do you say the party was held?"

"At the house of the deputy minister that Rafael's enterprise is responsible to. In Miramar, near the tourist shop on Fifth and Forty-Second.

"Who were the guests?"

"Let me think for a minute." She needed time and fiddled with her errant lock once more. "The owners of the house, Alberto and his wife, naturally. That's Alberto Fernández," she added as the Count pulled a small notebook from this back trouser pocket. "So you still carry a notebook in your back pocket?"

"Same old defects," he replied, shaking his head, for he couldn't imagine anyone remembering an old habit of his that he'd almost forgotten. What else should I be remembering, he wondered, and Tamara smiled, and he thought yet again what a burden memories are and that perhaps he ought not to be there; if he'd let on to the Boss, perhaps he'd have sent someone else, and then he thought he'd better ask to be taken off the job, that he shouldn't be there searching for a man he didn't want to find and conversing with the man's wife, that woman whose every nostalgic outburst aroused his desire. But replied: "I never liked carrying a satchel."

"Do you remember the day you had a fight in the playground with Isidrito from Managua?"

"I can still feel the pain. That joker really hit me." And he smiled at Manolo, who was brilliantly playing his cameo role as a peripheral spectator.

"And why did you thump each other, Mario?"

"You know, we started arguing about baseball, about who was best, Andrés, Biajaca and the people from my barrio or the guys from Managua, until I lost it and told him that anyone born outside my barrio was a son of a bitch. And, naturally, the joker went for me."

"Mario, I reckon if Carlos hadn't intervened, Isidrito would have killed you."

"And a good policeman would have been lost forever," he smiled, deciding to put his notepad away. "Look, just make me a list of the guests and tell me where everybody works and if you've got some way of contacting them. All those you remember. And were other important people there apart from the deputy minister?

"Sure, the minister was there, but he left early, at around eleven, because he had an engagement elsewhere."

"And did he talk to Rafael?"

"They said hello to each other but that was all. To each other, I mean."

"Uh-huh. And did he talk to anyone by himself?"

She thought for a moment. Almost closed her eyes and he looked away. He preferred playing with the ash on his cigarette and finally crushed the butt-end. He was at a loss what to do with the ashtray and was afraid to revisit the story of the Sargadelos vase. But he couldn't avoid Tamara's smell: she smelled clean and tanned, of lavender and wet earth and above all of woman.

"I think he spoke to Maciques, his office manager. They spend their lives talking of work; and at parties I have to put up with Maciques's wife; if only you could see her, she's taller than a flagpole . . . Well, you should hear her. The other day she discovered cotton is better than polyester, and now she says she just loves silk . . ."

"I can imagine what she's like. And who else did he talk to?"

"Well, Rafael was out on the balcony a good while, and when he came back in Dapena was just arriving, a Spaniard who's always doing business in Cuba."

"Hold on," he asked and looked for his notepad. "A Spaniard?"

"Well, a Galician actually. His full name is José Manuel Dapena. Some of the business he does involves Rafael's enterprise but particularly the Foreign Trade department."

"And you say they talked?"

"Well, I saw them both come in from the balcony. I don't know if there was anybody else."

"Tamara," he said and started playing with the catch on his pen, creating a monotonous tick-tack, "what are these parties like?"

"What parties?" She seemed surprised and at a loss.

"What are these parties like that you go to with ministers, deputy ministers and foreign businessmen?"

"I don't know what you mean, Mario; like any other party. People talk, dance, drink. I'm not sure what you're after. Keep your pen still please," she begged, and he knew she was upset.

"And don't people get drunk, swear and piss off the balconies?"

"I'm in no mood to play games, Mario, please." And she pressed her eyelids, although she didn't look tired. When she took her fingers away, her eyes shone even more brightly.

"I'm sorry," he replied and returned his pen to his shirt pocket. "Tell me about Rafael."

She sighed and shook her head at something only she was aware of and glanced towards the picture window that looked over the interior garden. How theatrical, he thought, and following her gaze he could just discern the artificial, slightly darkened colour of the ferns proliferating beyond the Calobar glass.

"You know, I'd have preferred another policeman. I find it hard going with you."

"So do I with you and Rafael. What's more, if your husband hadn't gone missing, I'd be at home reading and free until Monday. Now I just want him to turn up quickly. And you've just got to help me, right?"

She made as if to get up, but then sank back into the sofa. Her mouth was now a pencil line, the mouth of someone in disagreement, only softening when she looked at Sergeant Manuel Palacios.

"What can I tell you about Rafael? You know him too . . . He lives for his work. He didn't get where he is by only doing what he liked, and the best thing about him is that he enjoys working like a dog. I think he's a good leader, I really do, and everyone says he is. He's in great demand and always delivers. He also reckons he is successful. He spends his life travelling abroad, particularly to Spain and Panama, to sort out contracts and purchases, and it seems he's a good businessman. Can you imagine Rafael as a businessman?"

He couldn't either and looked at the sound system in the corner of the living room: turntable, double cassette deck, CD, equalizer, amplifier and two no doubt incredibly powerful speakers, and thought how music from there must really sound like music.

"No, I can't," he said and asked: "Where did that hi-fi system come from? It's worth more than a thousand dollars . . ."

She glanced back at Manolo and then straight at her old school friend.

"What's wrong with you, Mario? Why all these questions? You know nobody works like crazy just for the fun of it. Everybody is after something and . . . in this place if you can get steak, you don't settle for rice and eggs."

"Sure, to him that God gave . . ."

He searched for his pen but then left it where it was.

"All right, all right, forget it."

"No, I can't. If you had to travel in your work, wouldn't you travel and buy things for your wife and son?" she asked, seeking Manolo's approval. The sergeant barely raised his shoulders, was still holding his cup of coffee.

"Nil return on both counts: I don't travel abroad and don't have a wife and child."

"But you *are* envious, aren't you?" she responded quietly, looking back at the ferns. He knew he'd touched Tamara on a raw nerve. For years she'd tried to be like everybody else, but her background had won out and she always seemed different: her perfumes were never the cheap scents others used; she was allergic and could only use a few brands of male eau-de-cologne; her weekend party outfits seemed like those her friends wore but were made from Indian cotton; she knew when and how to cough, sneeze and yawn in public and was the only one who immediately understood the lyrics of Led Zeppelin or Rare Earth songs. He placed the ashtray on the sofa and looked for another cigarette. It was the last one in the packet and, as ever, he was alarmed by the quantity he'd smoked but told himself it wasn't true, he wasn't at all envious.

"I guess so," he demurred as he lit up and realized he hadn't the energy to argue with her. "But that's what I least envy about Rafael, I can tell you," he smiled knowingly at Manolo: "May St Peter bless these things."

She'd shut her eyes, and he wondered if she could have understood the level of envy he was experiencing. She'd come nearer, and he could smell her to his heart's content, and then she gripped one of his hands.

"Forgive me, Mario," she pleaded. "I'm very on edge with all this mess. You must understand that," she said, withdrawing her hand. "So you want a guest list?"

"Comrade, comrade," Sergeant Manuel Palacios finally piped up, raising his hand as if asking for permission to speak from the back of the class and not daring to look the Count in the eye. "I know how you must be feeling, but you must try to help us."

"I thought that was what I was doing."

"Of course. But I don't know your husband ... Before New Year's Day, did you notice anything strange? Did he act at all oddly?"

She lifted a hand and caressed her neck for a moment, as if very lovingly.

"Rafael was always rather odd. His character was like

that, extremely volatile. He was easily upset. If I did notice anything untoward, I'd say he seemed uneasy on the thirtieth. He told me he was very tired after all the end-of-year accounting but he was almost elated on the thirty-first, and I think he enjoyed the party. But work always worried him."

"And he didn't say anything or do anything that struck you as odd?" Manolo continued to avoid the lieutenant's gaze.

"I really don't think so. Besides, on the thirty-first he went to have lunch with his mother and spent almost all day with her."

"I'm sorry, Manolo," interjected the Count, who'd observed how the sergeant was rubbing his hands, warming to the task: he could go on questioning her for an hour. "Tamara, I'd like you to try to think of anything he might have done recently that may relate to what's happened. Anything could be important. Things he wouldn't usually say or do, if he spoke to someone you didn't know, whatever . . . And it's also important to get that list ready. Do you intend going out today?"

"No, why?"

"Nothing in particular, just so I know where you are. When I finish at headquarters I may pass by to pick the list up and we can talk more. It's not a problem. It's on my way."

"All right, I'll be expecting you and will get the list done, don't worry," she said, tussling yet again with her wayward lock.

"Look," he replied, tearing a page from his pad. "If anything crops up, you can get me on these numbers."

"All right, of course," she replied taking the paper, and her smile was radiant. "Hey, Mario, you're thinning out on top. Don't tell me you're going bald?"

He smiled, stood up and walked over to the door. Turned the door handle and let Manolo through first. Now he was opposite Tamara, looking her in the eye.

"Yes, I'm going bald into the bargain," he said, adding: "Tamara, don't worry for my sake. I've got a job to do and you must understand that, I suppose?"

"Yes, of course, Mario."

"Then, apart from you, tell me who would benefit from Rafael's death?"

She seemed surprised but then smiled. Forgot her lively lock and said: "What kind of psychologist were you going to be, Mario? I could bene . . . a sound system and the Lada downstairs?"

"I really don't know," he admitted and lifted a hand to wave goodbye. "I never get it right with you." And he left the house he'd not entered for fifteen years knowing he'd been hurt. He preferred not to see her waving farewell from her doorway. Walked to the road and crossed over without looking at the traffic.

"Walking warms you up," he declared as he settled down in the car, and he could not not look towards the house and see the farewell wave from that woman standing on her doorstep by the side of an aggressive concrete shrub.

"That egg's asking for a pinch of salt."

"What are you getting at?"

"Take care, Conde, take care."

"What do you mean, Manolo? You going to tell me off?"

"Me tell you off? No, Conde, you're getting on, and you've been in the force too long to know what you should and should not do. But I have my doubts about her."

"Go on, then, what's getting at you? Tell me."

"I'm not sure, but I really can't fathom her. She's too

42

poised for me. Even for you . . . So poised, put yourself in her place, husband missing, probably dead or up to his neck . . ."

"Uh-huh."

"Didn't you think she was a bit like, what the hell do I care?"

"And you reckon she's implicated?"

"Bloody hell, when the mule says it can't . . ."

"Come on, don't speak in riddles if you want me to get you . . ."

"All right, forget the riddles. I'll be as clear as daylight. You know, Conde, anyone watching you can see you slavering at the mouth when you look at that woman, and one look at her and you know she knows as well. That wouldn't be a problem if there weren't the slight matter of a husband . . . right? And as I said, something stinks."

"You think she knows something?"

"Could be. I'm not sure, but take care, guy. OK?"

"OK, Sergeant."

As he said "sergeant" he stretched out his hand and ordered him to stop the car.

"Near there," he asked when he spotted a patrol car by the kerb and two policemen picking a man up. He knew only too well what was happening and showed the two police his ID out of the car window. "What happened?"

"He was drunk and flat out there," one of the policemen explained, pointing to the entrance to the San Juan Bosco church. "We're taking him in to cool off at the station," he went on, almost dropping the man.

"Fine, help him out," said the Count, saluting and telling Manolo to drive on. It wasn't cold, but the Count felt his hair stand on end. Drunks who'd lost their way upset him as much as street dogs, and unconsciously he ran two fingers through his hair to check out Tamara's comment. Can it be true I'm also going bald? And when the car stopped by the Coca-Cola traffic light he took a peek at himself in the rear-view mirror. He probably was.

"Manolo," he said, without looking at his companion, "let's get on with the business. Drop me at Foreign Trade, and I'll find out who Dapena the Galician is and where we can find him if we need him, and you go and see Maciques and talk to him. Record the interview and take it gently please, you've been a bit heavy recently. Then we'll meet up at headquarters . . . But are you telling me you wouldn't fancy laying a woman like that?"

". . . I'd just like to ask whether I could record our exchange/that's all right, comrade, whatever you want . . . /so, you're René Maciques Alba and head up Rafael Morín Rodríguez's office, the citizen who disappeared from his home on the first/yes, comrade, on the first . . . /and how long have you been working for him?/ . . . well, it's almost the other way round, if I might explain, I was in charge of the previous director's office and when they appointed Rafael I continued in the same post, you understand, it was two and a half years ago, in June 1987, and I can almost remember that day . . . /and how did you get on with him/with Rafael? . . . well, you know, it's not the thing to say, but he and I were always like friends, right from the start, and how can one describe a friend, he was a fine leader, always concerned about his work and subordinates, the kind of person who's liked, who's very responsible . . . /you have any idea why he's disappeared?/any idea? not really . . . he and I went to the New Year's party held at the house of comrade Alberto, the deputy minister/what's his full name? deputy minister for what?/oh, of course, Alberto Fernández-Lorea, deputy minister for industry, he sees to anything to do with the commercial work of the ministry, and as I said, we and our wives went to his place in Miramar, and were there from around ten o'clock to just after two or three, time flies when you're at a party like that, and Rafael and I talked a bit and agreed to meet on Monday to prepare the contracts we had to send to Japan for an urgent deal/what kind of deal?/what kind? . . . a purchase, you know, bearings and other things to do with plastics and computers, you know the Japanese offer very good prices for this kind of thing?/and you say you didn't notice anything strange?/well, to be frank, I didn't . . . I've given it some thought but I don't think so, he danced, ate, drank, ate an enormous amount, that's for sure, he said the deputy minister did the best roast pork in the world/and was the enterprise in any difficulty?/not really, no . . . the accounts at the end of the year were very favourable, perhaps some worries at the amount of work we had on our plate, but that always worried him, and that's normal given he was in charge, do you see? and besides with the socialist countries in difficulty, life can only get more complicated from here on, you know . . . /do you have any idea where he might be?/well, was it lieutenant?/sergeant/that's right, sergeant, I don't have a clue about what might have happened, he led his normal life/did he have any problems at work?/at work? . . . none at all, sergeant, I told you, Rafael had everything very well taped/and did he have lots of women friends?/what do you mean, lots of women friends? who told you that, sergeant?/nobody, I'm just trying to find out where Rafael Morín is, did he like women?/I know nothing about his private life . . . /but you were friends, weren't you?/yes, we were, but more like work friends, you know? I'd pay the odd visit to his house, and he'd come to mine/did anybody at work have it in for him?/in what way? wanting to make his life difficult?/ yes, in that sense . . . / . . . no, I don't think so, there'll always be someone envious or resentful, they're more common than muck in Havana, that's true enough, but he wasn't the kind to create enemies, at least at work, which is where I knew him best/who is José Manuel Dapena?/oh, right, Dapena, a Spanish businessman/how did he get on with Rafael?/well, let me explain, Dapena owns a shipyard business in Vigo, and he helped us to import various things, though he wasn't really in the same line of business, more into the fishing industry/and what was he doing at the party?/at the party? I expect he'd been invited, right?/ invited by?/by the owner of the house, I expect, naturally/and what were relations like between Rafael and Dapena?/to be frank, they were purely business, I don't know if I should mention this but . . . /do please feel free/one day Dapena made a pass at Rafael's wife . . . /and did it lead to problems?/no, don't imagine that for one minute, it was all a misunderstanding, but Rafael found it difficult to tolerate him after that/and is the Spaniard a friend of yours?/he's no friend of mine, after what happened with Tamara, Rafael's wife, the Galician guy is one of those who thinks he's God Almighty because he's got dollars/and what happened to the previous head of the enterprise?/so what's the relevance of that? I'm sorry, sergeant . . . nothing, a spot of *dolce vita*, as people say, he set himself up, well, you know what it's like . . . /and was Rafael so inclined?/Rafael was quite the opposite to the extent that . . . /to the extent that what?/he was different, I mean/what time did you leave the party?/oh, right . . . about three/and did you leave together?/no, well almost, when I went, he was bidding farewell to the comrade deputy minister and . . . /and what?/no, nothing, I left . . . /you say you've no idea what might have happened to citizen Rafael Morín?/no, sergeant, not a clue . . ."

René Maciques must be around the fifty mark, balding, and wears glasses, the round sort, like a model librarian, thought the Count as he stared at the cassette recorder. Manolo's work highlighted the man's bureaucratic rhetoric and his strict ethics when it came to always defending his boss's back until the opposite is proved to be true, wherever he may be, and now at least we don't where the hell he's got to, he told himself. Nevertheless, the sphere of Rafael's relationships and friendships, the recorded interview with Maciques and his own conversation with Tamara were evidence of an important element in his search: Rafael was as squeaky clean as ever, and Conde shouldn't let his prejudices get the better of him. His memories were scars from wounds he'd thought had healed a long time ago and a case under investigation was quite another matter, and investigations have antecedents, evidence, clues, suspicions, hunches, intuitions, certainties, comparable statistical data, fingerprints, documents and many, many coincidences but nothing as tricky and treacherous as prejudice.

He stood up and walked over to the window in his cubicle. He'd looked out so often on that fragment of landscape that it had become his favourite vista. The leaves on the laurel trees moved slightly, rustled by a northern breeze bringing a patch of dark heavy clouds that were gathering on the horizon. Two nuns clad in dark winter outfits left the church and got into a VW Beetle with a naturalness that was simply post-modern. His empty stomach fluttered like the leaves on the laurel trees, but he didn't want to think about food. He thought about Tamara, Rafael, Skinny Carlos, Aymara in Milan and Dulcita, who was God knows where, about the twins' spectacular fifteenth birthday party and about himself, in that office which was so cold in winter and so hot in summer, contemplating laurel leaves and engaged in a search for someone he'd never have chosen to look for. Everything was so perfect.

He rested his fingertips on the icy windowpane and wondered what he'd made of his life: whenever he revisited his past he felt he was nobody and had nothing, only his thirty-four years and two abandoned marriages. He left Maritza for Haydée, and Haydée left him for Rodolfo, and he couldn't bring himself to look for her, although he was still in love with her and could forgive her almost anything: he was afraid and preferred to get drunk every night for a week, and in the end he couldn't forget that woman; and the terrible truth was he'd been magnificently cuckolded, and his detective instinct had never alerted him to a crime that had been months in the making before reaching its grand finale. His voice grew hoarser by the day because of the two packets of cigarettes he smoked daily, and he knew that apart from going bald, he'd end up with a hole in his throat and a check scarf round his neck, like a cowboy eating a snack, perhaps talking via an apparatus that would make him sound like a stainless steel robot. He hardly read nowadays and had even forgotten the day when he'd pledged before a photo of Hemingway, the idol he most worshipped, that he'd be a writer and nothing else and that any other adventures would be valid as life experience. Life experience. Dead bodies, suicides, murderers, smugglers, whores, pimps, rapists and raped, thieves, sadists, twisted people of every shape, size, sex, age, colour, social and geographical origins. A load of bastards. And fingerprints, autopsies, digging, bullets fired, scissors, knives, crowbars, hair and teeth extracted, faces disfigured. His life experiences. And the plaudits at the end of every case solved and the terrible frustration, disgust and infinite impotence at the end of every case that was filed unsolved. Ten years wallowing in the sewers of society had finally conditioned his reactions and perspectives, revealing to him only the sourest, most ornery side of life, even impregnating his skin with a stench of rot he'd never cast off and, worse still, one he only smelled when it was particularly offensive, because his sense of smell had gone forever. Everything as pleasant and perfect as a good kick in the balls.

What have you made of your life, Mario Conde? he asked himself daily as he attempted to reverse the time machine and one by one right his own wrongs, disappointments and excesses, anger and hatred, cast off his errant ways and find the exact point at which to begin afresh. But does it make any sense? he also wondered, now I'm almost bald, and he always responded in the same fashion: Where was I? Oh, I mustn't be prejudiced, but the fact is I love prejudices, he muttered as he rang Manolo.

The story was called "Sundays" and it was a true story, autobiographical to boot. It began one Sunday morning when my character's mum (my mum) woke him up, "Up you get, my boy, it's half past seven", and he understood how on that particular morning he couldn't eat breakfast or stay a bit longer in bed or play baseball later, because it was Sunday and he had to go to church, as he did every Sunday, while his friends ("they'll all perish in hell," said his/my mother) spent the only morning when there was no school dossing around the barrio and organizing handball or baseball games in the alley on the corner or on the wasteland by the quarry. I felt very anticlerical, I'd read Boccaccio and in the Prologue they'd explained what it meant to be anticlerical, and the fact I was forced to go to church made me anticlerical as well because I wanted to be a baseball player, so I decided to write the story, merely hinting at the anticlericalism, not being in your face about it, like the iceberg Hemingway talks about. That was the story I took to the workshop.

The feeling you are a writer is really fantastic. Although the workshop was more like a beggars' banquet. There was a bit of everything: from Millán and black Pancho, the only two known queers at school, to Quijá, the basketball team captain who wrote the longest of sonnets; from Adita Vélez, who was so pretty and delicate it was impossible to imagine her in the daily act of shedding a turd, to Baby-Face Miki, the school Romeo, yet to write a line and still looking for a chick to lay; from Afón the black, who almost never came to class, to Olguita the teacher of literature, who was in charge, and myself and Lamey, who was the life and soul of the workshop. People used to say "he's a real poet" because he'd published poems in *The Bearded Cayman* and wore white shirts with stiff collars and sleeves rolled back to the elbow not because he was a poet or anything of that sort, but because those

white shirts were all he had to wear to school and he
had to make the most of the splendid collars and
ties his father had worn as a sales rep in the fifties
in Venezuela when Lamey was born, who was consequently a Venezuelan living in La Víbora and he was
the one who had the idea of doing a literary workshop
magazine, and unawares he had let all hell loose.

We met every Friday afternoon under the carob
trees in the PE yard, and Olguita the teacher brought a
big thermos of cold tea, and night would creep up on
us as we criticized each other's stories and poems to
death and were hypercritical, always looking for the
other side of things, the historical framework, whether
it was idealist or realist, what was the theme and what
was the subject and other idiocies they taught us in
class to put us off reading ever again, although our
teacher Olguita never mentioned such things and
read us a chapter of Cortázar's *Hopscotch* every week;
you could see she really liked it because she would
be almost in tears when she told us this is literature,
and I thought she got more and more like *la Maga*,
and I almost fell in love with her, although I was
Cuqui's boyfriend and in love with Tamara, and besides
Olguita's face was pockmarked, and she was ten years
older than me, and she also agreed it would a good
idea to bring out a monthly magazine with the best
pieces from the workshop.

That was the other bone of contention: the best
pieces. Because we all wrote the most brilliant texts
and we needed a book to pack it all in, and then Lamey
said that with issue zero – and I was really surprised by
that number zero, if it was in fact number one, because
zero is zero and I couldn't get it out of my head, that it
was like a magazine with blank pages or at best a magazine that never existed, you following me? – we should

51

be very demanding, and he and Olguita selected the pieces, and they got our vote of confidence just this once. And they selected "Sundays"; and I couldn't keep my bum still, thinking I was really going to be a writer, and Skinny and Jose were very, very happy, and Rabbit was very, very envious: I would at last get into print. Issue zero also carried two poems by Lamey – power rules OK – and one by Lamey's girlfriend – power etc. – a story by Pancho, the black queer, a critique by Adita of the play performed by the school drama group, another story by Carmita and an editorial penned by Olguita our teacher to introduce issue zero of *La Viboreña*, the magazine of the José Martí literary workshop, at René O Reiné High School. So exciting!

Our little mag was to have ten pages, and Lamey got two reams of paper; we'd have a hundred copies, and Olguita spoke to the school office about the typing and copying side, and I dreamed every night I could see *La Viboreña* and believe that I was really a writer. To make sure it was ready, we spent one night collating and stapling pages, and the following day we stood outside the school entrance distributing it to people, Lamey didn't roll up his sleeves and looked like a waiter, and Olguita our teacher watched us from the steps and was proud and happy the last time I saw her laugh.

The following day the school secretary summoned us, classroom by classroom, to a meeting at two pm in the headmaster's office. We were writers and so naïve as to expect to receive diplomas as well as plaudits and other moral encouragement for that magazine that was so innovative when the headmaster told us to sit down; already seated there were the head of the Spanish department, who'd never come to the workshop, the secretary for the youth and Rafael Morín, who was gasping as if he'd had a mild attack of asthma.

The headmaster, who after twelve months and the Water-Pre scandal would no longer be in post, made a meal of it: what was the meaning of the magazine's motto: "Communism will be a sun-sized aspirin"? So socialism was a headache, was it? What was dear comrade Adita's intention when she critiqued the play about political prisoners in Chile, to rubbish the theatre group's efforts and the play's message? Why were all the poems in the magazine love poems with not a single one dedicated to the work of the Revolution, to the life of a martyr or to the fatherland? Why was comrade Conde's story on a religious theme and why did he avoid taking up a position against the church and its reactionary dogmas? And above all, he continued – we felt as if we were all drunk by this point – and he stood opposite skinny Carmita, you could see her shaking, and they all nodded sagely, why did you publish a story with the by-line comrade Carmen Sendán on the theme of a girl who commits suicide for reasons of love? (He said "theme" not "subject"). Is that the image we should be presenting of Cuban youth today? Is that the example we should be putting forward rather than one exalting purity, selflessness, a spirit of sacrifice to inspire new generations . . .? All hell had been let loose.

Olguita our teacher stood up, a bright red, allow me to interrupt you, comrade headmaster, she said looking at her head of department who avoided her venomous glance and started cleaning her nails and at the headmaster who stared back at her, because I have something to say on all this: and she said lots of things, that it wasn't ethical for her to find out about the subject of the meeting without prior notice (she said "subject" and not "theme"), that she was totally opposed to an approach which smacked of the Inquisition, that

53

she couldn't understand how there could be such a lack of understanding of the efforts and initiatives of these students, that only a bunch of political troglodytes could interpret the writing in the magazine in that way and, as I see there can be no dialogue, given these Stalinist accusations of which my comrade head of department clearly approves, please sign my resignation papers as I can't continue here, even though there are sensitive, good and worthy students like the ones here, and she pointed at us and walked out of the headmaster's office, and I'll never forget how bright red she went; she was crying, and it was as if she were no longer pockmarked and had become the most beautiful woman in the world.

We froze there, until Carmita started crying, and Lamey looked at the tribunal standing in judgement over us when Rafael stood up, smiled, smirked and sidled over to the headmaster, comrade headmaster, he said, after this nasty incident, I think it right I should speak to the students, because they're all excellent comrades and I think they must understand what you have just told them. Take yourself, Carmita, he said, and he put a hand on the skinny girl's shoulder, I'm sure you never thought through the consequences of your idealist story, but we must be on our guard, you must agree. I believe the best thing you can do now is to show how you can produce a magazine that reflects the needs of the times, in which we can emphasize purity, selflessness, the spirit of sacrifice to inspire the new generations (*sic*), right, Carmita? And poor Carmita said yes and nodded, not knowing she was saying yes forever, that Rafael was right, and even I wondered whether he was, but I couldn't forget Olguita our teacher and what they'd said about my story, and Lamey got up, please, he said, any complaints about him should be made to his rank-and-file committee and he walked out as well. It cost him a year's curtailment of rights and the worst possible reputation; he's always been an awkward, sarcastic, arrogant type, he's got even more bigheaded after the publication of those paltry poems, pronounced the head of department as she watched him leave. I wanted to die on the spot as I've never wanted to since, I was afraid, I was speechless, I didn't understand what I'd done wrong, I'd only written about what I felt and what had happened to me when I was a kid, that I preferred playing baseball on the street corner to going to Mass, and luckily I kept back five copies of *La Viboreña*, which never made it to issue number one, that was going to be about democracy, because Olguita our teacher, who was so nice and so beautiful, thought we should create that issue by taking a vote on the best we could reap from our rich literary harvest.

"You had a bite to eat?" Manolo nodded, gently rubbing his stomach, and the Count thought it wasn't a good idea to carry on without eating. "Look, I need you to go on the computer and get a list of all the investigations started in Havana over the last five days and which . . ."

"Every single one?" asked Manolo, sitting opposite the Count ready to challenge his orders. He stared at his face, and the pupil in his left eye began to shift till it almost disappeared behind the bridge of his nose.

"Hey, don't look at me like that . . . Can I finish what I was saying?" asked the lieutenant, who rested his chin on his hands, contemplating his subordinate with resignation and wondering yet again whether Manolo was squint-eyed.

"Go on, then," the other demurred, sharing in his boss's resignation. He turned to look out the window, and his left eye slowly returned to its normal position.

"Look, you see, to get a grip on this we need to know if it's related to anything, to whatever. That's why I want you to get to the computer data and your brilliant brain to select whatever might be connected to Rafael Morín's disappearance. Something might turn up, you know?"

"I get it, blind man's bluff."

"Manolo, stop being so fucking awkward. It needs doing. Off you go. I'll see you in an hour."

"You'll see me in an hour. In an hour? Hey, you're sending me packing on my hoss and you've not even told me what the sheriff said . . ."

"Not much at all. I spoke to the head of security at Foreign Trade, and it seems the Spaniard is purer than the holy mother virgin. Fond of whores and mean with them, but he sang the usual refrain: he's a friend of Cuba, has done good business with us, nothing out of the ordinary."

"And are you going to talk to him?"

"You know I'd like to, don't you? But I don't think the Boss will give us a plane to go as far as Key Largo. The guy went there on the morning of the first. Apparently everyone left on the morning of the first."

"I think we *should* see him, after what Maciques said . . ."

"He won't be back till Monday, so we'll have to wait. OK, I'll be back within the hour, my friend."

Manolo stood up and yawned, opening his mouth as wide as he could, moaning plaintively.

"I get so sleepy after lunch."

"Hey, you realize what I've got to do now?" the Count pursued his interrogation, only pausing to walk over to the sergeant. "I've got to see the Boss and tell him we're clueless . . . You want to change places?"

Manolo smiled and beat a quick retreat.

"No, that's down to you, it's why you earn fifty pesos more than me. You said in an hour's time, didn't you?" He accepted his lot and left the cubicle without waiting for the uh-huh of the lieutenant's farewell.

The Count watched him shut the door, then yawned. He thought how at that time of day he should be sleeping a long siesta, curled up under his sheets, after stuffing Jose's meal or going to the cinema; he loved to relax in matinee shadows and watch very squalid moving films, like *The French Lieutenant's Woman*, *People Like Us* or Scola's *We Loved So Much*. There's no justice, he muttered, and picked up the folder and his battered notebook. If he'd believed in God, he would have commended his soul to God before going to the Boss empty-handed.

He left his cubicle and walked along the corridor to the staircase. A light was on in the last office on the passage, the coolest and biggest on the whole floor, and he decided to make a necessary stop. He tapped on the glass, opened the door and saw the hunched shoulders of Captain Jorrín, who was also looking through his window at the street, resting his forearm on the window frame. Headquarters' old bloodhound barely turned round to say, Come in, Conde, come in; he stayed still.

"Hey, Count! Do you really think I should take early retirement?" the man asked, and the lieutenant realized he'd picked a bad moment. I'm a good one to be offering advice, he thought.

Jorrín was the most veteran detective at headquarters, a kind of institution or oracle to which the Count and many of his colleagues had recourse hoping for advice, predictions and omens of a tried and tested usefulness. Talking to Jorrín was a kind of necessary rite in every tricky investigation, but Jorrín was ageing and his question was painfully symptomatic.

"What's the matter, Maestro?"

"I'm gradually coming to the conclusion I should retire, but I'd like to know what someone like you thinks."

Captain Jorrín swung round but stayed by the window. He seemed tired, sad or even exhausted by something that was torturing him.

"No, I've no problems with Rangel, nothing of that sort. We've even been friends of late. I'm the problem, Lieutenant. The fact is this work will be the death of me. I've been struggling on for almost thirty years and don't think I can stand any more, any more at all," he repeated and looked at the floor. "You know what I'm investigating right now? The murder of a thirteen-year-old boy, Lieutenant. A brilliant kid, you know? He was training to compete in the Latin American Mathematics Olympiad. Can you imagine? He was killed yesterday morning on the corner of his street, and his bike was stolen. Beaten to death by more than one person. He was dead before reaching the hospital; they'd fractured his skull, arms, several ribs and lots more besides. As if he'd been run over by a train, but it wasn't a train, it was people after a bicycle. What's gone wrong, Conde? How is so much violence possible? I should have got used to such things, shouldn't I? But I never have, you know? And every time it hurts more, upsets me more. Ours is a fucking awful job, you know?"

"You're right," the Count replied, getting to his feet. He walked over and stood by his friend. "But what the hell can we do, Captain? These things happen . . ."

"But there are people walking around who can't even imagine that they do, Lieutenant," he interrupted the advice the Count was offering and looked back out of the window. "I went to the boy's funeral this morning, and I realized I'm too old to be still doing this. Fuck, you know, they're killing kids to steal their bicycles . . . It's beyond me."

"Can I give you some advice, Maestro?"

Jorrín acquiesced. The Count knew that the day old Jorrín took his uniform off, he'd embark on an irreversible decline that would end in death, but he also knew he was right and imagined himself, twenty years on, looking for the murderers of a young kid and told himself it was all too much.

"I can think of only one thing to say, and I think it's what you'd have said to me if I were in your situation. First find the boy's killers and then consider whether you want to retire," he pronounced before he walked towards the door, tugged at the door handle and added, "Whoever forced us to be policemen?" and headed down the corridor to the lift, infected by the maestro's anguish. He looked at his watch and was alarmed to see it was already two-thirty. He felt he'd journeyed through the longest of mornings when minutes were languid and hours slow and difficult to defeat; his eyes saw a watch by Dalí. He went into the Boss's office and asked Maruchi if he could see him when the intercom alarm went off. The young woman said: "wait", waved her hand and pressed the red button. A rusty tin voice, turned into a stutter by the intercom, asked whether Lieutenant Mario the Count was around or where'd he got to as he'd not yet put in an appearance. Maruchi looked at him, changed her tone and said: "I've got him right here" and changed key again.

"Well, tell him he's got a call, from Tamara Valdemira. Should I transfer it?"

"Tell her yes, otherwise she'll bite my head off," said the Count, walking over to the grey phone.

"Transfer the call, Anita," Maruchi requested and cut off, adding, "I think the Count has an interest in the case."

The lieutenant put his hand on the receiver, and it rang. He was looking at the Boss's chief secretary when the telephone rang loudly for a second time, and he didn't lift up the receiver.

"I'm a bag of nerves," he confessed to the young woman, who shrugged her shoulders, what do you expect me to do? And he waited for the third ring to finish. Then picked it up: "Yes, it's me," and Maruchi just stared at him.

"Mario, that you? It's Tamara."

"Yes, tell me, what's the matter?"

"I'm not sure, something silly, but it might be of interest."

"I thought Rafael had turned up . . . Go on."

"No, I was just looking in the library and saw Rafael's telephone book, it was there by the extension and, I don't know, maybe I'm being really silly."

"Get to the point, woman," he begged and looked back at Maruchi: you're all the same, his sigh suggested.

"Nothing really, kid, the book was open at the letter Z."

"Hey, you're not going to tell me that Rafael is Zorro and that's why he's disappeared?"

She stayed silent for a moment.

"You can't hold back, can you?"

He smiled and replied: "Sometimes I can . . . Come on then, what's Z got to offer?"

"Just that there are two names: Zaida and Zoila, each with a number."

"And who might they be?" he asked, clearly interested.

"Zaida is Rafael's secretary. I don't know about the other one."

"Are you jealous?"

"What do you think? I reckon I'm a little on the old side for reactions of that kind."

"You're never too old ... Did he usually leave that book there?"

"No, that's why I called. He always had it in his case, and his case is in its usual place, by the bookcase at the back."

"Go on, give me the two numbers," he said, and his eyes requested Maruchi note them down. "Zaida, 327304, that's El Vedado. And Zoila 223171, that's Playa. Uh-huh," he said, reading Maruchi's jottings. "So you've no idea who this Zoila might be?"

"No, I really don't."

"How's the list going?"

"Going. That's why I was in the library ... You know, Mario, I'm more worried now."

"OK, Tamara, let me investigate these numbers, and I'll call by. All right?"

"All right, Mario, I'll be expecting you."

"Uh-huh. See you."

He took the sheet of paper the secretary pointed his way and studied it for a moment. Zaida and Zoila sounded like a melancholy Mexican duo of *ranchera* singers. He should have asked Tamara about the relationship between Rafael and Zaida but hadn't dared. He jotted down the names and numbers on his notepad and smiled and asked Maruchi: "Hey, baby, do me a favour and give the people downstairs a call and tell them to look out the addresses for these numbers."

"Anything for you," replied the young woman, bowing to the inevitable.

"I so love willing women. When I get paid I'll buy you . . . And the chief?"

"Go in, he's waiting for you, as he usually is . . ." she told him and pressed the black intercom button.

He tapped the door with his knuckles before going in. Major Antonio Rangel sat behind his desk, officiating at a cigar-lighting ceremony. He was subtly angling the flame from his lighter, turning the cigar, and each movement of his fingers created a tranquil puff of blue smoke that floated before his eyes, embracing him in a compact scented cloud. Smoking was a transcendent part of his life, and people familiar with his fetish for a good Havana never interrupted him in the act of lighting a cigar. Whenever possible, they would give him well known brands as presents on the requisite day: a birthday or wedding anniversary, Father's Day or New Year's Day, the birth of a grandson or graduation of a son; and Major Rangel was gathering together a proud collector's cache from which he could select different brands for particular times of day, buttresses to shore up his state of mind and sizes according to the time at his disposal for a smoke. Only when he'd finished lighting his cigar and contemplated with professional satisfaction the perfect crown glowing at the end of his smoke, would he straighten in his chair and address his latest visitor.

"You wanted to see me. Didn't you?"

"Yes, I didn't have much choice in the matter, did I? Take a seat."

"When you're as stressed as I am and feel you can't think straight, the best thing is to light a cigar, not firing it up and wallowing in smoke, but smoking it properly, for each cigar is unique and offers you every ounce of goodness it has. When I'm smoking like this and doing other things, it's a waste of a six-inch Davidoff 5000 Gran Corona, which deserves to be smoked slowly and thoughtfully or simply when one can sit down to smoke and chat for an hour, which is the ideal lifespan of a cigar. The one I lit this morning was a disaster: first because mornings have never been the best time for a cigar of such quality and second because I didn't pay it proper attention and mistreated it, and however much I tried later on, I couldn't make amends, and it was as if I were smoking an amateur roll, it really was. I can't understand why you prefer to smoke two packets of cigarettes a day rather than one Havana. That transforms you. And I don't mean it has to be a Davidoff 5000 or another good Corona, a Romeo y Julieta Cedros N° 2, for example, a Montecristo N° 3 or a Rey del Mundo of whatever size but a good dark-skinned cigar that pulls gently and burns evenly: that's what one calls living, Mario, or the nearest one ever gets. Kipling said a woman is but a woman, but a good *puro*, as they call them in Europe, is much more. I can tell you the fellow was absolutely right, because I may not know much about women, but I know lots about Havanas. One is a fiesta for the senses, a riot of pleasure, my boy: it revives the sight, awakens taste, rekindles touch and creates the lovely taste that goes so well with an after-dinner cup of coffee. And is even music to the ears. Listen to it moving between my fingers and almost moaning as if prey to desire. Do you hear that? Then come the accompanying pleasures: seeing half an inch of ash mount up or removing the band when you've smoked the first third. Isn't that living? Don't look at me like that. I'm being perfectly serious, more than you might think. Smoking is a true pleasure, particularly if you know how. What you do is a vice, a cheap experience, and that's why you get frustrated and despair. Get this straight, Mario: this is a case like any other and you are going to solve it. But don't let the past prejudice you, right? Look, to help you over the hump, I'm going to make an exception. Well, you know I never give cigars to anyone, but I'm going to give you a Davidoff 5000 as a present. I will now tell Maruchi to bring you a coffee and you'll light up, the way I told you, and you can tell me what it's like. You'd have to be a real son of a bitch if this doesn't bring you back to life. Maruchi."

"*Saturday 30–12–88*

"Armed Robbery. Retail company Guanabacoa district. Guard seriously injured. Culprits arrested. Closed.

"Attempted murder. La Lisa district. Culprit arrested: José Antonio Évora. Victim: culprit's wife. In a bad state. Statement: admits responsibility. Motive: jealousy. Closed.

"Armed robbery, Parque de los Chivos, La Víbora, October Tenth District. Victims: José María Fleites and Ohilda Rodríguez. Culprit: Arsenio Cicero Sancristóbal. Arrested 1–1–89. Closed.

"Murder. Victim: Aureliana Martínez Martínez. Resident at 21, N°1056, e/A and B, Vedado, Plaza District. Motive: unknown. Open.

"Disappearance: Disappearance of Wilfredo Cancio Isla. Case open: possibly drug trafficking. Missing man found in a boarded up house. Accused of breaking into the property. Arrested pending investigation possible drug connections.

"Armed robbery . . ."

He closed his eyes and pressed his fingertips against his eyelids. The conversation with Jorrín had sharpened the hypersensitivity he'd not lost in all those years on the job and which helped him imagine each case individually. And that list of pointless crimes filled three computer printouts, and he reflected how Havana was turning into a big city. He puffed gently on the cigar the Boss had given him. Recently, he reflected, robbery and assault were on an upward curve, the siphoning off of state goods seemed irrepressible, and trafficking in dollars and works of art had become much more than a passing fashion. It's a good cigar, but none of this relates to Rafael. Tens of daily reports, of cases that were open, closed or still under investigation, astonishing connections linking a basic illegal beer-bar with an illegal betting shop, and the betting shop with counterfeit petrol vouchers, and the counterfeiting with a consignment of marijuana, and the drugs with a real store offering a selection of domestic electrical goods to purchase with dollars that couldn't be traced. If only this cigar helped me think, because he needed to think, after he'd told the Boss about his dealings with Rafael Morín and Tamara Valdemira, I had a doggish infatuation for that woman, Boss. "But that was twenty years ago, wasn't it?" the major asked, and he said: "Forget any idea I might take you off the case. I need you on it, Mario. I didn't call you this morning for fun. You know I don't like disturbing people just for the sake of it, and I'm not so romantic as to invent tragedies when they don't exist.

But this tale of the man who disappeared reeks. Don't let me down now," he said, adding: "But be careful, Mario, be careful . . . Remember there's a loose end somewhere, and who better than you to find it? OK?"

"What have you come up with, Conde?" Sergeant Manuel Palacios asked, and the Count saw fireflies flying in his eyes born from the pressure from his fingertips.

He stood up, returned to the window and meditated gloomily. It was three hours to dusk, and the sky had turned overcast, a warning perhaps that rain and cold were on their way back. He'd always preferred cold for work, but the premature darkness depressed him and took away any inclination to work that he might still harbour. He'd never before so wanted to be finished with a case, the pressures from above the Boss passed on to him made him feel desperate, and the image of Tamara's butt shifting beneath her yellow dress was both torture and a warning: be careful. Everybody seemed to see danger. Worst of all, however, was the feeling of disorientation that was stifling him: he was as lost as Rafael and didn't like working like that. The major had approved his first steps, authorized him to speak to the Spanish businessman and investigate the enterprise – yes, something might turn up there, he'd said – to interview people and check papers with specialists in economics and accounting from head-quarters; only he'd have to wait till Monday, and the major didn't want this to last till Monday. But as he smoked that silken-flavoured cigar he convinced him-self that Rafael Morín's disappearance owed nothing to chance and that he'd have to revisit all paths that might lead logically to the beginning of the end of the

66

story; the party and the enterprise, the enterprise and the party seemed like tracks that ran into each other.

"Tamara rang and told me about something that may be a lead," he finally told Manolo as he informed him about the telephone book. The sergeant read the names, numbers and addresses of the two women and then asked: "Do you really think this might lead somewhere?"

"I'm interested in Zaida the secretary and in finding out who Zoila might be. Hey, how many names starting with Zed you got in your telephone book?"

Manolo shrugged his shoulders and smiled. No, he didn't know.

"Zed barely has eight or ten pages in dictionaries, and almost nobody has a name that begins with Zed," said the Count, opening his own telephone book. "I've only got Zenaida. Do you remember Zenaida?"

"Hey, Conde, drop it, that girl's for other occasions."

The lieutenant closed his telephone book and returned it to his desk drawer.

"Women are always there for other occasions. Yes, get a move on, we'd better go see the Zeds. Get the car out."

Saturday night wouldn't turn out to be at all spectacular. A cold drizzle that would continue into the early hours had begun to fall, and the cold could still be felt in the closed car, and the Count longed for the powerful sun that had accompanied his waking up that morning. The rain had emptied the streets, and a grey pall of apathy shrouded a city that lived for the heat and retreated into itself at the slightest cold or drop of water. The languid tropical winter came and went, even in the space of a single day, and it was difficult to work out the time of year: a shit winter, he muttered as he contemplated the boulevard, darkened by clumps of trees, swept by a wind from the sea gusting along paper and dead leaves. Nobody dared sit on the benches on the path down the centre of the avenue the Count thought the most beautiful in Havana and that was now the exclusive preserve of a gritty individual zipped into his windbreaker and engaged in his evening jogging. What strength of will. On such an evening he would have taken a book to bed and been asleep by the third page. On such an evening, he recognized, the cold and the rain irritated people who were condemned to stay indoors: the most easygoing wives could transform a husband's slightest macho thrust into an issue of feminine honour and bring down a flowerpot on his forehead, between steaks, quite remorselessly. Luckily tonight the baseball series would resume after the end-of-year break, but he thought how rain might perhaps lead to the game being called off. His team, the Industriales, which kept him awake worrying at night, were playing in the Latinoamericano Stadium against the Vegueros to decide who would go through to the final championship playoff, because Havana had already qualified. He would have liked the chance to go to the stadium: he needed the group therapy that seemed so much like freedom, where you could say anything, calling the referee's mother a whore or even your team's manager a fucking idiot and then depart sad in defeat or euphoric in victory but relaxed, hoarse and raring to go. Recently the Count was scepticism incarnate: he even tried not to go to baseball games because the Industriales played worse and worse, and luck seemed to have forsaken them, and apart from Vargas and Javier Méndez, the rest seemed second-raters, too weak in the leg to really get them into the final, let alone win it. He had forgotten Zaida and Zoila by the time they drove out on the Malecón. There a briny drizzle met a heavenly shower, and Manolo cursed his fucking luck, thinking he'd damned well have to wash the car before putting it away for the night.

"You not been to the stadium for a long time, Manolo?"

"Why fuck on about the stadium, Conde? What's the point? Look how filthy the car's got, I'm an idiot, I should have gone down Línea," he lamented, turning down G in the direction of Fifth Avenue. They stopped in front of a block of flats and got out of the car.

"The stadium would cure you of such tantrums."

Zaida Lima Ramos lived on the sixth floor, in flat 6D, Lieutenant Mario Conde checked the details and, from the hallway, saw Manolo getting drenched as he took down the radio aerial and smiled:

"Crime prevention, Lieutenant. Last month one was lifted right in front of my house," said Manolo, and they walked towards the lift only to be greeted by a notice that said: BROKEN.

"That's a good start," scowled the Count, heading to the stairs barely lit by a few light bulbs in the exits to some of the floors. As he climbed he breathed through his mouth, panted, and felt his heartbeat quicken from lack of air and his leg muscles go numb with the effort. He thought for a moment how the long-distance runner on the Paseo had got it right, and on the fifth floor he leaned back on the stair-rail, looked at Manolo, at the two remaining flights to the entrance to the sixth floor and waved pathetically, wait, wait, he must catch his breath, nobody would respect a police detective who knocks on their door, tongue hanging out, tears welling up, begging for a glass of water. He wanted to sit down and mechanically retrieved a cigarette from his jacket-pocket but finally decided to let reason

69

triumph. He perched it on his dry, dry lips, didn't light up, and tackled the last flights on that endless staircase.

They came out into a passage that was also in semi-darkness, and found 6D at the far end. Before knocking, the Count decided to light up.

"How are we going to play this?" enquired Manolo before they started their questioning.

"I really want to know what the man's like at work, let's start there. And take it gently, as if it's no big deal, uh-huh? But if necessary, get a bit sharp and to the point."

"Shall we record her?"

He thought for a moment, pressed the bell and said: "Not yet."

The woman looked startled to see them. She was clearly expecting someone else: those two strangers on that rainy cold Saturday evening weren't part of her agenda. Good evening, said the police who introduced themselves, and she said yes, her voice trembling slightly, she was Zaida Lima Ramos. She let them in, even more at a loss, as she tried to smooth down her ruffled hair, perhaps she'd been in bed, she looked sleepy, and they explained the reason for their visit: comrade Rafael Morín, her boss, had disappeared.

"So I heard," she replied, settling into the armchair. She sat down, clasping her legs tight together, and tried to pull down a skirt that barely reached her knees.

The Count noted her thighs were downy, little eddies going upwards, and he tried to rein in the other eddy rising in his imagination. The woman was between twenty-five and thirty, with large dark eyes, a comely mulatta's ample mouth, and the Count decided that even without make-up and with tousled hair she was really beautiful. Her living room was small but was clean and tidy and everything sparkled. The Count registered the multipurpose shelves on the wall opposite the balcony with Sony colour television, Beta videoplayer, stereo recorder and picturesque souvenirs from several parts of the world: a mosaic from Toledo, a little Mexican statue, a miniature Big Ben and Leaning Tower of Pisa, while Zaida explained how Maciques had called on the afternoon of the first, that people were looking for Rafael, she hadn't the slightest idea where he might be and she'd called him several times since, the last time being that afternoon, she was worried, wasn't there any news of Rafael?"

"A nice apartment," the lieutenant commented and on the pretext he was looking for an ashtray his eyes took more liberties as he peered around.

"You gradually collect things," she smiled nervously, "and try to make a pleasant place to live in. The problem is that my son and his friends always turn things upside-down."

"You've a son?"

"Yes, he's twelve."

"Twelve or two?" asked the Count, really confused.

"Twelve, twelve," she repeated. "He just went out with some friends from the block. Just imagine, it's this cold and they want to eat ice-cream at the Coppelia."

"Well, the Chinese say, or at least some do, like one I know who's the father of a colleague, that it's good for you to eat ice-cream when it's cold." He smiled, and Manolo continued to act silent. If only he always acted like that.

"Would you like a coffee?" asked Zaida. She was cold or perhaps afraid and didn't know whether to fold her arms or struggle against her short skirt.

"No thanks, Zaida. We don't want to take up too

much of your time. You were expecting visitors, weren't you? We just want you to tell us a bit about your boss, what you know about him. Anything that might help us find him."

"I don't know, it's seems incredible, impossible Rafael's gone missing. I hope not, but I feel something terrible may . . . No, I don't even want to think about it. He's not gone into hiding, has he? Why should he? You know. It makes no sense. It's all very peculiar. I've been thinking about it these three days and just can't understand. I'll shut the balcony windows. Suddenly it's turned cold, and this house is like an icebox. The sea's right outside and I've got a bit of a headache, too much sleep I reckon . . . But I think I know Rafael well, right, I've worked for him for nine years, that's a fact, I started in the main stores at the ministry, he employed me as a typist and helped me loads. I had no experience and that was when the boy's father went off with the Mariel lot, when I found out he was already there. He was crazy to go like that. He ended up in Miami. He left with another guy, prepared everything behind my back, told me nothing, didn't even say goodbye to his son, well, it was terrible, I don't have to tell you, and, as I could type a bit, and had finished secondary school but had a small kid, and then problems with my family, I don't know, my mother was still angry with me because I'd got pregnant before getting married, and a gentleman who lives near here, on the committee, told me there was a job at his work, in the stores, they needed a typist and that it wasn't difficult, just payrolls and payslips and such like. Sorry I'm always rambling on. Well, the truth is I got started and, as things improved with my mum, I enrolled on a secretarial course at night school and Rafael helped me a lot. He gave me every Saturday off so I could take care of my problems and be with my son, because what with work and school all blessed day, for two years, and when I passed my exams, I got the post of secretary, it was already vacant but he'd kept it for me, because, anyway, I'd been doing the job for some time. Rafael. Just imagine, I've always seen him as a good friend and I don't know how my little story can help you, but he's a good friend, that's for sure, and I couldn't wish for a better, more human, more responsible boss, he looks after everyone, then and now in the enterprise, because, of course, the problem is he asked me to go and work for him in the enterprise where things are much more complicated. He needed people he could trust and it's a tremendous responsibility, almost everything's dollars and deals with foreign firms, you know ... A tremendous responsibility, but he had to have everything shipshape, as they say, and it was never any different, like now, and you know, best of all, as far as I can remember, he's never had problems with any of his workers, if you want, you can ask García, from the union and he'll tell you. No, and that's why I can't understand what's happened now, nothing's any different, we've had lots of work connected to the '89 development plan, and as we often finished late he'd get a driver to bring me home or drive me home himself. I can hardly believe Rafael isn't around someplace, I still can't ... something's happened to him, right? But, you know, just to show you, when Alfredito was six, Alfredito, my kid, got one hell of a temperature and I thought he was going to die, and Rafael acted better than if he'd been the kid's father, got him meat, got him a car to go to the hospital and gave me a full wage, well, that's beside the point, what *is* to the point is the way he behaved and I'm no exception. I always saw him behave like that with everyone, just you ask García, the union steward. The poor . . . Phone? Did he phone me on the first? No, the last time I saw him was on the thirtieth, because he didn't work on the thirty-first, he drove me back here and came up for a coffee and said he was very tired, exhausted was what he said, because we chatted for a while and he gave me a present . . . nothing really, a New Year's Eve gift, you know, we'd been working together for so long, side by side. He's more than my boss, you know, closeness brings on love, right? And he looked so tired. What on earth do you think can have happened?"

"No, don't tell me what you're thinking, wait before you tell me," he begged Manolo as they walked out of the building. A fine monotonous drizzle was still falling, and darkness had descended on the city. "Let's go to Seventy and Seventeenth and see what surprises Zoila has in store."

"You don't want anything to prejudice you?" queried Manolo as he slotted the aerial back in place.

"Hey, man, just give me a break. Leave the aerial in peace, we'll be getting out in a minute."

Manolo carried on as if he'd heard nothing, and while the Count got in the car he put the aerial back. He knew the lieutenant was beginning to get on edge and that it was best to ignore him. You don't want to know what I'm thinking? Well, I won't tell you and stick that . . . But I am thinking lots of things, he said loudly as the car sped up Línea towards the tunnel, and the Count scrawled some notes on his battered writing pad. He started playing with the catch on his pen again and without so much as a by your leave switched off the car radio Manolo had turned on. Nonetheless, Sergeant Manolo confessed he preferred working with his half-neurotic lieutenant and had reached that conclusion when he was a greenhorn cop assigned to a team investigating the theft of various pictures from the National Museum and the forensic worker in the group had said: "Look, the guy who just arrived is the Count. He's in charge of this operation. Don't be put off by anything he says, because he's crazy, but he's a good guy and I think he's the best detective we've got" as Manolo saw for himself on several occasions.

"And might I know your thoughts on the matter?" asked the sergeant, staring at the road ahead.

"No."

"You in crisis, my friend?"

"Yeah, sure. On the verge of a nervous breakdown. Well, I know Rafael Morín and can smell where this is coming from, but there are lots of loose ends and I don't want to prejudge anything."

The car advanced down Nineteenth, and Manolo decided to smoke his first cigarette of the day. I envy this fellow as well, thought the Count, imagine smoking just when you feel like it.

"If you're agonizing about reaching the wrong conclusions, then you really are in crisis," Manolo declared as he turned into Seventy on his way to Seventeenth.

"That's the one," said the Count when he saw house number 568. "Stop here, and if you remove the aerial again, I'll file a disciplinary report, you hear me?"

"Got you. But at least wind up the window properly, if you don't mind?" Manolo shouted as he closed his as tight as it would go.

The light was on in the hallway, but the house door and front windows were shut. The Count knocked, two, three times and waited. Manolo, now by his side, put on his rainproof jacket and tried to zip it up. The lieutenant knocked again and glanced at his colleague still fiddling with his zip.

"Those zips are useless, pal. Let's go, nobody's at home," he said as he hammered on the wooden door again.

The knocks echoed in the distance, as if around an empty house.

"Let's talk to the committee," the lieutenant went on.

They walked along the pavement, looking for the sign for the local Revolutionary Committee, and finally spotted one on the corner, almost hidden by a jungle of box-hedges and dwarf palms in the garden.

"That's the worst of this cold. I'm getting hungrier and hungrier, Count," Manolo lamented his afflictions and begged his boss to make it short and sweet.

"And what do you think I've got in my belly? After what I drank last night, today's fasting and the cigar the Boss gave me, I feel like I've got a dead toad in my gut. I feel as if I'm about to throw up."

He tapped on the glass in the door, a dog started barking, and now Manolo was on edge.

"I tell you, I'm going back to the car," he said, reviewing his unique record of bites on duty.

"Don't be silly, kid, stay still." The door opened.

A black and white dog ran out, ignoring his master's orders. Lion Cub, he called him, fancy calling that funny-coloured mongrel Lion. It was curly tailed and half mulatto, and had ignored Mario Conde and gone straight to sniff Manolo's shoes and trousers, as if they'd once belonged to him.

"He's harmless," the proud owner of the well-behaved dog reassured them. "But he's a good guard dog. How can I help?"

The Count introduced himself and asked for the head of the committee.

"Yours truly, comrade. Would you like to come in?"

"No, that's not necessary. We just want to know if

you've seen Zoila Amarán today. We're looking to ask her a few . . ."

"Is there something the matter?"

"No, just a routine enquiry."

"Well, my friend, I think you're up against it. You'll need a lasso to get a hold on Zoilita, because she hardly shows her face around here," the committee head observed. "Hey, Lion Cub, come here, leave the comrade alone or he'll lock you up," he said with a smile.

"Does she live by herself?"

"Yes and no. Her brother and his wife live in her place, but they are doctors and have just been posted to Pinar del Río, and they visit every two or three months. So she lives by herself and I heard, you know, you find these things out without trying. I think it was today when I was getting bread from the corner store that she'd told someone she was going away and she's not been sighted for three days."

"Three days?" asked the Count, smiling at the relief on Manolo's face when Lion Cub finally lost interest in his shoes and trousers and scampered into the garden.

"Yes, three days or so. But, you know, to be frank, and this is a fact: ever since she's been a kid – and I've watched her grow up right here – Zoilita's been a tearaway, and not even her mother, the late Zoila, could keep track of her. I even thought she'd turn out a tomboy, but no way. OK, she's not done anything wrong, has she? She might be half-mad, but I can honestly say she's not a bad girl."

The Count listened to the man expressing his opinions while he searched his jacket pocket for a cigarette. His brain wanted to weigh up the fact Zoila hadn't been back home for precisely three days, although suddenly he was feeling weary of all this, of Zaida and

Maciques defending Rafael, of Zoila and the Spaniard Dapena, who'd also vanished on the first, of Tamara and Rafael, but he replied: "No, don't worry, there's nothing wrong. We only wanted to find out a couple of other things: how old is Zoilita and where does she work?"

The committee head rested his forearm on the doorframe, watched Lion Cub shit copiously and pleasurably in the garden and smiled.

"I don't remember her exact age; I'd have to look on the register . . ."

"No need, more or less," said Manolo, coming back to life.

"About twenty-three, I'd guess," he said. "As you get older, a twenty-year-old seems much the same as a thirty-year-old, you know? And as for your other question: well she works at home, makes arty-crafty objects from seeds and shells and earns good money and only works when she has to. You can imagine, around New Year she rakes it in. You can't find anything to buy then, you know?"

"Very good, comrade, many thanks," said the Count, stemming the flow of words that threatened to drown them. "We'll just ask you for one favour. When she comes, call us on this number and leave a message for Lieutenant Conde or Sergeant Palacios. Is that OK?"

"On the contrary, comrades, it's a real pleasure. We are here to serve you, naturally. But, I must say, Lieutenant, it's strange you won't come in for a sit-down and a cup of freshly made coffee? I thought when two policemen visited a Revolutionary Committee that always had to happen."

"So did I, but not to worry. There are also police who are scared of dogs," said the Count as he shook the man's hand.

"That was nice of you," griped Manolo as they walked to their car. He was wearing his jacket open to the cold air. "You're very witty today. As if not facing up to dogs were a sin."

"That must be why they bite you. Look what a sweat you're in, kid."

"Yes, it's all very well to go on about adrenaline, smell and your fucking mother, but the fact is they always go for me."

They got into the car; Manolo took a deep breath and put both hands on the wheel.

"Well, we now have some idea about who Zoilita is. The plot thickens."

"The plot thickens, but it makes no odds. Look, let's divide up now. I'll go to collect the guest list for the deputy minister's party and you put two people on task to find out about Zaida and Zoilita. Particularly Zoilita. I want to know where she's got to and what she's got to do with all this."

"Why don't we switch tasks? I'll collect the list, go on."

"Hey, Manolo, you can play with the chain but leave the monkey in peace. No more griping," he said and looked into the street. He was fascinated by the steady flow of white lines the car was devouring, and only then did he notice it had stopped raining. But the pain from his hungry misused stomach now met the pressure from the urine filling his bladder. "What else are you thinking of doing?"

Manolo kept staring at the road ahead.

"I'm talking to you, Manolo," insisted the Count.

"Well, I reckon there are too many bloody coincidences, and Zoilita's much too much of a coincidence, don't you think? And I reckon you should talk to Maciques. That man knows more than he's letting on."

"We'll see him at the enterprise on Monday."

"I'd see him before then."

"Tomorrow if there's time, OK?"

"Hey, let's have some music, I'm going to piss myself."

"You can piss yourself, but I can't put any music on."

"What's a matter, man, you still shaking because of that mongrel?"

"No, it's your fault we can't listen to music. They stole our aerial from in front of Zoilita's place."

His favourite song had always been "Strawberry Fields". He'd discovered it one unexpected day in 1967 or 1968 in his cousin Juan Antonio's house; it was horribly hot, but Juan Antonio and three of his friends were older, in eighth grade, and they'd squeezed into his cousin's bedroom, he recalled, as if they were going to pray to the prophet: they were sitting on the floor around an ancient RCA Victor gramophone, it even had termites, and an opaque, unidentified record was turning on the deck. "It's a copy, idiot, of course it's not got a label," said Juan Antonio as bad-temperedly as ever, and he also sat on the floor because nobody wanted to speak, not even the women. Then Tomy moved the arm and placed it lovingly on the record, and the song began; he understood nothing, the Beatles didn't sing as well as they did on real records, but the big lads hummed the words, as if they knew them, and all he knew was that "field" was park, "centerfield" was centre of the park, he concluded, but that would come later. He felt as if he were experiencing a unique act of magic, and when the song finished he asked, go on, play it again, Tomy. And he started singing again and didn't know why: he didn't want to accept that that melody was flagging up his nostalgia for a past when everything was perfect and straightforward, and although he now knew what the lyrics meant, he preferred to repeat them unthinkingly and just feel as if he were walking through that field of strawberries he'd never seen, the one his memories were so familiar with, to be alone with that music. "Strawberry Fields" always came like that, out of nowhere, and pushed everything else out. He sang along, picked up on any phrase and felt better; he no longer saw the dark or gloomily overcast sky or the image of Rafael Morín speechifying on the podium at school. He didn't want to smoke and listen to Manolo recounting his latest amorous conquest, as he drove him to Tamara's house, "Strawberry fields forever, tum, tum, tum . . ."

"The book was right there."

Time is an illusion; nothing had changed in the library: the complete set of the *Espasa-Calpe Encyclopaedia*, the one most packed with knowledge, its dark blue spines and gilt letters still shiny despite the years that had gone by; Tamara's father's Doctor in Law certificate still fearlessly enjoying its privileged position, even above Victor Manuel's two pen-and-ink drawings he'd always coveted so much. The dark tome of Father Brown stories, with the leather covers that his fingers caressed, brought on another bout of melancholy; old Doctor Valdemira recommended them to him so many years ago when the Count could never have imagined he'd become a colleague of Chesterton's little priest. And the mahogany desk was immortal, broad as a desert and beautiful like a woman. A handsome writing desk. Only the leather on the swivel chair seemed rather tired, it was over thirty years old and genuine bison; that was the place occupied by the person responsible for night-time revision before an exam, the privilege of the one who knew most. The day Mario Conde first entered that room, he had felt small, helpless and terribly uncultured, and his memory could still recreate that painful sensation of intellectual inadequacy he'd yet to cure himself of.

"I've often dreamed of this place. But in my dreams I never remembered your father having a telephone here, or did he?"

"No, never. Daddy hated two things to the point of sickness: one was the telephone and the other television, and that shows how very sensitive he was," she recalled as she flopped down into one of the armchairs in front of the desk.

"And do those two phobias relate to this redbrick fireplace in a Havana library?" he asked as he bent down over the small hearth and played with one of the tongs.

"It had logs and everything. It's pretty, isn't it?"

"Sorry to sound rude . . . Given it never snows in Cuba, pray what is the point?"

She smiled sadly.

"It was the cover to a safe. I found that out when I was twenty. Daddy was a real character. An eccentric."

He put the tongs down and sat in the other armchair next to Tamara. The library's only source of light was from a small Art Nouveau lamp on a bronze stand embellished by small bunches of deep purple grapes, and she was bathed in an amber light that endowed her face with a warm humanity. She wore a tracksuit as deep blue as the *Espasa-Calpe*, and her clumsy ballerina body seemed to relish that garment which sheathed and shaped her.

"Rafael had the extension installed some seven or eight years ago. *He* couldn't live without the telephone."

He digested Rafael's decision and felt his shoulders sag, exhausted by an overlong day when he'd only heard talk of Rafael Morín. So many people had talked to him that he'd now begun to wonder whether he'd really known him or whether he was a circus freak with a thousand faces, all linked by a family air, but quite distinctive. He'd have preferred to speak about other things, would have felt good telling her he'd sung "Strawberry Fields" all the way to her house. He was in the mood to make that kind of confidence or to tell her he thought she'd only got better and better, tastier and tastier, but finally decided she might think such confessions a touch cheap and vulgar.

"I never heard about your father's death. I'd have gone to the funeral," he said finally, because the old diplomat's presence was tangible in that room.

"Not to worry," she said, swaying her head, which sufficed to stir her lock of hair and make it flop over her forehead. "It was a tremendous shock, you can't imagine. It was hard accepting Daddy had died, you know?"

He nodded and wanted to smoke. Death always brought on a desire for a smoke. He found an earthenware ashtray on the desk and was happy it wasn't Murano glass or a Moser or a Sargadelos, hand engraved from Doctor Valdemira's collection. In the meantime, she'd stood up and walked over to the mini-bar built into one of the library bookcases.

"I'll join you for a drink. I think we both need one," she pouted as she poured liquid from an almost square bottle into two tall glasses. "I don't know about you, but I like it neat, without ice. Ice only cuts a good Scotch whisky down to size."

"It's Ballantine's, isn't it?"

"Yes, a special reserve Rafael had," she said, giving him his glass. "Good health and good luck."

"Health for you and pesetas for the safe, because you have beauty in good supply," he replied, savouring the whisky and feeling its warmth run down over his tongue, throat, empty stomach, and he began to perk up.

"Who is Zoila, Mario?"

He opened his jacket and took a second sip.

"Was he carrying on with other women?"

"I'm not sure, but the truth is I was less and less interested in following Rafael's tracks and have no idea what he did with his life."

"What do you mean?"

"That Rafael was hardly ever at home. He was always in meetings or travelling, and I wasn't interested in keeping track of him, but now I want to know. Who is Zoila?"

"We don't know yet. She's not been home for several days. We're investigating her."

"And do you really think that Rafael is . . .?" and she seemed really shocked.

He was at a loss and felt uneasy. Her look demanded an answer.

"I don't know, Tamara, that's why I asked you about his womanising. You're the one who should be telling me."

She sipped her drink and then tried – unsuccessfully – to smile.

"I'm really at a loss, you know. All this is like a bad joke and sometimes I think no, it's not a nightmare, no, Rafael is on his travels again, that nothing is

84

happening, nothing will happen, and any minute he will walk through that door," she said, and he couldn't stop himself: he looked at the door. "I need security, Mario, I can't live with insecurity, do you understand?"

She asked the question, and of course, it was easy to understand her security, he thought, as he watched her take another sip and felt the warm flow of whisky and lowered the zip on his coat to a frankly dangerous level: he wanted to look, tried to concentrate on his drink but couldn't and looked because he felt an erection coming on. Why might that be? He tried to explain the mystery: people didn't swoon when they saw Tamara walk down the street yet he stopped breathing, had never been able to see off the desire that woman provoked. So now he crossed his legs in order to submit his urges to the obligatory application of the universal law of gravity. Down, boy.

"I don't think Rafael was, I really don't. Perhaps he bedded a woman from time to time? Look, quite frankly, I don't really know, but I expect he did. You love doing that kind of thing, don't you? But I don't think he'd dare to go into hiding with a woman. I think I know him too well to imagine him trying that."

"I agree. I don't think he would," he insisted, quite convinced; he wasn't going to leave all this in the air, and Zoilita wasn't the Duchess of Windsor. Some things I don't know but I am sure of that much, he thought.

"And what else have you discovered?"

"That Dapena the Spaniard went crazy when he saw you."

Her eyes opened. How can she open them so wide, he wondered, and then she raised her voice, sounded upset, annoyed, not what you call poised.

"Who told you?"

"Maciques."

"What a gossip . . . And they go on about women."

"And what happened between you and the Spaniard, Tamara?"

"Nothing. It was a misunderstanding. So is that all you've found out?" And she took another sip.

He rested his chin on the palm of his hand and got another whiff of her. He was starting to feel so good it was frightening.

"Right, not so very much. I think we've spent the day going round in circles. This job is trickier than you can imagine."

"No, I can, and particularly since I'm one of the suspects."

"I never said that, Tamara, you know I didn't. Technically you're a suspect because you're the person closest to him. You last had news of him, and God knows how many reasons you have or might have to want to get Rafael off your back. I told you this is an investigation and might be quite upsetting."

She finished her drink and put the glass down next to the light that was illuminating her.

"Mario, don't you think that's a silly thing to say to me?"

"And why did you always call me Mario and not the Count like everybody else in the class?"

"And why change the subject? I'm really worried you can think such things about me."

"How else can I put it to you? You know, do you think it's one big party spending your life like this? That's it a hoot working with murderers, thieves, fraudsters and rapists and that you're always going to think the best of people and be as nice as pie?"

She forced her lips into a brief smile while her hand

86

tried to tidy away the disrespectful twisted lock that insisted on darkening her forehead.

"The Count, right? Tell me, why did you join the police? So you could grouch and whinge all day long?"

He smiled: he couldn't stop himself. It was the question he'd most been asked in his years as a detective and the second time of asking that day. He thought she deserved an answer.

"That's an easy one. There are two reasons why I am a policeman: one I don't know, and the other has to do with destiny which has led me this way."

"And the one you know?" she insisted, and he felt the woman's expectations rise and was sorry to disappoint her.

"It's quite simple, Tamara, and will probably make you laugh, but it's true: because I don't like bastards going unpunished."

"How very self-righteous of you," she replied after considering all that lay behind his answer and picking up her glass. "But you're a sorry policeman, and that's not the same as a sad policeman . . . Would you like another?"

He studied the bottom of his glass and hesitated. He liked the distinctive taste of Scotch whisky and would always be ready to fight to the death for a bottle of Ballantine's, and he felt so good, next to her, surrounded by those wise library shadows, and she looked so ravishing. And answered:

"No, that's OK, I've not had breakfast yet."

"Do you want something to eat?"

"I do and need it bad, but thanks all the same, I've got a date," he almost lamented. "They're expecting me at Skinny's."

"As thick as thieves as ever," she smiled.

"Hey, I didn't ask after your son," he said as he stood up.

"Just imagine, with this palaver . . . No, around mid-day I told Mima to take him to his Aunt Teruca's, over in Santa Fe, at least till Monday or till we know something. I think he'd find this upsetting . . . Mario, what on earth has happened to Rafael?" And she now stood up and folded her arms over her chest, as if the spirit of the whisky had suddenly abandoned her and she felt very cold.

"If only we knew, Tamara. But get used to the idea: whatever it is, it's nasty. Can you give me the list of guests at the party?"

She didn't react, as if she'd not heard him, and then unfolded her arms.

"Here it is," she replied, looking for a piece of paper under a magazine. "I put down all the ones I remember, I don't think I missed anyone out."

He took the sheet and walked over to the lamp. He slowly read the names, surnames and positions held by the guests.

"There's nobody like me there, is there?" he asked and then looked at her. "No sorry policeman?"

She folded her arms back over her chest and stared into the fireplace, as if asking it to do the impossible and bring forth heat.

"I realized this morning how much you've changed, Mario. Why are you so bitter? Why speak of yourself self-pityingly, as if everyone else was a bastard, and you were the purest and the poorest?"

He took her abuse and felt he'd got it all wrong about her; she was still an intelligent woman. He felt weak and vulnerable and needed to sit down, drink another whisky and talk and talk. But he was afraid to.

"I don't know, Tamara. Let's talk about it some other time."

"I think you're trying to run away."

"A policeman never runs away, he simply ups and takes his happiness with him."

"There's no cure, then."

"And no getting better."

"Well, please tell me if you do find anything," she said as they walked down the passage. She still had her arms folded, and Mario Conde, after winking at the ruddy exuberant Flora framed and hanging on the best wall in the room, wondered how Tamara Valdemira could possibly spend her time in a house that was so empty. Looking at herself in the mirror?

Skinny Carlos is in the centre of the group. Arms splayed out, head tilting to the right, as if crucified, although at the time he didn't think he'd ever be bearing a cross. He always fixed it so he was in the centre, in order to be the centre, or perhaps we nudged that way to turn him into the group's navel, where he and we could feel good. He could deliver a joke a minute, make a wisecrack about the silliest thing that would drop from anyone else's mouth like a lead balloon and earn a couple of polite smiles. He wore his hair long; I don't how he managed to get through school-gate inspections; he was still very skinny, although we were in thirteenth grade and that day we'd done our university pre-enrolment. For his first choice he'd put civil engineering; he dreamed of building an airport, two bridges, and most of all, creating the design for a contraceptive factory, with distinctive production lines according to size, colour, taste and shape, able to meet all the requirements of the Caribbean, the place on earth where people screwed the best and the most, for that was his obsession: getting laid. His second choice was industrial engineering. Between Skinny and Rabbit, Dulcita was then Skinny's fiancé, and if Skinny hadn't been crucified, he'd surely have been touching her up and she'd be smiling, for she too liked a touch of porn. Her skirt, with the three white stripes on the hem, was the shortest of the lot, well above the knee: she was the most expert at rolling it up round the waist as soon as she set a foot outside school; her knees were rounded, her thighs compact and long, her legs appeared well-thrown and handmade, and her buttocks – as Skinny would say, using one of his catastrophically poetic similes – were as hard as hunger at five am, and yet all that was balanced out, compensated as it were, he added, by her not having an inch of tit. Dulcita is smiling happily because she's sure she's going for architecture to work with Skinny on his projects, and she'll do the designs. And as second choice, she chose geology, since she was crazy about going into caves, especially with Skinny, to satisfy their joint obsession: a good lay. At the time Dulcita was perfect: she'd kill to help you, a terrific friend, sharp, intelligent and never stopped for anything: she'd bail you out in an exam or soften a girl up for you. She was top mate, a real good gal, and I never understood why she went to the United States. When they told me, I couldn't believe it; she was one of us, what's happened . . .? Rabbit can't avoid displaying his teeth. God knows whether he ever laughed, with those teeth-and-a half you never knew; he too was very skinny and had gone for a history degree as his first choice and for teaching history as a second, and at the time he was quite convinced that if the English hadn't left Havana in 1763, Elvis Presley would probably have been born in Pinar del Río, or River Pine City, or whatever the hell he'd have said, in those cane-cutter's boots that were his school shoes, for going out every night as well as to Saturday-night parties. He was really thin, because he had no choice in the matter; in his place they chewed cable, not literally, but real cable, the ones Goyo brought from his work as an electrician; he'd say, spaghetti cable, cable and chips, cable croquettes. Tamara looks serious though she always looks best like that: she's more ... beautiful? The light brown lock of hair hanging languidly and rebelliously over her forehead and her right eye giving her airs of Van Gult's *Honorata*, and there right next to Dulcita, they'd say Dulcita was always better, but Tamara's something else, more than beautiful, nice and tasty, as delicious as the crack of a baseball cleanly hit, hot enough to give Mahomet a hard-on: but, no, you felt like eating her bit by bit, clothes and all, I told Skinny once, even if I'd shit rags for a week. And you also felt like sitting with her on a manicured lawn one afternoon, all alone, and leaning your head back on her bounteous thighs, lighting a cigarette, hearing the birds chirp and enjoying happiness. She'd chosen dentistry as her first choice and medicine as second, and it's a pity to see her looking so serious, as if the future dentist had teeth that would never visit a dentist, and Rabbit would be her first customer, when I get you in my chair, she'd say, I'll do my doctorate trying to get your buckteeth under control. My awful face hasn't changed a bit: I'm on the far right, next to Tamara naturally, as always whenever possible; and look, with my trousers cut round the knee so my mum can turn the leg upside down, with the knee which is broader at the bottom and the bottom which is narrower sewn at the knee, it being the only way to get a spot of flares, which were the rage then. And gym shoes without socks, both patched over the toes: mine are crooked and always poked a hole through the same place: I'm also smiling, but it's a forced smile, only halfway across the lips, on my starving scary face, with bags under my eyes, and I'm thinking I'm sure I won't get literature, for they've almost shut down literary studies this year, I'm in a good position but it's a lottery and I so much want to get in, and I put down psychology for second choice and not dentistry. That was Tamara's fault, for I can't stand the sight of blood so perhaps history would be a better option like for Rabbit, I don't know, a psychology degree leads to somewhere, but I never knew how to decide. Taking decisions was always torture, and it makes sense that I didn't feel like laughing in that photo we took coming down the steps at high school, on the eve of our final exams that we were all going to pass because in thirteenth grade they don't fail anyone, unless there's another Viboragate scandal and they set special exams in order to fuck us up, as happened to thirteenth grade last year, to Dulcita who's so intelligent but is repeating a year because of all that, but we would pass, for sure. On the back of the photo it says June 1975, we were all still very poor – that is, almost all of us – and very happy. Skinny is skinny. Tamara is more than beautiful, Dulcita is one of us, Rabbit is dreaming of changing history, and I'm on my way to being a writer like Hemingway. The photo has yellowed with age: it got wet one day and one corner is cracked, and when I look at it I get a real guilty conscience because Skinny is skinny no more and Rafael Morín is the invisible presence lurking behind the camera.

He pressed the bell four times, thumped on the

door, shouted. There was nobody at home, and he jumped up and down, the almost palpable lavatory had aroused an urgent desire to piss, he couldn't hold on and thumped on the door again.

"I'm hungry, so hungry and nearly pissing myself," the Count blurted out before greeting her or kissing her on the forehead and then rushing to lower his head to receive her womanly kiss. It was a tradition from the time when Skinny Carlos was very skinny and the Count spent every day in that house, and they played ping-pong and tried with dubious success to learn how to dance and studied physics in the early hours before their exams. But Skinny Carlos was skinny no more, and only he persisted in calling him that. Skinny Carlos now weighed in at more than two hundred pounds and moved around in fits and starts in a wheelchair. In 1981, in Angola, he'd got a bullet in the back, waist-high, and it severed his spinal cord. None of the five operations he'd undergone since had improved things, and Skinny awoke each morning with a new pain, another nerve or muscle that had been stilled forever.

"Hey, my boy, you look bloody awful," said Josefina when she saw him coming out of the lavatory and handed him a glass of watery coffee.

"I'm on my last legs, Jose, and incredibly hungry." And gave her the glass back after taking only one sip of coffee.

Much relieved and cigarette already lit, he entered his friend's room. Skinny was in his wheelchair, in front of the television and looking worried.

"They say they're seeing to the ground, and the game will go ahead. Hey, no, for Christ's sake, no," he protested as he saw his friend unwrapping a bottle of rum.

"We need to talk, my brother, and I need two shots of rum. If you don't . . ."

"Fuck, you'll be the death of me," rasped Skinny, and he started to swing his chair round. "Don't give me any ice, that Santa Cruz is so sweet."

The Count left the room and came back carrying two glasses and a corkscrew.

"Well, how are things going?"

"I've just been to Tamara's, Skinny, I swear to you, the wench is hotter than ever. She doesn't get older. She just gets better."

"Women are like that. Do you still want to marry her?"

"Fuck off. You're right about this rum. It's really good."

"My friend, take it gently today. You look really shit."

"It's a combination of sleep deprivation, hunger and incipient baldness," he said, pointing to his receding hairline before taking another sip. "No news, the man's still missing and no clue as to where the fuck he's got to or why he's vanished, whether he's dead or alive . . ."

Skinny was still edgy. He glanced at the television where they were showing music videos until the baseball game started. Of the people the Count knew, Skinny was, and by a long chalk compared to himself, the one who most agonized over baseball, ever since he'd been skinny and centerfield in the high school team. The Count had only seen him cry twice, and twice it had been brought on by baseball and his lament was a bolero, with big tears and sobs, and he became inconsolable.

"Well, doesn't life take funny old turns?" Skinny Carlos remarked as he looked back at his friend. "You looking for Rafael Morín."

"Not that many turns, Skinny, you know. He's exactly the same, an opportunist bastard who's really wheeled and dealed to get to where he's got."

"Hey, not so, my friend," retorted Skinny after lighting his cigarette. "Rafael knew what he wanted and went for it, and was made of the right stuff. It wasn't for nothing that he got the best marks at high school and then in industrial engineering. When I went into the civil side, he was already being talked up like the star act at the circus. He was phenomenal: almost top marks right from year one."

"Are *you* going to start defending him now?" asked the Count, looking incredulous.

"Hey, I don't know what's happened now, nor do you, and you're the policeman. But things aren't so simple, pal. The fact is he was good at school and, you know, I for one reckon he didn't need to cheat at the exams when the Viboragate scandal broke."

The Count ran a hand through his hair and couldn't repress a smile.

"Fucking shit, Skinny, Viboragate. I thought nobody remembered that."

"If I wasn't on my hobbyhorse, I think I would have forgotten it," replied Skinny, pouring more rum out. "You get me going. You know, Miki dropped by this afternoon. He came to see me because he's going to Germany and wanted to know if I needed anything, and while he was about it he asked me to lend him ten pesos. But I told him about the Rafael business, and he said you should make sure you go to see him."

"Why? Does he know something?"

"No, he only found out when I told him and it was then he said you should contact him. You know Miki's always been a bit of a mystery."

"And did Rafael survive Viboragate with a clean bill of health?"

"Pour yourself some more if it improves your thinking. Right, he didn't have problems, when the headmaster got the push, he was already at university, and the guy who almost got the rap was Armandito Fonseca, the student president for that year, right?"

"Naturally, the shit went close, but it didn't stick. Didn't I tell you?"

Skinny shook his head, as if trying to say "you're beyond the pale" but then added:

"That's enough of that, Conde, you don't know if he was involved or not, and the fact is they didn't accuse him of fixing marks or letting out exam papers or anything like that. What always bugged you was that he fucked Tamara and you only jerked off thinking of her.

"And what made *your* hands so sore, too much groping in the playground?"

"And it also bugged you a lot, you told me as much, the fact we couldn't study in Daddy Valdemira's library anymore because Rafael had claimed that as his own . . ."

The Count stood up and walked over to Skinny Carlos. He stuck out his index finger and placed it between his friend's eyebrows.

"Hey, are you with the Indians or the Cowboys? You know, I can't curse your mother because she's getting my dinner ready. But I can piss on you, easy as pie. Since when have you been a card-carrying time-server, hey?"

"I hope he gets it where it really hurts," said Skinny, slapping the Count's arm and starting to laugh. It was a body-shaking guffaw, rising from his gut, shaking all his huge, limp, almost useless body, a deep visceral laugh that threatened to kill off his wheelchair, flatten walls and hit the street, turn corners, open doors and make Lieutenant Mario Conde collapse in stitches on his ass on his bed begging for another shot of rum to deal with the bout of coughing. They were laughing as if they'd just learned how, and Josefina, drawn by the din, looked at them from the doorway, and her face was deeply gloomy behind the hint of a smile: she'd have given anything, her own life, her good health which was now beginning to fail her, for nothing to have happened and for those men who were laughing still to be boys who always laughed like that, even if they had no reason, if only for the pleasure of laughing.

"All right, that's enough," she said and walked into the room. "Time to eat. It's almost nine o'clock."

"Yes, mother darling, I'm the walking wounded," said the Count and went over to Skinny's wheelchair.

"Hey, just wait a minute," asked Carlos when the music stopped on the telly and the presenter's over-eager smile appeared on the screen.

"Dear viewers," said the woman, who wanted to look enthused and so happy at what she was about to say, "conditions are practically right in the Latino-americano Stadium to kick off the first game in the Industriales-Vegueros playoffs. While we wait for that interesting game to start, we will continue with our musical offerings."

She concluded, froze her synthetic smile and pre-served it stoically for the video of another song, by another singer no one was interested in, which now filled the small screen.

"Come on, let's go," Skinny suggested, and his friend pushed his wheelchair toward the dining room. "Do you think the Industriales stand a chance?"

"Without Marquetti and Medina and with Javier Méndez injured? No, wild man, I think they've had it," opined the Count, and his friend shook his head disconsolately. He suffered before and after each game, even when the Industriales won, for he thought that if they won that one, they were more likely to lose the next, and he suffered eternally, in spite of all his promises to be less fanatical and to ditch baseball: it wasn't what it used to be, he would say, when Capiró, Chávez, Changa Mederos and Co played. But both knew they were incurable and the one most infected was Skinny Carlos.

They went over to the table and the Count analysed Josefina's offering: the traditional black beans; pork steaks in breadcrumbs, well done but juicy all the same, as the golden rule for fillets required; the grains of rice separating out in the dish, as pure white and tender as a virgin bride; a green salad, artfully displayed with a careful combination of red and green, the golden glow of ripe tomatoes and bunches of fried, curved green plantain. And on the table another bottle of Rumanian wine, red, dry and almost perfect plonk.

"Jose, for heaven's sake, what have we got here?" asked the Count as he bit into a fried plantain and spoiled the beautiful salad by plundering a slice of tomato. "A plague on anyone who mentions work," he warned and began to pile a mountain of food on his plate, determined to down at one sitting breakfast, lunch and dinner on a day that looked to be never-ending – or whatever – and then he gorged himself.

Mario Conde was born in a bustling dusty barrio that, according to family lore, was founded by his paternal great-great grandfather, a madcap islander who preferred to set up home, create a family and await death on barren land far from the sea and rivers and far from the arm of the law which was still pursuing him in Madrid, Las Palmas and Seville. The barrio where the Condes lived had never been elegant or prosperous, yet it expanded exponentially with the offspring of that crooked, absolutely plebeian Canary Islander who was so infatuated with his new name and his Cuban wife that he fathered eighteen children and forced them all to swear, each at the appropriate moment, to beget at least ten children and compelled the females to give their whelps the first surname of Conde as their badge of distinction in the barrio. When Mario celebrated his third birthday and his Granddaddy Rufino the Count first told him of Granddad Teodoro's adventures and his desire to found a dynasty, the kid also discovered that a pit for fighting cocks could also be the centre of the universe. At the time baseball was a vice he'd picked up in the barrio, while fighting cocks were an endemic pleasure. His Granddaddy Rufino, an enthusiastic breeder, trainer and gambler when it came to fighting cocks, took him to all the local pits and yards and taught him the art of preparing a cock to win every time: by first showering it with the finest, most sporting attentions a boxer could ever receive, and then anointing it with oil the moment before it stepped in to the arena so it would never be caught by its opponent. Granddaddy Rufino's philosophy of never playing unless you were sure you would win gave the lad the satisfaction of seeing the cock he'd first met as a very ordinary egg die an old bird, winner of thirty-two contests and coverer of an innumerable quantity of hens as lively, if not livelier than himself. In those easygoing times of school in the mornings and work with cocks in the afternoons, Mario Conde also learned the meaning of the word "love": he loved his granddaddy and was so miserable he was ill when old Rufino died, three years after the official outlawing of cockfights.

Now he'd satisfied the need for cold water that had almost dragged him from his bed, the Count began that Sunday morning by indulging in memories of his grandfather. Sunday was the day for fights in the most popular pits, and that was why he liked Sunday mornings. Not the dreary endless afternoons after a siesta when he would feel tired and sleepy till nightfall, nights weren't any better, everywhere was packed out and he'd always take refuge at Skinny's. However, there were other things that made Sunday nights tedious and drawn-out: there was no baseball game, and it was torture to hit the rum when Monday loomed menacingly. Mornings were a different story: Sunday mornings started with lots of hustle and bustle as in the story he wrote when he was at high school. It was a time to talk to everyone, and friends and relatives who lived away always came to visit the family, and you could set up a game of barehanded baseball and end up swollen-fingered and panting at first base, or play dominos or simply shoot the breeze on the street corner till the sun chased you inside. For some ancestral reason he couldn't explain and because of the large number of Sundays he spent with Granddaddy Rufino or his band of sporting cronies, Mario Conde enjoyed Sunday at leisure in the barrio more than any of his pals, and after a cup of coffee he'd go and buy bread and the newspaper and generally never returned home till it was time for a very late Sunday lunch. His women had never understood that necessary ritual, why can't you stay at home the odd Sunday, there's lots to do, but Sunday is for the barrio, he told them, leaving no room for argument, when some friend asked: "Hey, has the Count left yet?"

And that Sunday he got up after slaking a dragon's thirst, with memories of granddaddy still floating around his head, and went onto the porch after putting the coffee pot on to boil. He was still wearing his pyjama trousers and an old padded coat, and he noticed the streets were quieter than usual for a Sunday because of the cold. The sky had cleared during the night, but an annoyingly biting wind was blowing, and he reckoned it had gone below fifty and was perhaps the coldest morning of the winter. As usual he regretted having to work on a Sunday. He had thought he'd go and see Rabbit and then lunch at his sister's, he recalled, and he waved at Cuco the butcher: How's life treating you, Condesito? He too must work that Sunday morning.

Coffee bubbled up like lava from the innards of his coffeepot, and the Count put four spoonfuls of sugar into a jug. Waited for the pot to percolate all the coffee, poured it in the jug and stirred slowly, relishing the hot bitter smell. Then returned it to the pot before pouring the coffee into his thermos and serving himself a large cup of coffee. He sat in his small dining room and lit the first cigarette of the day. He felt terrifyingly alone and decided to ward off melancholy by thinking what to do with the list of guests at the deputy minister's New Year party. He anticipated he had a number of tricky interrogations ahead, the kind he'd rather avoid. Zoilita still hadn't put in an appearance – he'd not had a call from headquarters – and she'd been gone four days, like Rafael. He couldn't go to the enterprise till the following morning, and that blocked one avenue he was keen explore. He'd not heard anything from the provinces, or from the coastguards, who could have contacted him at any time, so there was still no trace of the man who'd vanished into thin air. And what about the Spaniard Dapena? *Mañana*: the usual story. Hunting tit in Key Largo . . . But he did have work that Sunday and, sipping a cup of coffee that aroused his palate and intellect, he decided to give himself more time for thought: he wanted to put himself in Rafael Morín's shoes, although he'd never before believed that was even remotely possible; he should feel what a person like that felt, should want what he wanted, which was a sight easier, and generate at least one idea about his startling disappearance, but he couldn't. Rafael wasn't one of the criminals he encountered daily, and it was giving him detective's block. He preferred home-grown wide boys, smugglers of whatever, traffickers in the unusual and fences of the most exotic merchandise, he knew their habits and could discern a logic to guide his investigations. Not now: now I'm lost on the prairie, he said, crushing his cigarette end in the ashtray and deciding it was time to call Manolo and go out onto the street, on a Sunday that seemed ideal for shooting the breeze on street corners, catching a little sun and listening to stories told time and again by his old friends.

He poured himself a less generous second cup of coffee, thanked his stomach for sparing him a punitive ulcer, lit up again and walked into his bedroom, congratulating himself on the quality of his lungs. He sat on his bed, by the telephone, and watched Rufino, his fighting fish, embark on a solitary circular dance. He then looked at his empty room and felt he too was circling round and round, in an attempt to find the tangent to take him out of that infinite circle of anguish.

"We're well and truly fucked, Rufino," he said, then dialled Manolo's number and heard it ring. "Hello," said a woman's voice as she picked up the receiver.

"Alina? It's the Count, how are you?" he enquired fearfully, for he was familiar with that lady's stress with telephones and before she could reply he jumped in: "Your son up yet? Get him on that phone, tell him I'm in a hurry."

"Ah, Manolito. Hey, Count, he stayed over at Vilma's, his current girl friend, you . . ."

A good catch, he felt like saying, but he took the easy option:

"Look, Alina, do me a favour. Call him and tell him to pick me up in half an hour. It's urgent business. You OK? See you and thanks, Alina." He sighed and hung up.

He drank his coffee slowly. Was fascinated by the ease with which Manolo switched girlfriends and persuaded them to let him sleep over. He, however, was enduring a long spell of solitary, and although he'd have preferred not to, he thought of Tamara, saw her in the tight-fitting tracksuit or yellow dress, marking out her knickers, and she was mouth-watering. Perhaps Manolo and the Boss were right: he should watch out for himself, and he thought he'd prefer not to see her or talk to her again, to keep her far from his mind and avoid frustrations like the previous night's, not even the drinking session with Skinny had tamed his desires, and he'd finished off the night by masturbating in honour of that unforgivable woman. Only then had he been able to get to sleep.

This is where Rafael Morín came from, he muttered as he walked towards the room at the back. Fame and paint had long deserted the big house on the Avenue of October Tenth, now a creaking sweaty ruin, where each room in the ancient mansion was an individual home with a communal bathroom and washhouse at the back, flaking walls with generations of graffiti, an ever-present smell of gas and a long overburdened washing line on that Sunday morning. "The pit and the peak," quipped Manolo, and he was right. That dark promiscuous rooming house seemed so remote from the residence on Santa Catalina that one could easily think they were separated by oceans, mountains and deserts and centuries of history. But Rafael Morín had been born on this shore, in room number seven, right at the back, next to the communal bathroom and washhouse now occupied by two women unafraid of the cold or life's other contingencies.

They greeted the women and knocked on the door of number seven. The latter looked at them, recognized their business and policemen's airs, had no doubt heard of Rafael's disappearance and returned to their washing only when the door opened.

"Hello, María Antonia," said the lieutenant.

"Hello," the old woman replied, and her eyes had a scared, hunted-animal look. The Count knew she was barely sixty, but life had dealt her such hard knocks she seemed more like eighty, long-suffering and with no will to keep going.

"I'm Lieutenant Mario Conde," he said, showing his card, "and this is Sergeant Manuel Palacios. We're responsible for your son's case."

"Please do come in and ignore the mess, I'm like that . . ."

The room was smaller than Tamara's father's library yet contained a double bed, a cabinet, a sideboard, an armchair, a dressing-table chair and a colour television on a small wrought-iron table. A curtain hung down by the television, and the Count imagined it must hide the way to the kitchen and perhaps an inside lavatory. He tried to see the mess she'd warned about and saw only a blouse draped on the bed and a linen bag and ration book on the sideboard. In one corner of the room stood a Virgen de la Caridad del Cobre lit by the blue flame from a languishing candle.

The Count sat down in the chair, Manolo took the armchair and María Antonia teetered on the edge of her bed and asked: "Is it bad news?"

The Count looked at her and felt ill at ease: that luckless woman's life must gravitate round her son's triumphs, and Rafael's absence perhaps robbed her of her only reason to exist. María Antonia seemed extremely fragile and sad, so much so that the Count caught himself sharing her sadness, and he wanted to be far from that spot, immediately.

"No, María Antonia, there's no news," he said finally and repressed his desire for a smoke. There were no ashtrays in the room. He decided to fiddle with his pen.

"What an earth has happened?" she asked, although she was really talking to herself. "I don't understand it at all. What can have happened to my son?"

"Madame," said Manolo, leaning towards her. "We're

105

doing all we can, and that's why we've come to see you. We need your help. OK? When was the last time you saw your son?"

The woman stopped nodding and looked at the sergeant. Perhaps she thought he looked very young, and she rubbed her long bony hands gently together. The room was damp, and the cold sticky.

"He came at midday on the thirty-first to bring me my New Year present, that perfume over there," and she pointed to the unmistakable bottle of Chanel N^0 5 on the sideboard. "He knew my only weakness was for perfumes and was always giving them to me as presents. For Mother's Day, for my birthday, for New Year. He used to say he wanted me to smell sweeter than anyone else in the barrio, just imagine. And at night he called my neighbour's phone to wish me good luck. He was at that party he'd gone to, and it must have been around ten to twelve. He always rang me, from wherever he was, last year he called from Panama, right, I think it was Panama."

"And did he have lunch with you?" continued Manolo, shifting his skinny rump onto the edge of the armchair. He liked asking the questions and when doing so he'd hunch up, like a cat whose fur was bristling.

"Yes, I made him beans and sausage, the way he liked it, and he said neither his wife nor mother-in-law could cook them the way I did."

"And how did he strike you? The same as usual?"

"What do you mean, comrade?"

"Nothing in particular, María Antonia, did he seem at all nervous, worried or different?"

The old lady looked up at the Virgin and then rubbed her legs, as if trying to relieve pain. Her hands were white, and her nails spotless.

106

"He was always stressed by problems at work. He said: you won't believe this, mummy, but I've got to spend the afternoon at the office, and he left around two."

"And did he seem anxious or on edge?"

"Look, comrade, I know my son very well: I gave birth to him and brought him up. He ate the beans and sausage at around one, and then we both washed up and lay on this bed and talked, as we always did. He liked stretching out on this bed, my poor son. He was always tired and sleepy, and his eyes would shut as we spoke."

"And what time did he leave?"

"At around two. He washed his face and told me he was going to a party that night, that he had lots of work on, and gave me two hundred pesos so you can buy yourself something for New Year's Eve, he said and he went to clean his teeth and comb his hair and gave me a kiss and left. He was as loving towards me as ever he was."

"Did he always give you money?"

"Always? No, just occasionally."

"Did he mention any problems he was having with his wife?"

"He and I never spoke about her. It was a kind of agreement between us."

"An agreement?" asked Manolo, leaning forward even more on the edge of the armchair. The Count thought: "Where's he taking this?"

"The fact is I never liked that woman. Not that she'd ever done anything, or that I had anything special against her, but I think she never cared for him as a husband should be cared for. She even had a maid . . . Forgive me, this is family business, but I think she always looked after Number One."

"And what did he say when he left?"

"He said he was going to work, as usual, that I should look after myself and sprayed me with the new scent he'd brought me. He was always so kind, and not because he was my son, I swear, just ask any of the old neighbours around here, and they'll all tell you the same: he turned out much better than anyone could have imagined. This isn't a good barrio, I can tell you, and I came here when I was still single and I'm still here, where I married, gave birth to Rafael, brought him up by myself in the direst of circumstances and, forgive me, I don't know what you think, but God and that Virgin over there helped me make a good man of him. They never had to call me from school, and in that drawer you'll find more than fifty diplomas he won as a student, his engineering degree and certificate for getting top marks in his year. All his own effort. Haven't I a right to be proud of my son? His destiny turned out so different to mine, or his father's, who never got to be more than a plumber. I don't know where my boy got his intelligence from, but when you think how fast he climbed the ladder and how he no longer lived in a rooming house and had a car and travelled to countries I didn't even know existed and was somebody in this country ... My God, what an earth has happened? Who can want to hurt Rafael who never hurt anybody, anybody at all? He's always been a revolutionary, from when he was a young boy. I remember how he was given responsibility at secondary school and was often president, at high school as well as university, and nobody from the ministry helped him. Nobody was levering him up; he got where he got, by himself, one rung at a time, by working very hard. Just for this to happen. But God can't punish me like this. My son and I don't deserve it.

What has happened, comrades? Tell me, say something. Who can want to threaten my son? Who can have hurt him? For God's sake . . ."

I think it was two or three weeks to the end of classes, then came the exams and after that the second year of high school would start, which is almost like the third, and almost like already being at university, and nobody could bug us about the length of our sideburns or our moustaches or about the virtues of short hair and all that stuff that makes you want to get out of school, however much you like going round with your schoolmates, having a girlfriend from there and so on. That was the worst of all: wanting time to pass quickly. Why should we? And we were lined up in the playground, it was June, the sun was burning our backs, and the headmaster spoke: we would win all the honours in all the competitions, we would be the most outstanding high school in the whole of Havana, in the country, practically in the universe, because we'd been best at working in the countryside, had won the Intercollegiate Games, two prizes in the National Amateurs Festival and ninety percent of us would get to university and nobody would shift us from first place, and we clapped, hurray, hurray, we shouted and thought how wonderful we were, how unbeatable. And the headmaster said there was more good news to come: two comrades had won medals in the National Mathematics Competition, hurray, hurray, more clapping, Comrade Fausto Fleites, hurray, hurray, a gold medal in the category of eleventh grade, and, hurray, hurray, Comrade Rafael Morín, a silver medal in the thirteenth grade category, and Fausto and Rafael climbed onto the platform where all the speeches were being made, real

109

champions, arms aloft in salute, smiling, naturally, they'd showed they were tremendous wavers of the flag, and Tamara kept on applauding after almost everyone else had stopped, even jumped for joy and Skinny asked, hey, pal, is this for show or did our girl-friend there really not know? And right, she just must have known, but she was too, too happy, as if she *had* just found out, jumping for joy, swinging her butt, in a way that even showed through the voluminous spoil-sport tunic she was wearing, and Rafael walked over to the microphone, and I told Skinny, be prepared, you animal, under this scorching sun and the way he likes to gab, but I got it wrong, I almost always get it wrong: he said he and Fausto were going to dedicate their prizes to the teachers in the maths department and to the school management team, but anyway he exhorted students to give it their all in the final examinations and stay in the forefront of the results table etcetera, etcetera, and while he was talking I looked at him and thought he was a fantastic guy after all, bright and dapper, silver-tongued and blue-eyed, with a girl-friend like Tamara who was always so well turned out and I muttered, fuck, I reckon I do really envy the bastard.

"What do you think, my friend?" asked Manolo as he switched on the engine and the Count smoked the final remnants of the cigarette he'd not dared light at María Antonia's.

"Drive to headquarters, we've got to talk to the Boss and see whether we can't interview today the deputy minister responsible for the enterprise," said the Count as he took one last look down the almost lugubrious passageway to the home which was Rafael Morín's birthplace. "Why didn't he find a way to get his mother a house?"

The car proceeded along the Avenue of October Tenth towards Agua Dulce, and Manolo accelerated down the hill.

"Just what I was thinking. Rafael Morín's lifestyle and that homestead don't fit."

"Or are too good a fit, right? Now what we need to know is where he got to on the afternoon of the thirty-first, or find out if he really was at the enterprise and why he told Tamara he'd be here with his mother."

"You'll have to catch up with Morín or find a *babalao* to read the bones and clear the way, right?" the sergeant replied as he stopped the car at the traffic lights on the corner of Toyo. On the pavement opposite, the queue to get the vital Sunday bread ration was a block long. "Hey, Conde, Vilma lives just round that corner."

"And how did you get on last night?"

"Just great, that girl's a scorcher. You know, I'll probably get married, the whole bit."

"Uh-huh. You know, Manolo I've heard that one before, but I wasn't asking you about Vilma and your sex life but about work, but just watch it. If you and your carryings on get you AIDS, I'll visit you in hospital once a month and bring you some good novels."

"What's got in to you today, Maestro? You woke up as sharp as a razor."

"Take it easy. Yes, I woke up really going for it. I'm up to here with Rafael Morín and when I heard his mother talking I felt sick, as if I'd done something wrong . . ."

"All right, but don't take it out on me," the sergeant protested, as if he felt hard done by. "Look, El Greco and Crespo have been looking for Zoilita all night, and we agreed they'd report to me at ten am, so they'll be expecting me. I asked for a report on all missing persons over the last two years, and I'll get that at eleven, and we can see if there's another case like this or whatever, Conde, but all this is quite crazy."

"When we get to headquarters, also phone the guy responsible for security at the enterprise and see if Rafael went there on the afternoon of the thirty-first. If it turns out he did, get him to arrange for us to see the person on duty."

"All right. Can I tune into some music?"

"Where did you get that aerial from?"

"If you've got friends . . ." He shrugged his shoulders and smiled. Switched on the car-radio and looked for a music programme. He tried two or three and finally plumped for "*Oh, vida*" sung by the pure voice of Benny Moré in a programme entirely devoted to his music.

"I think you're exaggerating, Conde," Manolo commented as they listened to "*Hoy como ayer*" and drove through the Plaza de la Revolución. "You may not like it but this is just another case, and you can't spend your day going from one bad mood to another."

"Manolo, my grandfather used to say 'Born a donkey die a horse . . .' That's progress enough for me."

"Lieutenant, the major says you should go to see him as soon as you get here. He's up in his office," said the duty officer, and the Count returned his salute.

On Sunday morning the peace and quiet in the street also permeated headquarters. All the routine cases, those which had gone on too long and didn't look as if they'd ever be solved, those which followed normal procedures and were of no great import, were adjourned for the day, and the detectives disappeared

112

and left headquarters eerily calm. Secretaries, office workers and researchers, identikit and forensic workers took the day off, and for twenty-four hours headquarters lost the stormy frenetic pace it had the rest of the week. Only those on permanent duty or engaged in urgent investigations were working in that building, which seemed bigger, darker and less human on Sunday mornings, when it was possible to hear the click of the dominoes with which the policemen condemned to guard duty attempted to relieve their boredom. Only the Boss had worked every Sunday for the last fifteen years: Major Rangel demanded that every thread in the fabrics being woven by his subordinates pass through his hands, and he followed the movement traced by each investigation with the passion of a man possessed, from Monday to Sunday. The Count knew that the warning from the duty officer was more than an order, it was a diktat from his chief, and he asked Manolo to look out the reports and expect him in the incubator in half an hour.

The peace in the building persuaded him he should wait for the lift. The lights indicated it was on its way down, fourth, third, second, and the door to the cage opened like the theatre curtain the Count always imagined, and he now practically collided with the man getting out.

"Maestro, weren't you going to make Sunday a day of rest?"

Captain Jorrín smiled and slapped him on the shoulder.

"And what about yourself, Conde? You want to win a refrigerator?" he quipped as he took him by the arm and pulled him towards the Department of Information. The Count tried to explain the Boss was expecting him but told himself the major could wait.

"How's your case going, Captain?"

"I think it's going real well, Conde," said Jorrín the veteran, almost smiling. "A witness has come forward who can probably identify one of the boy's killers. We now know there were at least three and according to our witness they're very young. We're going to do the identikit portrait now."

"You see, Maestro, there's always light at the end of the tunnel, right?"

"Yes, I know. But that doesn't solve everything . . . Just imagine if we finally get our hands on the murderers, and they turn out to be under eighteen. Already murderers, just imagine. That's the real problem. It's not just a boy who's been kicked to death, but the fact that there are three others who will end up inside for a good few years and they'll never become the people they should have turned into. They're killers."

The Count studied the wrinkles furrowing Captain Jorrín's face and felt his arm in the desperate grip of a man who'd spent half a life hunting criminals.

"At the start I thought we'd react like doctors," he said, staring him in the eye. "That with time we'd get used to the blood."

"No, I hope that never happens. These things must hurt, Count. And if one day they don't, that's the time to give up."

"Good luck, Maestro," he said, opposite the Department of Information, and rushed off towards the staircase.

Maruchi's table was also enjoying the Sunday magic: it was completely clean, and apparently sad and abandoned, without the flower the young woman brought daily. When he was by the office door he heard the major's voice, knocked softly and heard him say: "Come on in."

114

The Boss sat behind his desk, in civilian dress, wearing a grey-and-white striped pullover that emphasized his handsome chest and showed off his muscular neck. The major's eyes pointed him to a chair while he continued on the phone. He was talking to his daughter; something was amiss, "Don't be upset, Mirna, after all . . . All right, yes, phone your mother and tell her I'll pick her up to go and have lunch with you, a good idea." He added "give the kid a kiss from me, right" and hung up. All that time he spoke in a warm charming tone, never grumbled, the most pleasant sample the Count had ever heard from his broad repertoire of voices.

"What a bloody mess," rasped the major after retrieving the Davidoff 5000 he'd just lit. "Another one who's gone missing: my son-in-law. But we know where *he* is. He's gone off with a nineteen-year-old bimbo. And my stupid daughter still loves him. Can you believe it? That's why I don't think I'll ever retire. You can have a thousand problems here, staff problems, calls from on high, cases that prompt them, but I prefer this madhouse to being at home and having to sort out the hassles there. Do you know what Mirta, my other daughter, wants? You'll never bloody imagine . . . She met an Austrian at university with hair down to here, who's travelling the world saying there's a hole in the ozone layer here and the sea's being polluted there, and she says she's going to marry him, that he's the most sensitive man in the world and she'll go anywhere to be with him. Do you know what that means? Well, I don't even want to contemplate the prospect, but I can tell you one thing for nothing, Conde, she'll not marry him. And now this business with my son-in-law."

"I thought Austrians were an extinct species. Have you ever seen an Austrian?"

The major looked at his cigar.

"No, the truth is I'd never seen one before clapping my eyes on this fellow."

The Count smiled, and although he wasn't sure whether he should, he chanced his arm: "Look, just tell your daughters you have a lieutenant who's available and single, a fine upstanding lad, with a good brain, who's looking for a partner and better still if she's the major's daughter."

"You know," replied the Major, unsmiling, "that's all I need . . . You know, it's turned cold, hasn't it?"

"Who told you to act the hero and wear only a pullover?"

"I left my coat in the car; I didn't think it would be so bad. How's your case going?"

"So, so."

"Like how?"

"I don't really know. We've got several leads, but only one going anywhere: we don't know where Rafael Morín was on the afternoon and evening of the thirty-first. He told his wife he was going to his mother's and his mother that he was going to the enterprise, and his secretary says the thirtieth was the last day they worked. We're also investigating a woman he knew called Zoila and nobody knows where she's been since the first. And the other lead is that it seems he was having an affair with his secretary."

"And what if he lied so as to cover up what he was doing on the afternoon of the thirty-first because he was up to no good, and it's got nothing to do with his disappearance?"

"Uh-huh. What I want to do is talk to deputy minister Alberto Fernández-Lorea. Today, if possible. I can't get the party out of my head, and I need you to ring him."

"You can ring him."

"I'd prefer you to. Remember I'm only a sad police-man, as someone told me yesterday, and he's a deputy minister."

The major leaned back in his chair and began to rock. He puffed on his cigar and exhaled a blue curl of smoke. He was enjoying himself. Mario Conde, mean-while, pulled one of the major's telephones to his side of the desk and started to dial a number.

"Take this, the phone's ringing in Fernández's house," he said and waved the phone. The major grunted and accepted the inevitable.

"I don't think anybody's there," he retorted, and just as he was starting to put the phone down he stopped and said: "Yes, I can hear you, is that Comrade Fernández-Lorea's house?" He got a positive response and then told him he was needed for questioning. "Yes, today if it's no bother . . . Of course . . . In an hour's time? That's fine, see you then and many thanks. Lieutenant Mario Conde. Yes," and hung up.

"Satisfied?"

"Pass my message on to your daughters," said the Count, as he got up and straightened his pistol.

"Call me at home tonight and tell me what's new," the major demanded in a decidedly authoritarian tone. "Lots of luck," he added and gazed once more at the wonderfully pure ash of his Davidoff.

The Count went down to his second-floor cubicle. Sergeant Manuel Palacios was waiting for him, seated in his chair behind his desk.

"No clues from the list of missing people, Conde. They're all mad or geriatric, husband and wives who've done a bunk, youths hiding from their parents, chil-dren kidnapped by divorced parents and only one case in October of a woman forcibly abducted by an unrequited lover. And there's only one case of disappearance that's still open: a twenty-three-year-old who's been missing from April of last year, although people suspect he employed primitive means to leave the island," explained Manolo, and his voice and eyes looked bored. "I also spoke to the head of security at the enterprise, and luckily it was his wife who also works there who was on duty on the twelve to eight shift, and Rafael Morín didn't pay a call, though René Maciques did."

"Maciques, the friend . . . And Zoilita?"

"She's another kettle of fish. From what Greco and Crespo found out, that girl is a tasty item and people like to get a lick. They still don't know where she's fucking holed up, for she gets around, is a real mover and is on file as a hooker, but no criminal record as yet. She's just as likely to be on the arm of a Mexican as with a Bulgarian living in the block of flats for Soviet Bloc bureaucrats or spending a fortnight at the International in Varadero, but all her boyfriends have cars, money and good positions. You can imagine. And when she gets bored she makes china plates and other ornaments that aren't at all bad. Nobody saw her the day she left, and nobody knows what she did for New Year's Eve. She's not checked in at any hotel, and her brother hasn't the slightest idea where she might be."

The Count listened to the tale of Zoilita's goings on and thought he'd really like to talk to her. He stood up and walked over to the window.

"We must find her. I have a real hunch that nympho is up to something with Rafael Morín."

"Should we put a search out for her?"

"Yes, dig her out from under the ground or the guy she's with or wherever the fuck," growled the Count, and he thought of Tamara again. Damn Tamara, he

118

told himself and remembered that at some stage he should speak to Baby-Face Miki. He could see the pure blue sky from his window and finally told Manolo: "Go on, put a search out for her and see you downstairs. A deputy minister is expecting us to call."

He lived on Seventh and Thirty-Eighth, in a three-storey building with a redbrick façade and big balconies that looked out on the boulevard. A path of flagstones embedded in the earth crossed the green sward of well-clipped lawn and led to an elegant building that was modern despite being thirty years old, and also somewhat humble in comparison to the surrounding mansions. The Count and Manolo silently climbed up the steps and rang the bell to the flat that occupied an entire second floor: the first high-pitched fanfare from Mendelssohn's *Wedding March* rang out the other side of the door. Manolo laughed and shook his head.

"Do come in, please. I was expecting you," said their host when he opened the door, and the Count thought: I know him. Alberto Fernández-Lorea was a man nearing fifty, but he still looked in good shape. I bet he doesn't smoke and goes for runs in Martí Park, thought the Count who was trying to remember where he'd seen him before. The deputy minister's athletic body, his lank abundant hair parted down the middle and the build of a man in his prime might have suggested Vargas Llosa's Scribe on the crest of the wave, and that would have been spot on.

The deputy minister invited them to sit down and excused himself for a moment – "I'm sorry, if you don't mind" – and walked over to the unpolished wood partition separating the living room from what was probably the kitchen-diner. It was a very large living room, perhaps disproportionately so, from what the Count could see of the flat, and he recalled how it was there Rafael Morín had danced and eaten, talked and laughed in what was probably his last public appearance. It was a splendid space, and through the balcony windows you could see the high branches of a leafless Royal Poinciana, and the Count thought how in summer the tree would be a joy to the eyes when orangey flowers bedecked every branch.

Fernández-Lorea came back, and the Count was quite sure his face was more than familiar, but where *have* I seen this guy before? He racked his brains: the extra information might be a bonus.

"Well, please feel free to start," the deputy minister suggested, and his voice resounded several decibels above what was necessary for such a meeting. He'd settled down in an armchair with plastic piping and rocked gently to and fro. "We're all very worried about the whereabouts of Comrade Rafael Morín."

The Count contemplated the man's languid eyes and felt he could say nothing: he was thinking about how he should address him. Comrade Deputy Minister sounded hollow, officious and too smarmy; Fernández by itself, simply impersonal; Alberto, beyond the pale, an expression of nonexistent intimacy, and he wanted that exchange which had started so tentatively to be over and done with.

"Comrade Deputy Minister Fernández," he said finally, and the very sound of those words made it feel like an exercise in self-flagellation, "you know, this is a very unusual case, disappearances as such hardly exist in Cuba so we've been forced to spread our net as wide as possible. For the moment, we've discounted the idea of a kidnapping or any illegal departure from the country . . ."

"No, such things are out of the question as far as Rafael is concerned. I'm sure he's had an accident or

120

something else untoward has happened," the deputy minister commented and apologized theatrically for his interjection. "Do please go on."

"At this stage," the Count continued and then looked at his colleague, "there are only two possibilities: one that so far seems very unlikely, which is that Rafael has gone into hiding because of something we're unaware of. And the other is that he has been murdered, for something we're also unaware of, but experience tells us it could be anything, the most banal motive. In any case the night before he disappeared he came here with his wife to say farewell to the Old Year and perhaps your party holds the clue that will take us to Rafael. That's why we're here."

The deputy minister looked towards the partition and shifted a foot rather nervously. The Count then scented the indiscreet aroma of good coffee and thanked him in advance.

"Well, Comrades," Fernández-Lorea finally asserted, Solomon-like, still rocking away, "the truth is I don't know what help I can be. It's true what you say about nobody ever going missing in Cuba, and yet the slightest thing gets lost. It even adds a little piquancy, don't you agree? Perhaps what you're after is my opinion of Morín, and I can give you that, no problem. I think Rafael is the best young manager on our board, which is responsible for supplying raw materials to industry and negotiating the foreign sales of some of our products. I first met Rafael just under two years ago, when I was moved from foreign affairs to the ministry, and to be quite candid, as soon as I saw him in action I had no doubt that one day he would occupy my post, and I," he lowered his voice to a tone more in keeping with a meeting of three and began to speak confidentially, "I would be grateful to him for that, because I wasn't born to do these things. The post I now hold now came by chance rather than choice, I can be quite candid on that front, because I prefer the peace and quiet of an office preparing market studies to the daily whirlwind of a ministry, that gets more difficult to stomach by the day, and the more things happen in the socialist camp the worse it will get, and we don't know how it will all end. Besides, it requires a use of diplomatic procedures that have never been my forte."

The deputy minister gently rubbed his hands together, and Lieutenant Mario Conde felt embarrassed and almost disappointed, because Alberto Fernández-Lorea sounded genuine, despite his pompous turn of phrase. After all, he thought, there have to be people who don't want to be like Rafael.

"I'm very afraid of failure and doubly so of looking ridiculous," the man went on after taking another look at the screen, "and I don't know whether I have the ability to cope with the responsibility I have and wouldn't like to finish up a cast-off. On the other hand, that young man's work capacity is extraordinary, and his career is at its best point ever. What do I mean? That Rafael Morín was quite first-rate in what he did and had something I lack: he was ambitious, and I am using that word in its best sense."

The coffee finally emerged from the kitchen. It arrived in three cups on a glass tray that also carried two glasses of water. Behind it walked a woman. "Good afternoon," she said just before entering the living room. She too was on her way to fifty and in a hurry to arrive and looked fully the part: wrinkles fanned out aggressively from around her eyes, and her neck drooped flabbily. She was an exhausted woman reflecting none of her husband's warm sporting sheen.

"My wife, Laura," the deputy minister introduced

122

her. They greeted her, and he wanted to be more precise: "Mario Conde and . . ."

"Sergeant Manuel Palacios," Manolo came to his rescue.

The woman offered them their coffee, and only the Count took two sips to clean his palate. It was strong bitter coffee, and the lieutenant repeated his thanks.

"It's a blend of Brazilian which I got as a present and coffee from the corner store. That way it lasts longer, and I think this mixture makes it taste better, don't you? Because at the end of the day a coffee's quality depends not just on its purity, but also on a taste that has been created over the years. A few months ago, in Prague, I was invited to drink Turkish coffee vaunted the best in the world yet I found it difficulty to finish the cup. And as a coffee-drinker I even drink the stuff brewed opposite the Coppelia," she added as they nodded in agreement.

The Count savoured his coffee and thought Manolo must be feeling what Fernández-Lorea experienced in Prague: he preferred his coffee very sweet and very weak, the Oriente province style his mother still favoured.

"And you said he was ambitious?"

"Yes, and I added that I meant that in the best sense of the word, Lieutenant. At least in my opinion," he said, taking a packet of cigarettes from his pocket. "Would you like one?"

"Thanks," said the Count as he accepted a cigarette. So he's a smoker as well, he thought. "And what do you know about Rafael Morín's private life outside of work?"

"Really very little, Lieutenant. I have enough to cope with at work without worrying overly about that side of things, which I've never considered important, I'm sorry."

"But you *were* friends," interjected Manolo, who couldn't stand any more of this, the Count thought, watching him perch like a skinny cat about to attack.

"To an extent we were. We'd meet in lots of places for work reasons and got on well as colleagues. But we'd hardly known each other two years, and it was a work-based relationship, as I explained to the lieutenant."

"And on the thirty-first?" the sergeant continued. "Did you notice anything strange? Did you know he'd run into a problem with Dapena, the Spanish businessman?"

"I knew about the Dapena incident and thought it long dead and buried. I don't know what you can have heard. And on the thirty-first he was his usual self, talking about work, joking or dancing. It's the second time we've seen the Old Year out here, a group of us get together and get a pig from Pinar del Río, and I roast it on the next-door neighbours' spit. You can imagine, my father was a head chef and something rubbed off. I think I'm an accomplished pig-roaster."

"So he didn't seem anxious about anything?"

"Not that I could see. He didn't drink much either; he said he was feeling queasy."

"And he didn't have any problems at the enterprise, something that could force him to go into hiding?"

The deputy minister looked at the Count, perhaps trying to see what lurked behind such a question. His eyes shone more brightly, as if he'd seen a red light flashing. He took his time answering.

"Well, there are many kinds of problem, but for someone like Rafael Morín to decide to go into hiding, there's only one kind. To my knowledge, there's only one kind of problem, but anyway Major Rangel asked me for permission to investigate the enterprise, and you'll start tomorrow, I believe." He opened his arms, and Manolo nodded.

"I hope it isn't that sort of problem, because it could be terrible, but the enquiry will have the last word on that count, so don't ask me to put my hands in the fire now. Rafael Morín still continues to be an excellent comrade, and I'll think the contrary only when I'm told, or better, shown the contrary. Let's wait on that."

"One last question, Comrade," the Count now interjected to avoid another salvo from Manolo. He sensed the deputy minister's alarm was all too palpable for it to be mere speculation. Perhaps Fernández-Lorea had anticipated something, perhaps even knew something. "We don't wish to take up any more of your time, particularly on a Sunday. What funds were at Rafael Morín's disposal to make purchases abroad? I mean for handing presents around, apart from the ones he took home."

Fernández-Lorea expressed classic astonishment: he raised his eyebrows and then shifted one foot, as if expecting another round of coffee. However, his voice boomed at thrice the level for a public meeting.

"Funds, Lieutenant, of the kind you describe: none whatsoever. He travelled on expenses as a company director and with money for marketing purposes, depending on the type of deal he went to sign or the new market he was going to explore. Our enterprise had in that sense a degree of leeway, for it was often a matter of buying a very specific product, often manufactured in the US, for example, and it couldn't do that via traditional channels, but through third parties, as we sometimes did in Panama, just to cite one example. And you know, almost everywhere in the world business is done by wining and dining, and you have to give presents, and the embassy or whatever commercial office is put at our disposal doesn't always have a car available . . . He handled that money, sometimes a substantial amount, and although we are very careful, because the books are checked periodically, statements of account and expenditure on expenses drawn up and two audits a year, the accounts aren't often as exact as we'd like, for many reasons, and that's where trust is the key factor. And he was trustworthy, according to all the reports I got. On the other hand, Lieutenant, many businessmen we work with hand out presents as a matter of course when a good contract is signed. I myself was given a BMW in Bilbao only two months ago, and my Lada was in the repair shop . . . Well, and as the comrades who work at this level are always trustworthy, if it's not too large, if it's something quite personal, the comrade keeps whatever it is."

"And have there been problems with comrades over this kind of perk?"

"Yes, regrettably, there have."

The Count sensed Fernández-Lorea was speaking of a subject that grew more distasteful with each word and was about to thank him when Manolo piped up.

"I'm sorry, Comrade Fernández, but I think your information can be a great help to us. For example, who assigned these allowances, marketing expenses and whatever for Rafael Morín?"

Manolo put the question, and the Count didn't know whether to laugh or cry or both at once, but when they got out of there he'd find a mule and give it a good kick: Manolo had hit the right button.

"He generally assigned them himself and was his own boss at the enterprise," Fernández-Lorea disclosed before getting to his feet.

126

"What happened to the previous boss?" Manolo continued. "The one Rafael Morín replaced."

"He was removed for more or less that kind of reason, mishandling expenses and internal fraud, but I really can't believe Rafael is involved in that. At least it's what I'd prefer to think, because I'd never be able to forgive myself. Do you think that may be why he's gone missing?"

"We got him, fuck if we didn't get him!" Manolo almost shouted as he transmuted joy into speed. They were driving along Fifth Avenue, and the Count rested his hands on the car's glove compartment.

"Take it easy, Manolo," he told the sergeant and waited for the speedometer to creep down to forty-five. "I think we'll soon find out why Rafael Morín has scarpered."

"Hey, and did you notice? Fernández's a spitting image of Al Pacino."

The Count smiled and looked at the leafy promenade down the centre of the avenue.

"Shit, you're right. As soon as we got there, I thought I knew him from somewhere: he *is* just like Al Pacino. Did you see the film where he played a Grand Prix driver?"

"I can't recall any particular film at the moment, Conde. Tell me where we're headed."

"Well, right now we're going to have lunch and then we'll try to see the enterprise's accountant. Let's see whether La China, our Chinese Patricia, can go with us, and she can speak to him. The good side to all this is the fact it's turning out so bad."

127

Lunch was the reward and big plus for working on Sundays. As they cooked for some twenty people, Sunday lunch used to bring unexpected surprises that bordered on the refinements of a good restaurant. That Sunday they'd prepared chicken rice with the heavy juicy consistency of yellowish perfumed paella. As well as fried ripe plantain and a lettuce and radish salad to accompany an offering that climaxed in a dessert of rice pudding soused in cinnamon. Even the yoghurt was flavoured, and there was a choice: strawberry or pineapple.

The Count, who'd had a second helping of chicken rice and was smoking his second after-lunch cigarette, looked out of his cubicle window but saw nothing. Rafael was speaking from the podium at school, and he was listening to him, alone in the playground, when Manolo came in, swearing in every direction.

"Don't get too excited, Conde, there's no accountant around at the moment. He left yesterday for the Soviet Union on a training trip."

"This is linked to Rafael Morín, I bet you. But not to worry, it can wait till tomorrow. Besides, I don't expect the accountant would tell us very much. Come on, let's go."

"Let's go? If the accountant . . ."

He tried to protest but the Count was already on his way out of his cubicle and heading silently to the parking lot.

"Go up G in the direction of Boyeros," the Count ordered as he sat in his seat.

"And will you tell me where we're headed?" asked Manolo, unable to fathom the lieutenant's attitude, though he did recall that first comment he heard about him: "The guy's mad, but . . ."

"We're heading to see García, from the union, but

don't worry, we'll finish early today. I particularly want you to hear what I imagine García will tell us about the great Morín . . . Then you can go home."

They turned down Rancho Boyeros and stopped at the traffic light by the bus terminal.

"And what do we do if Zoilita appears?"

"You'll break the sound barrier and come for me like a shot. I'll go to see Tamara, I need to talk to her, and then I'll drop in on a school friend who wants to see me, who lives two blocks from Skinny, and I'll stay there. You'll find me at one of these places. What you really must do is speak to China and tell her we have to go to the enterprise early in the morning."

"Straight on, right?

"No, turn into the Plaza de la Revolución. García lives in Cruz del Padre, right by the stadium," said the Count, and he remembered how the previous night the Industriales had lost the first game in the series with Vegueros, and if they lost again that evening, his conversation tonight with Skinny wouldn't be a very constructive experience, at least lexically speaking. The sustained rumble issuing from the sports ground was a promise of emotions the Count would have liked to enjoy. But someone has to work on Sunday.

"You know, comrades, Comrade Morín may have had the odd problem with expenses and the things you've mentioned, you know more than I do about that and you may very well be right, but I, Manuel García García, won't believe it till I see it, and sorry if that sounds like I'm doubting you . . . And it's not because I'm pigheaded or anything of the sort. I've known Rafael, I mean Comrade Morín, for a long time and trust him wholeheartedly, and if I have to call myself to account later on his behalf, then so be it, but what you say is very serious and you have to find some evidence, don't you? Look, there are people at the enterprise who probably don't think like me, some say he over-centralized things, that he was a control freak and he did come in for criticism at a mass meeting and he went along with it, because he certainly knew how to be self-critical and he referred to the issue of central-ization several times, but the fact was in the long run everything started to pass through his hands again, and I sometimes think that lots of people were happy for him to take all the decisions and also that it was the only way he knew how to manage. But the same indi-viduals who criticized him agreed things always turned out fine on the day and that helped his reputation, which is what I think really matters. We in the union never had problems with him, and I've been on the executive from before he joined the enterprise, so you know, I know this union backwards. Besides, in the party cell he once told me our attitude was on the pas-sive side, and I said, but, Comrade Rafael, we're up-to-date with our subs, we meet our quotas for volunteer work, we do all the activities on our programme and address people's concerns in regular meetings, what else can the union do? Don't you agree, comrades? There haven't been any problems at the enterprise since three specialists in the foreign currency depart-ment caused a stink because they never travelled abroad, that was before I got to be general secretary, you know, some two years ago if my memory serves me correctly. I could see it was about those guys' ambition to visit capitalist countries, but in a meeting with the party and the union, Comrade Rafael explained how administrative decisions were a matter for the adminis-tration and that the administration had its reasons to reach that decision, and shortly after those comrades were transferred to one of the new corporations being set up. And one day Rafael, I mean Comrade Morín, said to me, and he didn't like fiddles: 'You know, García, all they wanted to do was travel.' Yes, he got on wonderfully with every comrade, and it's true what Zaida told you, he showed concern for everyone: I'm a mere head of services and he gave me a refresher trip to Czechoslovakia, well, not exactly, but he put me forward and spoke a lot on my behalf at the mass meeting. And his influence carried, obviously. . . Well, we weren't personal friends, what I mean by a personal friend, you know, he came to my place a couple of times when my mum fell ill and then he mobilized the whole enterprise for the wake and the funeral. And, although I sometimes tell myself he was a bit strange, you never forget that kind of gesture and you have to be grateful, because there's nothing worse on this planet than being ungrateful. So you must forgive me, I won't believe it till I see it. Why was he a bit strange? Nothing really, things I thought silly, just manias he had, like making sure he had lots of vegetables to eat and when he was at the enterprise getting his office cleaned twice a day or telling his driver to put tinted glass in his car so nobody would see who's inside, you know? Really trivial things. Besides, you ask anyone, even the people always criticizing him, they're all very worried about what's happened and nobody can explain a thing . . . Comrades, is it true he was killed by people trying to rob him?"

"And aren't you fed up of hearing people praise Rafael? Do you think we might be wrong, that in fact he is a great leader and not into any kind of fraud and it's all fine and dandy with his allowances and market-ing expenses? Don't you think he's God the Father, all-caring, beyond reproach, Mr Nice, ruling the roost and bestowing favours, sympathy and trips abroad as if he were God Almighty? Or do you think he was a total bastard, a control freak who loved wielding power?"

"Conde, Conde, watch it, you'll have a . . ."

"Don't worry, my friend, getting steamed up is becoming my normal state of mind."

"All right then, shall I drop you off at your friend's?"

The Count nodded, wondering what he'd to say to Tamara now and if it was really necessary to go back to see her. The idea of confronting that woman again irritated and riled him: he wanted to leave the universe of Rafael Morín behind, but Tamara acted like a magnet drawing him into the centre of his world, encouraging him to return to the scene, like the classic murderer.

"Hey, Manolo, it's still early. Let me buy you a drink. I need to cool down."

"Isn't the game you're playing a bit dangerous, my friend?"

"Yeah, the lottery. And I won a wristwatch," he said and then smiled.

"We've been whipping ourselves far too long."

"Turn down Lacret and park on the corner before you get to Mayía."

Sergeant Manuel Palacios did as he was told and eased the car in between a lorry and a taxi. A space Mario Conde could never have entered even on a bicycle. They locked the doors. Manolo disconnected the aerial, and they walked towards Mayía Rodríguez, where there was a surprisingly clean, well-lit bar that was almost always empty around midday. Bottles lined the top of the freezer, bottles of Santa Cruz rum, their labels boasting of a fake royal lineage, a few Havana Club creams and an absinthe no Creole drinker dared ask for even in times of direst shortages.

"Two doubles of Carta Blanca rum, my friend," the Count placed his order with the barman and went over to the bench where his friend had already taken a seat. Just a few regulars were in the bar fighting off Sunday lunchtime lethargy by drinking rum from those little jam-jars which forced you to throw your head right back to get at the last drop, while the barman's cassette recorder played a selection of boleros for daytime drinkers: Vicentico Valdés, Vallejo, Tejedor and Luis, Contreras were recounting a long chronicle of heart-breaks and tragedies that went better with rum than with ginger ale or Coca-Cola. It was inevitable: the Count was always casing no-hopers in high-noon saloons and trying to imagine why each individual was there, what had gone wrong with their lives for them to invest time and money year after year listening to the same sorrowful songs that only aggravated their lone-liness, their disenchantment, the neglect and betrayal they'd suffered, and pour me another, bro, downing gut-rot and firewater as their hands began to shake from the dosage. He exhausted his last efforts as a would-be psychologist and in the process psycho-analysed himself though without sticking the knife in, wondering what he was doing there and dodging his real answers: simply because I like dossing around, feeling damned and forgotten, asking for another drop, bro, listening to others chatter, talking to myself and feeling time go painlessly by. He'd sometimes ask for a drink in order to think a case through or forget it, or to celebrate or remember or just because he felt happier in that kind of place than in a bar with tall glasses and colourful cocktails, one of those elegant bars he'd not seen the inside of in a million years.

"What would you like to do now, Manolo?" he asked his colleague, who was quite taken aback by such a question after just one shot.

"Don't know, have a few here and then head off to Vilma's and get a bit of quiet till the morning, I suppose," he replied with a shrug of his shoulders.

"And if you weren't off to Vilma's, I mean?"

Manolo scrutinized his glass like a connoisseur, and the pupil of his left eye progressed smoothly towards the bridge of his nose.

"I think I'd like to listen to music. I always like listening to music. I wish I had a good hi-fi system, with all those equalizers and fucking gadgets and a couple of those speakers, so I could stretch out on the floor with my head between them, my ears right up against them, listening to music for hours on end. Just imagine, man, my old dad couldn't even give me a hundred and forty pesos to buy myself a guitar! I'd have been the happiest soul on earth playing that guitar, but you land up the son of a bus driver with a wage that has to look after six people, and happiness has to come in at a sight less than a hundred and forty pesos."

The Count thought how right you are, happiness could be a very expensive business and ordered another double. He looked out on the cold sunlit street, where few cars drove by, and felt completely at ease with his conscience. It was a good time to have a few drinks and sleep with a woman, as his colleague was about to, or catch a bus with Skinny and suffer for four hours in the stadium. It was a good time of day to be alive and happy, with or without a guitar, his throat reacting gratefully to each sip of rum – the familiar gentle heat of white rum – he thought how he'd often been happy and would be again some day, that loneliness isn't an incurable disease and perhaps one day he'd rekindle old expectations and own a house in Cojímar, right on the coast, a house made of wood with a tile roof and a writing room and never again be in thrall to murderers and thieves, attacked and attackers, and Rafael Morín would vanish from his nostalgic reveries and only good memories would surface, the way they should, the ones time rescues and protects so the past isn't a nasty horrible burden and you don't have to walk to the bridge and throw your love in the river, as in the Vicentico Valdés song they were now listening to.

"Listen to that," he said to Manolo with a smile. "Just what you want to hear after you've downed a couple: 'To the river I'll go to throw your love in the river/ watch it fall into the void/float off on the stream . . .' Almost what you call beautiful!"

"If you say so," nodded the sergeant, looking back at his glass.

"Hey, Manolo, are you or are you not squint-eyed?"

Manolo smiled, keeping his eyes on his glass, his left eye in free float.

"One day on, one day off," the sergeant replied and downed his drink. He looked at his colleague and pointed to his empty jar. "And what would *you* like to do right now?"

The Count also downed his drink and hesitated a moment before answering:

"Spend time with your big hi-fi, stretched out on the floor listening to 'Strawberry Fields' ten times on the trot."

I never took to that outfit. It made you look like a hoodlum – a jailbird – protested Alexis the Yankee, and it was true: the purple socks, cap, wording and sleeves on a chicken-yellow khaki background, the trousers that were far too wide and which we couldn't narrow as people normally did because Antonio the Fly, our teacher-cum-manager, made it plain that when the championship was over we would have to return everything, in the same or a better state than when we got it, what a fucking joke, as if anyone would want to hang on to outfits that earned us a great nickname: "The Víbora Violets". The championship involved six high schools and, as usual, we got a bad deal. After Water-Pre we got shat on from all sides, from the camps for rural labour to our baseball outfits, we always got the worst, because they dug deep and discovered first that we topped the exam league tables as a result of fraud and second that we won the cane-cutting competition because someone at the central store gave us cane cut by other schools, and then they discovered a whole string of other things.

Andrés, our usual first baseman, refused to have anything to do with the game after he injured himself and couldn't play for the National Youth Team. They let me take first base, despite being only the eighth batter in the line-up, in front of Arsenio the Moor, who was condemned to be last as he was a fuck-up dressed as a player – or jailbird – in one of those uniforms.

When we came out to warm up it was already dark and they'd switched on the lights, and the Habana High School team ran onto the field, enormous blacks about to slay us alive as they already had other teams, but we were cocksure and shouted at the pre-game huddle, we're going to beat the skinny liquorice sticks, fuck 'em, said Skinny, and even the Moor and I thought we would. The worst bit was our gear, because the stadium had had a fresh lick of paint, the floodlighting was great and half of the terraces were full of people from Havana and the other from Víbora, and there was a fantastic din, and we wore this disguise that belonged to the days when one played baseball in a bowler hat and gaiters.

And our team had Skinny, Isidrito the Joker – our pitcher for the day – and Pello and me – dubbed Foul, because all I ever hit were foul balls – and almost everyone from our class went to the games, starting with Tamara, who was in charge of the Achievement Committee because participation in activities counted and The Inter-School Games were an activity, and people always preferred a baseball game to the other kind – a museum visit or yawning through a performance of the school choir, for example. And the class invented a chorus they shouted whenever we played: "Violet team, Violet team/go for the brass", but the opposition went one better and sang: "Violet team, Violet team/the donkey's prick up your ass", so the cure was worse than the illness. Anyway, I was thrilled to be in the team, playing under the lights and feeling you could see things from a different angle: because sure it's not the same watching the players from the terraces as wearing the gear and watching the people on the terraces. It's something else.

"Balls, gentlemen, balls is what you need to win at this game," Skinny shouted from the bench when the game was about to start, but it was never just a game for him when it was baseball, and the veins on his neck bulged, he was so skinny. "And we're more than well-endowed, right?"

And we had to say yes or he might have a fit, and as we were the home club and came out first, the Havana fans started to boo and the Víbora mob cheered, and then I looked towards the terraces and truly saw things

137

differently. I saw Tamara wave a purple handkerchief, and I stopped wanting to play when I spotted the former Student Federation president, next to Tamara, like a police dog. Rafael Morín laughed his usual sparkling, self-satisfied laugh, like the day he told us "I'm Rafael Morín", looking down at us in his flash check shirt, and us below in gear that made us look like jailbirds.

But even so it was the best game I ever played. That day Isidrito had downed two quarts of undiluted milk, which he said was good for pitching straight and the fact was he was throwing really hard and farting like a lord . . . And the Joker starting striking out the Havana darkies, and almost nobody got on their base, and if they did, it didn't matter, because they weren't scoring. And we were the same, or worse, because Yayo Butter, Havana's pitcher, was red-hot and struck out seven of us in a row, and the crowd on the terrace went quieter and quieter; the game became really serious, was keeping its big outburst for the last innings, right?

We were zero-zero in the eighth inning, when it was Skinny's turn to bat, for he was fifth up, and he hit a drive past the shortstop and he got to second. All hell was let loose: people started shouting "Violeta, Violeta", and Skinny went "Balls, we've got balls" till the umpire had a go at him for swearing. And it was all down to that bitch destiny, because Isidrito, who was sixth up and never blew it, made a pig's ear out of it, was the first out, and Paulino the Bull's Testicle, who was seventh, rolled it into Yayo's hands who leisurely stroked it over his balls before throwing it to first base, and Paulino was the second out. Then it was my turn to hit.

I was shitting myself, legs shaking, hands sweating and everybody went dead silent, and even Skinny, who knew me well, didn't shout at me and I think he reckoned the innings was done for. Then I picked myself up, spat into my hands and rubbed them with earth and remembered I should lift the bat right back, raise my elbow, grip tight when I started my swing, a deep, deep silence, and Yayo Butter pitched it straight, a mean fucking fastball, and I said here we go, lifted my bat back, raised my elbow, gripped tight, shut my eyes and swung. And it was Sodom and Gomorrah: fuck! It was one hell of a hit right down the middle of the field, real hard, like I'd never hit before, and it was like seeing the ball flying in slow motion, flying till it hit the fence right under the scoreboard, and I started to run hell for leather, and it went so far I could go to third, almost enough for a homerun, they screamed, Skinny scored, then ran to third base and scooped me up in his arms, Isidrito who hadn't spoken to me from the day we'd had that fight, kissed me he was so excited, and the whole team came to hug me, and I deserved it, right? I was over the moon, the fans were going crazy, and I looked to the terraces to see things differently and felt I would die: Tamara and Rafael had left . . .

In the ninth innings the La Habana lot scored twice and beat us two-one. But it was the best game of my life.

Before he knocked on the door, he glanced at his watch: ten past four. If she'd been having a siesta, she'd be up by now. Perhaps she was watching the Sunday matinee film, he thought, then thought he didn't exactly know why he'd come or else he knew only too well and didn't want to give it another thought. Lam's sham figures rested under the shadow of a ceiba-tree, possibly quite deliberately planted next to the concrete jungle, and the well-pruned hedges and lush hibiscus created the atmosphere of a colourful artificial wood he really liked. In fact, as he had reminded Manolo, it wasn't a house for policemen, and the pain of nostalgia the place provoked was so intense, his temples and chest felt ready to burst. He was pleased he'd had a couple with Manolo; when and after he'd pressed the bell, he felt calm and relaxed.

The ring of the bell echoed round the huge house, and while waiting he lit a cigarette and adjusted the regulation pistol in his belt, the weight of which he'd never accepted, and finally she opened the door and greeted him with a smile: "Well, if it isn't the Prince of the City. I watched that film last night and pitied the policeman. Recently all the police I've seen have looked sad. Though that guy doesn't look much like you." And she stepped back to let him in.

"Lately I don't feel much like myself," he retorted as she shut the door, and they headed for the television room. "Do you want to see the rest of the film?"

"No, I saw it three months ago. Rafael brought the video, but as I was bored . . ." She settled down in a plush armchair that matched his. "I felt drowsy. I slept very badly last night."

The curtains were closed, and the room got little of the cold light from outside. He searched for an ashtray and finally spotted a metal one, of the lidded variety to hide the ash and cigarette ends. It was annoyingly clean and shiny, and he moved the lid two or three times before enquiring:

"Who cleans this place, Tamara?"

"A lady who's a friend of Mummy's. She comes twice a week, why?"

"Nothing really, I just pollute ashtrays."

She smiled almost sadly.

"Nothing new there, right, Mario?"

140

"So here we are again, Tamara," he lied, not feeling the slightest remorse, and wondered how much of the truth his old comrade knew.

"That's what I'd imagined. My mother-in-law called this morning and told me you'd been round to see her. The poor woman was in tears."

"It's to be expected. And then I spoke to Fernández-Lorea, who confirmed what an excellent fellow your husband is. And with García, from the union at the enterprise, and he insisted on singing Rafael's praises like everyone else. I was quite won over."

"That's good then," she replied, and her almond eyes shone even more brightly. But he knew she wouldn't start crying. "You're always prospecting for mud."

"Can I tell you something? I don't swallow all this. I know Rafael, and I'm sorry but I saw him do two or three things I never liked."

"What kind of things?" she asked and started tangling with her wayward lock.

"No, nothing serious, don't worry, but enough to make you wary."

"And what did Alberto tell you?"

He contemplated the *Flora* by Portocarrero ladying it on one of the walls. Read on one side "For you, Valdemira, from your friend René" and decided that he liked the blues the maestro used when painting Flora's hair, that looked colder yet more alive and noted that, like all Floras, she also viewed the world through trustingly tender eyes.

"Nothing new of note. We're trying to find Zoilita, who's still not put in an appearance. And tomorrow we'll start at the enterprise to see if anything turns up there."

And she crossed her legs and studied him as if he were suddenly a very alien being she was seeing for the first time. But he could only look at her legs and dress, nothing more than a very long white pullover revealing almost all the front of her thighs.

"Why did you leave that day at the baseball game?"

"What do you mean?" she asked, taken aback.

"Oh, nothing. I want to find your husband and find out why he went missing . . . And I want to know how you're feeling."

She made an effort to tame her impertinent lock and rested her head on the back of her chair.

"Quite at a loss. I've been thinking a lot," she said before standing up. He watched her walk towards the library, and the mere sight of her brought to mind his masturbatory frigging of the previous night and he was almost ashamed he liked that woman, when she returned with two glasses and a bottle of Ballantine's. She pulled a coffee table over and poured out two big chestnut-coloured shots, and the unmistakeably oak smell hit the Count.

"What are you scared of, Tamara?"

"Scared of?" she asked looking back at him. "Nothing. What about you, Mario?"

He felt the whisky's dry heat on his tongue and thought he should take his jacket off.

"I'm scared of everything, every little thing. That maybe Rafael's dead or maybe he's not and that he'll turn up and everything will get back to normal. That the years are passing me by, putting an end to any likelihood I'll ever fulfil my dreams. That Skinny will die and I'll be left alone and will feel even guiltier. That tobacco will be the death of me. That I don't do my job properly. That I'll be really lonely, incredibly lonely . . . That I might fall in love with you, Rafael's wife, you who live in such a clean perfect world and whom I've wanted all my life," he said and looked at

142

Flora, so pristine and remote, and felt now he'd started he couldn't stop.

The precise day his life changed, Mario Conde was wondering how destinies are forged. A few days before he had read Thornton Wilder's novel *The Bridge of San Luis Rey* and thought how he too could have been one of the seven individuals that destiny led to converge on the old bridge of the Vice-Regency of Peru at that precise moment, among millions of precise moments when its weary supports decided wearily to give way. The seven fell into the abyss, and he was obsessed by the image of seven individuals flying above the condors, and the strictly police investigation through which another individual sought out reasons for the impossible convergence of those men and women who'd never before coincided anywhere on earth and had now gathered to die on the bridge of San Luis Rey. He'd gone to the Psychology Faculty offices to tell them he was leaving the university and wasn't yet thinking about Destiny, when the deputy dean saw him and asked if he was resolved to abandon his studies, and he said he was, that he had no choice. She asked him to wait a moment and went out, and he waited fifteen minutes and a man came and introduced himself as Captain Rafael Acosta, who started off asking him what's your problem, my lad, and he thought what have I done to warrant an interrogation? It's down to money, comrade; I need work right now. So why don't you make an effort? the captain asked and he was even more at a loss. I need to work, he repeated, and I really don't like the degree course, and they started talking and he started to be less afraid when Captain Acosta suggested he entered the Academy, because he'd come

143

out an officer and would get a wage from month one. I'm not a party member, he'd said. Doesn't matter, we know who you are. I've never been a leader, he'd said, I'm very laid back, and I love the Beatles, he thought, and again it didn't matter. He'd never thought of becoming a policeman or anything of the sort, what on earth use will I be? You'll find out later, persisted Captain Rafael Acosta, the important thing was to join, afterwards he could even study at university in the evenings, this degree or whichever you want to, and you'll have time to think about it, and didn't give it another thought: he said yes. Was that Destiny? he'd wondered ever since because he'd never imagined becoming a policeman, let alone a good policeman, as he'd been told he was, you need common sense, lots of common sense, a colleague explained, and they never assigned him to the Re-education Section, as he'd requested when he finished at the Academy, but to the General Information Department, classifying cases, *modus operandi*, different types of criminals, until he shut himself up in the computer room with an old file, read and reread papers and data, racked his brains till his head ached and forged a striking metaphor by joining two disconnected distant leads that had been rattling around loose in a murder case that had been under investigation for four years. Was that Destiny? he wondered now and remembered with pleasure his first stint in Criminal Investigations, when he didn't have to bother about uniform and could wear jeans and even grew a beard and moustache after working the Boss round, and felt he was foraying into the world to right wrongs and was full of optimism. Those days of euphoria now seemed distant and had soon given way to routine, for that is what being a policeman is, they'd enlighten him, common sense plus routine, as he'd

144

later tell new recruits, repeating Jorrín's patter, knowing how to make a start every day, even though you didn't want to start again and again. If it hadn't been for Destiny, he'd never have discovered the case waiting to be solved by him alone, because he wouldn't have said yes to Captain Acosta; because his father wouldn't have died before he'd finished his degree; because they'd have given him literature and not psychology when he finished at high school; because he wouldn't have enjoyed those books by Hemingway when he caught chickenpox late when he should have got it years earlier with all the other kids on the block; because he'd liked to have been a pilot, and they wouldn't have expelled him from military school for launching a verbal and physical attack on a colleague who'd mercilessly mocked his desire to fly, and so on *ad nauseam*, because perhaps he'd never have been born or, Great Granddad Teodoro, the first of the Condes, wouldn't have thieved or ever have landed up in Cuba. That was why he was a policeman and Destiny had placed him in Rafael Morín's life and in yours, Tamara, a life so remote from yours, it was difficult to think they'd once thought they were equals. But life changes, like everything else, and he was no longer crazy and irresponsible, only as neurotic as ever, incurable, sad, lonely and sentimental, without wife or children perhaps forever, knowing his best friend might die, that nothing could be done for him, and carrying that pistol that weighed on his belt and which he'd only once fired away from the practice-ground, in fact, almost sure he'd miss his target, because he couldn't shoot anyone, yet he did shoot and was on target. But he could remember how on that precise day that changed his life he'd asked himself what is this thing called Destiny and got a single

145

response: say yes or say no. If you can . . . I did have a choice, Tamara.

"Pour me another," he asked, taking another look. She'd listened to him while drinking her whisky, and her eyes glazed over. She poured two more shots before admitting: "I'm afraid too", and it was almost a sigh that rose from the depths of that armchair. She'd left her troublesome lock over her eyes, as if she'd got used to living with it, to seeing it before she saw anything else in the world.

"Afraid of what?"

"Of feeling empty inside. Of ending up on my back talking about cotton and silk, of not living my life, of thinking I have everything because I'm used to having everything and there are things I think I can't live without. I'm afraid of everything and don't even under-stand myself anymore, and I could quite easily want Rafael to be here, so everything could stay easy and orderly, as wish he might never reappear so I can strike out on my own, without Rafael, Daddy, Mima, my son even . . . And it's nothing new, Mario, I've felt like this for some time."

"Let me tell you something. I just remembered what Sandín the gypsy's aunt said when she read your palm. Do you remember?"

"Of course I do, I've never forgotten: 'You'll have everything and nothing.' Could that have been on my palm ever since? Was that my destiny, as you say?"

"I don't know, because she got me all wrong: she said I'd travel a long way and die young. She mistook me for Skinny Carlos, or possibly not, perhaps we're the ones who got it wrong . . . Tamara, do you have it in you to kill your husband?"

146

She took a long sip, then stood up.

"Why do we have to be so complicated, my sorry policeman?" she asked as she stood in front of him. "Every woman at some stage wants to kill her husband; that much you must know. But in the end few do. Least of all big cowardly me, Mario," she announced before taking a step forward.

He gripped his drink, held it against his stomach, tried not to touch her thighs. He felt his hands shaking, and breathing became a difficult conscious act.

"You never before dared tell me you liked me. Why now?"

"How long have you known?"

"Forever. Don't belittle the female intellect, Mario."

He leaned his head back and shut his eyes.

"I think I'd have dared if Rafael hadn't beat me to it seventeen years ago. After that I couldn't. You can't imagine how much I loved you, the number of times I dreamed of you, the things I imagined us doing together. But none of this makes any sense now."

"Why are you so sure?"

"Because we drift further apart by the day, Tamara."

She shook her head, took another step forward and touched his knees.

"And what if I said I'd like to go to bed with you right now?"

"I'd think it was just another one of your whims, that you're used to getting what you want. Why do this to me?" he asked because he couldn't fight it, his chest throbbing, his mouth dry and his glass about to slip from his wet palms.

"Didn't you want me to say that? Wasn't that what you wanted me to say? Are you always going to be afraid?"

"I think so."

"But we will go to bed because I know you still want me and that you won't say no."

He looked at her and put his glass on the floor. He felt she wasn't the same woman, she'd changed, was a woman in heat, had that smell. And he thought now was his chance to say no.

"And if I say no?"

"You'll have had yet another chance to create your own destiny, by saying yes or no. You like decisions, don't you?" she asked, taking the final step possible, the one placing her right between his legs. Her smell was irresistible, and he knew she was more desirable than ever. He could see her nipples under her pullover, threatening, inflamed by cold and desire, no doubt as dark as her lips, and caught a glimpse of himself, at the age of thirty-four, on the rim of the pan, nourishing his most ancient of frustrations with saliva and without passion. He then stood in the intimate space she'd left him to take his decision and looked at the inevitable lock of hair, her moistening eyes, and knew he should say no forever, I can't do it, I don't want to do it, I can't, I shouldn't. He felt a stupid emptiness between his legs, and that was another form of fear. But always fighting against Destiny was futile.

They didn't touch each other as they walked towards the hall and went upstairs to the rooms on the second floor. She went first and opened a door, and they entered more palpable shadows around a bed perfectly draped in a brown overlay. He didn't know if he was or wasn't in her room, his ability to think had evaporated and when she pulled her pullover over her head and he finally saw the breasts he'd been dreaming of for the last seventeen years, he did think they were more beautiful than he'd ever imagined, that he could never have said no. But as much as he desired her, he wanted Rafael Morín to pop up at that precise moment, just to see that perpetual smile wiped from his face.

He smoked and tried to count the lights on the chandelier. He knew he'd killed another dream but must accept the consequences. Inaccessible Tamara, the more beautiful of the twins, now slept the sleep of a carefree lover, and her round heavy buttocks brushed against the Count's hips. I don't want to think, he told himself, I can't spend my life thinking, when the telephone rang, and she gave a start on the bed.

She clumsily tried to slip into her long pullover and finally made it to the passage where the telephone was still ringing. She came back to the bedroom: "Hurry. It's for you." She seemed confused and anxious.

He wrapped a towel round his midriff and went out. Tamara followed him to the door and watched him talk.

"Yes, who is it?" he asked, then listened for more than a minute before adding: "Send a car and I'll come straightaway."

He hung up and glanced at her. Went over to her, wanted to kiss her but first had to tussle with her wayward lock.

"No, Rafael hasn't turned up," he said, and they started on a long peaceful kiss, tongues gleefully intertwining, saliva mingling, lips beginning to hurt. It was their best kiss, and he said: "I've got to go to headquarters. They've found Zoila. I'll call you if anything involving Rafael crops up."

Zoila Amarán Izquierdo watched them enter the cubicle. Her eyes hovered between indifference and suspicion, while Mario Conde savoured her lusty femininity. The young woman's skin wore a healthy animal sheen; and her mouth, her face's most striking feature, was fleshy, shamelessly attractive. She was a self-confident twenty-three-year-old: the Count anticipated it wouldn't be easy. That girl was streetwise and then some: she'd been hardened through contact with all kinds, and one of her sources of pride was that she could say I don't owe anybody anything, and I've a fine set of what it takes, as she must have been called on to demonstrate more than once. She liked the good life and wasn't worried about flirting with the illegal to get it, because, apart from having what it takes, she had a sharp enough brain to avoid crossing boundaries that were too dangerous. No, it wouldn't be easy, he warned himself after taking one look and concluding she was one of those women who are so beautiful you felt like kissing the ground they walked.

"This is Zoila Amarán Izquierdo, Comrade Lieutenant," said Manolo, and he walked over to the woman who stayed seated in the middle of the cubicle. "Our colleague spotted her returning home in a taxi and asked her to come to headquarters for questioning."

"We only want to ask you a few things, Zoila. You're not under arrest, and we want you to help us, OK?" explained the Count as he headed towards the door, seeking out an angle from which she'd have to twist round to see him.

"Why?" she asked keeping still, and her voice was equally beautiful, clear and resonant.

The Count signalled to Manolo to start.

"Where were you on the thirty-first?"

"Do I have to answer that?"

"I'd like you to, but it's not compulsory. Where were you, Zoila?"

"Round and about, with a friend. This is a free sovereign country, they tell me?"

"Where?"

"Oh, in Cienfuegos, a house belonging to a friend of his."

"And the name of those friends?"

"What's this all about, for heaven's sake?"

"Please, Zoila, name names. The quicker we get this over with, the quicker you leave."

"Norberto Codina and Ambrosio Fornés, I think, all right? Can I go now?"

"That's fine, but there's still . . . Wasn't there another friend by the name of Rafael, Rafael Morín?"

"I've already been asked that, and I said I don't know who he is. Why should I?"

"Isn't he a friend of yours?"

"I don't know him."

"Where does your Cienfuegos friend live?"

"Around the corner from the theatre, I don't know the name of the street."

"Are you sure you don't remember Rafael Morín?"

"Hey, what *is* all this about? Look, I'll clam up if you like and that will be the end of that."

"All right, just as you like. You clam up, but we can keep you shut up here, awaiting investigation, on suspicion of kidnapping and murder and . . ."

"What *is* all this about?"

"It's an investigation, Zoila, you know? What's the name of the friend who went to Cienfuegos with you?"

"Norberto Codina, I told you."

"Where does he live?"

"On Línea and N."

"Does he have a phone?"

"Yes."

"What number?"

"What are you going to do?"

"Ring to find out if it's true you were with him."

151

"Hey, the guy's married."

"Give me his number, we're the souls of discretion."

"Please, comrades. It's 325307."

"Give him a call, Lieutenant."

The Count went over to the phone on the filing cabinet and asked for a line.

"Look at this photo, Zoila," Manolo continued and handed her a copy of the Rafael Morín photo they were circulating.

"Yes, well, what has happened . . .?" she asked, trying to catch the Count's whispered exchanges with Manolo.

"Don't you recognize him?"

"Yes, I went out with him a few times. Some three months ago."

"And you don't know his name?"

"René."

"René?"

"René Maciques, why?"

The Count hung up and walked over to his desk.

"Zoila, are you sure that's his name?" the lieutenant asked, and the girl looked at him with the slightest hint of a smile.

"Yes, I am entirely sure."

"She was with Norberto Codina," stated the Count before returning to the door.

"You see. I told you so."

"Where did you meet René?"

Zoila Amarán Izquierdo signalled her total incomprehension. It was clear she understood nothing but was scared of something, and now she really did smile.

"In the street, he picked me up."

"And why did he call you on the thirty-first, if not the first?"

"Who? René?"

"René Maciques?"

"I don't know, I'd not seen him for ages."

"For how long?"

"I'm not sure, October time?"

"What did you know about him?"

"Well, very little, that he was married, that he travelled abroad and when we stayed in hotels he always booked the rooms."

"Which hotels?"

"You can imagine. The Riviera, the Mar Azul, that kind of hotel."

"What did he say his line of work is?"

"Was it foreign affairs? Or foreign trade, something like that?"

"I don't know, you tell me."

"Well, I think it's foreign affairs."

"Did he have lots of money?"

"How else do you think you pay at the Riviera?"

"Watch what you're saying, Zoila. Give me an answer."

"Of course he had lots. But as I told you we only went out a few times."

"Didn't you meet up again?"

"No."

"Why not?"

"Because he went abroad. A whole year in Canada, I think."

"When was that?"

"Around October, I told you."

"Did he give you presents?"

"Little things."

"What kind of little thing?"

"Perfume, bracelets, a dress, that sort of thing."

"From abroad?"

"Yes, from abroad."

"So he had dollars?"

"I never saw any."

"How did you get to see each other?"

"Simple, he always had lots of work on, and when he had a chance he'd call me at home. If I wasn't busy, he'd come for me. In his car. Naturally."

"What kind of car?"

"He had two. Almost always the newer one, a private Lada, and sometimes in another Lada, state-owned I think, with tinted glass."

"Zoila, now I want you to think carefully what you say: for your own good and for the good of your friend René Maciques. Where might he get so much money from?"

Zoila Amarán Izquierdo leaned her head to one side to look at the lieutenant, and her eyes tried to say how the hell should I know? Then she looked at Manolo and replied:

"You know, comrade, you don't ask that kind of question on the street. I'm not a whore because I don't go to bed for money, but if someone shows up with money and invites you to a meal at L'Aiglon and to a beer by the pool and then wants to hang out at a night club and go up to a room overlooking the Malecón, you don't dig any further. You enjoy yourself, comrade. Things are very bad these days, and you're only young once, right?"

Of course you're only young once, he thought, so much was obvious. A warm lazy voice and cloudless sky-blue eyes were the only visible reminder of the attributes of the mythical Baby-Face Miki, the lad who set the record for the number of girlfriends in one year at high school in La Víbora: twenty-eight all told,

154

snogged to a woman and some explored more thoroughly. Now he didn't have enough hair to attempt Afro curly waves but plenty enough to declare his bankruptcy and assume his baldpated fate. His beard was an explosion of reddish grey stubble, like the last Viking in a comic. His previously handsome face now had the consistency of a poorly kneaded biscuit: uneven, cracked, with mountains and valleys of poorly distributed, prematurely aged flab. He laughed and displayed the jaundiced sadness of his teeth, and if he laughed a lot, his smoker's lungs regaled him with a two-minute coughing fit. Miki was a warning, the Count told himself: his appearance was evidence that they would soon hit forty, were no longer spring chickens able to greet every morning afresh, and had good reason to be exhausted and nostalgic.

"This is a disaster area, Conde. Mariíta left me a month ago, and look at this pigsty." And his spread-eagled arms tried to embrace the endless mess in his living room. He picked up two glasses soiled by several generations of dirt and put them back in almost the same spot. Cursed the absent woman five times and went over to the record player. Without thinking, he took the LP on the top of the pile and put it on the turntable. "Listen to this and die: *The Best of the Mamas and the Papas* . . . It's not fair, the bastards sing so sweetly, right? With Mariíta I'm on my fifth divorce and third kid, and I get more miserable by the day. They share out my pay, and I can't even afford a smoke. Talking of which, give me a cigarette. Do you think anyone in this state can write? No shit, you don't feel like writing, let alone living, but it's important not to give up, though sometimes you get tired and do give up a bit. It's not easy, Conde, not easy at all. Listen to that . . . 'California Dreams', that's from when we were at secondary school. Oh, to be that young again. I listen to this song and I swear I even feel like getting married again. And have you finally got down to writing something?"

The Count shifted a pair of trousers and two shirts from an armchair and could sit down. He was intrigued by the fact that, apart from Lamey, Miki was the only writer spawned by that literary workshop at high school, which Miki basically attended to see what he could pull. But at some stage the bright spark had expressed his enthusiasm for literature, set his lights on becoming a writer and somehow or other had made it. Two books of short stories and one novel published: he was what was considered a prolific writer, although in a vein that the Count could never have tapped had he had the time or talent to defeat the defiantly white page. Miki wrote about literacy campaigns, the first years of the revolution and the class struggle, whereas he would have preferred to write a story about squalor. Something squalid and moving, because even though he'd not experienced many squalid things that were also moving, he'd more need of them than ever.

"No, I'm not writing."

"What's wrong?"

"I don't know, I try occasionally but nothing comes."

"It happens, right?"

"I think so."

"Give me another cigarette. If I'd got any coffee, I'd invite you, but I'm up shit-creek. Not even ciggies, you hound. How's it going, any sign of the guy yet?"

"No, he's not put in an appearance," said the Count trying to make himself comfortable in the sofa-chair, despite the spring that kept poking into him.

"When Carlos told me you were after Rafael, I almost pissed myself laughing. You must agree it's funny."

"It's not funny at all as far as I'm concerned."

Baby-Face Miki crushed his cigarette on the floor and coughed a couple of times.

"Rafael and I had some trouble five or six years ago. Did you know that? No, most people don't, and the old crowd from high school I keep bumping into ask me about him and think we're still good pals. It used to annoy me no end lying to the effect that everything was fine. You can't spend your whole life making out everything's fine . . . Don't you have the slightest fucking clue what might have happened to Rafael? Do you reckon he's gone off with a little number and will turn up acting as if butter wouldn't melt in his mouth?"

"I don't know, but I don't think so."

"What's up, man? You're very downbeat. Look, I have this strange thing with Rafael: I sometimes think I still like him, because once we were as close as brothers, and at others I pity him a little, just a very little, and then I feel indifferent, as if I don't care a fuck what's happened to him, because I didn't deserve all the trouble he got me into with the party check-up."

"What trouble?"

"Well, that's why I told Carlos you should make sure you saw me today. Listen, Conde: I know Rafael is up to his neck in something big. I don't know if what I'm going to tell you will be much use, maybe, you'll tell me. And if I'm telling you, it's because you're the policeman in charge of this case, because if it were someone else, he'd never find out. Look, the trouble came about because when they were vetting him for the party, Rafael gave them my name as a person they could ask, and the couple doing the audit on him did come to see me. I remember it happened when I'd left the Youth Organization, and they told me it was just routine, that if I'd known Rafael well from his time as a student that was all they needed. Imagine, had I known him? Then they started to question me, and I answered, and everything went just fine. Well, kid, two months later Rafael showed up here in a right rage: he said it was my fault they'd deferred his joining the party, that I shouldn't have said his mum went to church or that he went to see his father when he came back to the country, that his old man was more fucked than a dog without teeth, a poor sucker who was still a third-rate Miami plumber, although he and his mother told people his father was a drunkard and dead. And what most got his goat was that I said he still loved his dad and was very pleased they'd seen each other again after twenty years, because since we'd been at primary school he'd been traumatized by what happened to his father and the fucking fact he'd left the island. You know, I looked for the human side of the story . . . I only wish Yoly was here to tell you. He went mad, shouted in my face that I was a cunt, that I was jealous of him plus a few excremental pleasantries. But that's not the worst of it, and don't look at me like that. The worst is that I went to the office where he worked and talked to the guys who questioned me because I didn't think any of what I'd said was that bad, and that's what they said, that it was just another element in his dossier, and of no great consequence because they could understand he'd wanted to see his father but that they had deferred his entry into the party because he'd shown signs of arrogance and been in a silly dispute with the union, I don't remember what, but they were sure he'd get there, blah, blah, blah. That was the spot of trouble."

"I had a vague idea about all that. Sounds just like him," said the Count, and he anticipated Miki's desires.

Gave him a cigarette and lit his. "But what's all that got to do with the trouble he's causing now?"

"It has to do with the fact that, in his eyes, I'm a liar. The truth is that he thought I'd told the investigation that he accepted the suitcase of clothes his father had brought and that they went to the Diplomat Shop and that I even gave him one hundred and fifty pesos for jeans that were too big for him. But I said nothing of the sort but said what I said to defend him, not because I'm naturally a liar, but because those days all that was lethal ammunition to militants and I'd invented a sentimental tale about him and his . . ."

"Hell, Miki . . ."

"Hey wait a minute, don't start on me, I don't need your absolution. I didn't ask you to come here to make a confession to you. The nitty-gritty is that Rafael came back here on the afternoon of the thirty-first, at about three pm, after years of ignoring me. Now you're interested, I bet, Conde. I know you only too well."

"Why did he come, Miki?"

"Now wait another minute, let me turn the record over, the one Rafael gave me for New Year. He knew I'm addicted to the Mamas and the Stones . . . I was very, very surprised to see him round here, but I was really pleased, as I'm not one to harbour a grudge. Well, I borrowed a packet of coffee from my next-door neighbour, and we drank the pint of rum I had left, and we chatted as if nothing had ever happened. We raked over a stack of shit about secondary school, high school, the barrio, the usual. Rafael had a chip, you know? In the end he was the one who envied me, and he told me so right where you're sat now. He told me I'd always done what I damned well wanted and lived as I wanted: fancy, me as fucked as I am, with three books published that I reckon are pure cow dung

159

I don't even like opening. When I told him that he laughed his head off. He always thought I was joking."

"But what did he want, man? Why the hell did he pay you a call?"

"He came to say he was sorry, Count. He wanted me to forgive him. You know what he said? He said I'd been his best friend."

Mario Conde couldn't help himself: yet again he had visions of Tamara stripping off and felt sure he was being sucked into a deadly quagmire.

"Was he a cynic or just an asshole?"

Miki repeated the exercise of crushing his cigarette end on the floor but destroyed it carefully, and after he'd destroyed it, kept stomping his foot down.

"Why talk like that, Count? You're another one with a chip, right? That's why you'll never be a mediocre writer like me, or an elegant opportunist like Rafael or even a good person like Carlos. You will never make it anywhere, Conde, because you want to sit in judgement on everyone but yourself."

"You're talking shit, Miki."

"I'm not talking shit at all, and you know it. You're afraid of yourself, and you'll never face up to it. Why aren't you a real policeman? You're always going off at half cock. You're the typical representative of our hidden generation, as a professor of philosophy at the university once told me. He said we were a face-less, aimless, gutless generation. That we didn't know where we stood or what we wanted and so preferred to hide. I'm a lousy writer, I don't want to get into trouble over what I write: I know that much. But what are you?"

"Someone who doesn't give a fuck about what you just said."

Miki smiled and held out a hand. The Count

gave him the last cigarette from the packet he then crumpled into a ball and lobbed at the window.

"That LP is really good, right?" asked the writer, enjoying the smoke from his cigarette.

"Hey, Miki," asked the lieutenant, looking his old schoolmate in the eye, "was that record of yours at high school just another of your lies?"

He never heard the bullet, and first he thought, my waist's been opened up, but hardly, because he lost his balance, and by the time he hit the ground he was already unconscious, and he only recovered consciousness two hours later, when he learned what real pain was, when he was flying in a helicopter to Luanda, with a drip in one arm, and the doctor said: Don't move, we'll soon get there, but he didn't need to be told, for he couldn't move any part of his body, and the pain was so intense he passed out, and his next memory was from after his emergency operation in the Luanda Military Hospital.

Once he'd heard that story, the Count repeated it to himself so many times he'd turned it into a film and could visualize every detail of the sequence: the way he fell facedown on the hot sandy ground that smelled remotely of dry fish; the sound of the helicopter, and a very young doctor's pale face saying: Don't move, the 0187 is about to land, and he could also see the inside of the aircraft, he must have felt cold, and remembered seeing an immaculately white cloud scud by in the distance.

After he'd had another operation in Havana, Skinny told him the story of his only engagement with an enemy he'd not even seen. Josefina looked after him by day, and the Count, Pancho, Rabbit and Andrés took it in turns by night and chatted till they fell asleep and even Mario Conde convinced himself that that had been his war, though his hands never held a gun and the face of his enemy was self-evident: a bedridden Skinny. He already knew it was unlikely his friend would walk again: the easy, carefree, cheerful relationship they'd enjoyed till then had been tarnished by a feeling of guilt the Count never managed to exorcize.

"Why do you have to get like that, you wild man?"

"What do you expect me to be like after what those wankers did to you? The cowardly assholes. And when they lost on Saturday I imagined this was coming, because it seemed that luck was on their side but they couldn't score and left everybody on base and the Vegueros won with just a couple of ridiculous runs. And feel pleased you didn't see today's game: they belted fifteen hits in the first inning, went ahead nine-one, and in the second, the one they really had to win, they lost nine-zero. Hell, how can you spend your whole life waiting for these wankers to win a championship when they always open their legs like hookers when they really need to concentrate on winning? But I get like this because I'm an idiot, I should just give up watching bloody baseball . . ."

"So you don't want a shot of rum?"

"Take it easy, Count, take it easy. Give it here," and he grabbed the glass the Count had put next to the ashtray, as if making a real sacrifice.

"Hey, and what got into you, buying rum?"

"Conde, I'm in a right state. Either you drink rum or piss off as if I'd never seen you."

"I'll drink rum, but let's change the subject, because I'm not the team manager, right?"

"If you say so."

Skinny poured himself another shot and seemed to

have declared a truce. His deep breathing returned to normal.

"How you getting on with the Rafael thing, my brother?"

"It's getting better. We've got a good lead."

"Did you see Miki?"

"Uh-huh. I've just come from his place. He was really odd. I thought he was more in need of a priest than a policeman."

"And did you forgive his sins?"

"I consigned him and his three books to hell. For being a liar and a bad writer. Pour me some more, quick."

"And what's the lead?"

"That lots of money passed through Rafael's hands and he'd probably run into difficulties with finances at the enterprise. Guess what the bastard did when he picked up a chick? He'd tell her his name was his department head's: see the kind of dick-head our pal is."

"We'd all do the same, kid," replied Skinny, gulping his rum down anxiously. The Count did likewise and didn't even think how good the rum was. "You had something to eat?"

"No, I don't feel like food. Let me down a few shots and then go to sleep."

"Did you see the twin today?"

"Yes, around midday. Nothing new to report. I drank two whiskies with her . . ."

"Yours is a hard life, isn't it?"

The Count opted for another rum rather than to start another argument with Skinny. That's what he's after, the bastard, he's lost it after the baseball, he told himself, and used his feet to take his shoes off. He was beginning to feel comfortable, slumped in an armchair,

163

Jose was looking at television in the living room and he suddenly remembered the Mamas and the Papas and felt an urgent need to listen to music.

"I'll put something on," he said and walked over to the sideboard where the cassette player stood. He opened a drawer and studied the cassettes Skinny had numbered and put in order. The complete Beatles; almost all of Chicago and Blood, Sweat and Tears; several tapes of Serrat, Silvio and Pablo Milanés; and one of Patxy Andión, selections from Los Brincos, Juan and Junior, Formula V, Stevie Wonder and Rubén Blades. What a mixture, hell, and he chose the tape of a record sung in English by Rubén Blades that he'd given Skinny as a present. He switched on the deck, gulped down a generous measure and poured out Skinny and himself some more rum. Now the pain had gone from his back and butt that had been tortured by Miki's armchair.

He liked that record and knew Skinny did, and they felt morbidly carefree singing the ballad "The Letter", the epistle a friend writes to another who knows he's going to die, and they drank and drank like thirsty pilgrims. The bottom of the bottle was beginning to show; and Skinny moved his wheelchair over to the glass cabinet and pointed to the pint left over from the day before, and they thought great, we've got another pint of rum, we can handle it, and they wanted to down all that alcohol.

"This rum's delicious, right?" asked Skinny, smiling.

"You're coming out with the usual drunken shit."

"But what did I say wrong, kid?"

"Nothing, that it's good rum blah blah. Of course it's good, you beast."

"And what's this drunken shit? You can't open your mouth in this place now . . ."

He protested and started drinking again, as if wanting to clear his throat. Mario looked at him and saw a man so fat and so changed he didn't know how long he could count on Skinny, and the residue from all his nostalgia and failures started to rise to his brain as he tried to imagine Carlos standing up and walking, but his brain refused to process that pleasant sight. And it was the last straw.

"When was your last embarrassing moment, Skinny, I mean really embarrassing moment?"

"Hey, kid," Skinny smiled and held his rum up to the light, "so I'm the pickled one around here, am I? And what are people who start to ask such things – cosmonauts?"

"Kid, try to be serious."

"No, you beast, I don't make a habit of counting these things up. Living like this," and he pointed to his legs but smiled, "living like this is embarrassing enough, but what do you want me to say?"

The Count looked at him and nodded, of course, it was embarrassing, but he knew how to set things straight.

"What was your most embarrassing moment?"

"Hey, just what are you after? You tell me yours."

"Mine . . . Wait a minute. When I was learning to drive and turned into a service station, I braked badly and knocked over a tank containing fifty-five gallons of petrol. The bastards there all clapped."

"And from all the shit in the past?"

"Well, every time I remember, I feel really sick . . . I don't know why. I feel the same when I remember the day Mad Eduardo put the boot into the camp-leader's face and I was afraid I'd insult Rafael's mother."

"Yes, right, I remember that . . . Look, I get sick as

shit whenever a nurse has to take my cock so I can pee in the pot."

"And the day I crouched down at university and my trousers split and my underpants had two holes as big as . . ."

"And the day we went to eat in Pinar del Río, you, me and Ernestico, when we were picking tobacco, and I said, well I'm going to put clean pants on, you never know when you might pull a country girly and it turned out the ones I'd put in my case were all brown patches."

"And you still worry about that? I feel real fucking bad when I remember that second-year meeting, when they wanted to kick some guy out of the class because he'd been accused of being a queer, and I didn't stand up and defend him, because I was scared they'd mention the Venezuelan girl who was going out with me at the time, you remember, Marieta, she of the small butt and big tits?"

"Hey, sure, tell me more . . . Kid, one day a nurse came from the clinic to give me an injection. It was very late, and I didn't hear her come in and she caught me with my prick flying high from that magazine Peyi lent me."

"That's fucking terrible," and to round the session off they had recourse to another bottle. "Just like the day I went to grab the rail on the bus when the driver braked suddenly, and I grabbed that woman's tit, and she whacked me and called me everything from bastard downwards, and people started shouting, groper, groper . . ."

"And fuck, what about the day the Rank-and-File Committee designated me and another girl to persuade people not to come to school with such long hair, and I went along with it, though it wasn't in the rules? Shit, the things they forced you to do."

"Wait a minute, you just wait one minute, I've one to beat you, you beast, the day I spoke, *señor,* with a lilt so they'd think I was Venezuelan and would let me in the Capri with Marieta. Incredible, how embarrassing . . ."

"Hey, and I'd rather not remember the day, yes, a drop more rum, the day when black Samson stole my tin of condensed milk in the cane-cutting camp and I knew he'd done it but played dumb so I wouldn't have to fight him."

"Shit, life's one bowl of shit . . . And what happened to me today, Skinny, I can't, I'll die of embarrassment, of rum, I'll die," and he shut his eyes in order to keep a hold on his brain's battered remnants of lucidity so as not to die of embarrassment yet again and confess, "Skinny, Tamara invited me to lay her, because, you know, she had to make the first move, because I was shit-scared, and we went upstairs and yes, her tits are just like we imagined, and we got into bed, and not a flicker, not a bloody flicker, and then it perked up and I came just like that, brother, we'd hardly started, and she said, not to worry, these things happen, not to worry. Hell, Skinny, things happen that make you want to commit suicide you're so embarrassed. Give me that bottle of rum, Skinny, come on, hand it over."

Each morning seemed to dawn as if ripe for Armageddon. An apocalyptic clap from an eardrum-shattering bell that heralded the end of the world: even Rabbit had no option but to wake up. Their leader enjoyed ringing that bell all round the camp, and what's more he shouted "On your feet, up you get, on your feet", and even if we were on our feet or standing up holding our hands to our heads, he went on ringing that bell, ding-dong dong-ding, up and down the huts, until one day a righteous, mud-caked boot flew out of the darkness and smashed into the camp-leader's nose. He fell on his backside and dropped the bell, and those who hadn't seen the big boot wondered, happy and relieved, why on earth he'd stopped.

Within a quarter of an hour we were all lined up on the wasteland between the huts and the refectory. Eight brigades, five from eleventh grade and three from thirteenth, in front of the general staff of the camp. It was an hour before sunrise, bitterly cold, and we could feel the dew falling, and knew something bad was in store. When Baby-Face Miki, one of the brigade leaders for thirteenth grade, walked by, he muttered: "Speak and die . . ." The camp leader held a towel to his nose, and I could almost see the shafts of hatred winging from his eyes. Behind me Pancho had wrapped himself in a blanket, but they'd forced him into the open air and he wheezed like a pair of rusty bellows and when I heard him I thought I too would soon be gasping for air.

The school secretary spoke: there'd been a very serious act of indiscipline, which would lead to the guilty individual's expulsion, and there'd be no appeals or let-offs, and if he had any civic spirit he should step up. Silence. How could there be such an act of indiscipline in a camp for high school students? This wasn't a farm for re-educating kids from reform school. That kind of person, he added, was like a rotten potato in a sack of healthy ones: it corrupted and rotted the rest; they always used potatoes as an example as we never saw an apple. Rabbit looked at me, starting to wake up. Silence. Silence. Did nobody dare expose the miscreant who was tarnishing the prestige of the whole cohort that would not now win the league table after expending so much effort cutting cane? Silence. Silence. Silence. Skinny raised his eyebrows; he knew what was coming. All right then, if the guilty person wouldn't step forward and nobody had civic spirit enough to denounce him, then everyone would be punished until that person was found, for things couldn't continue as normal . . . A cosmic silence followed the secretary's speech, and the smell of coffee being prepared in the kitchen became the first, most subtle of the tortures we'd suffer out in that cold. Pancho was still out of breath.

Then the oracle from Delphi spoke: "I'm here as a student," said Rafael, "as a comrade and your representative elected by mass vote, and I know, just as you do, that someone here has committed a serious breach of discipline and could be taken to court for grievous bodily harm . . ." "Listen to him," said Rabbit . . . ". . . for which we sinners will have to pay . . ." He had to have his Biblical touch. ". . . and it really affects us in the inter-camp competition, where we were almost sure of first place in the province. Can that be right because of a single person's indiscipline? That the labours of one hundred and twelve comrades, yes, one hundred and twelve, because I'm now excluding the guilty party, should bite the dust? You know me, comrades, there are people here who've been with me for three years, you elected me president of the Student Federation and I'm just an ordinary student like the rest of you, but I can't approve of things like this, that besmirch the prestige of the revolutionary Cuban student body and force the school management team to take disciplinary measures against you all." More silence. "And I ask you, since you are clinging to male pride and such like: Is it manly to throw a boot in the dark at the camp's supreme head? Similarly: is it manly to hide in the crowd and not show your face, knowing we will all suffer? Speak up, comrades, speak up," he asked, and I shouted "Fuck your mother, you pansy!" at the top of my voice so everybody heard me fuck his mother, except the words didn't reach my lips because I was afraid of fucking Rafael Morín's mother there, in that cold, with Pancho all asthmatic, and Baby-Face Miki walking up and down the lines saying "Die", the smell of coffee killing me and the camp leader pressing a towel to his nose because of a boot that had been flung his way.

When the Count entered headquarters he felt nostalgic for the peace and quiet of Sundays. It was barely five past eight. But it was Monday, and every Monday the world seemed to be coming to an end as if headquarters were preparing to evacuate before the outbreak of nuclear war: people couldn't wait for the lift and rushed up the stairs; there was no space in the parking lot and exchanges of greetings were limited to a quick

170

"All right then?", "See you" or a garbled "Good day"; and suffering from the aftermath of his headache and dismal night, the Count preferred to respond with a wave of the hand and wait patiently in the queue for the lift. He knew he'd feel much better in half an hour, but the painkillers needed time to impact, although he wasn't reproaching himself for not taking them the night before. He felt so pure and liberated after talking to Skinny that he forgot he'd never told him what happened with Tamara and also that he should set his alarm clock. Another episode in the nightmare in which Rafael Morín was chasing him to put him behind bars opened his eyes at exactly seven am and he felt like dying at least twice: when he got out of bed and his headache kicked off and when, seated on the pan, he ruminated over the nightmare he'd been suffering all night and the terrible feeling of being chased that still floated in his brain. Then he burst spontaneously into song: "You're to blame, for all my sadness, for all my heartbreaks . . ." unable to fathom why he'd chosen that wretched bolero. He must be in love.

The lift stopped on his floor, and the Count looked at the clock on the wall: he was ten minutes late and wasn't inclined or in the mood to invent some excuse. He opened the door to his cubicle and was blessed by Patricia Wong's smile.

"Good morning, friends," he greeted them. Patricia stood up to give him the usual kiss, and Manolo looked at him distantly and didn't open his mouth. "What a nice smell, China," he complimented his colleague and stopped for a moment to contemplate, as he always did, that impressive woman who was half-black and half-Chinese. Almost six feet tall and one hundred and eighty pounds distributed carefully with the best

171

of intentions: her breasts small and no doubt very firm, hips like the Pacific Ocean, and buttocks that inevitably provoked a desire to touch or mount them and jump up and down, as if trampolining, to check out whether such a prodigious rump was for real.

"How are you, Mayo?" she asked, and the Count smiled for the first time that day on hearing that "Mayo" which was for Patricia Wong's exclusive use. Besides, she helped his headaches with her little jars of Chinese pomade and fed his most hidden, never acknowledged superstitions: she was like a good luck charm. On three occasions Lieutenant Patricia Wong, the detective in the Fraud Squad, had presented him on a plate the solution to three cases that seemed about to evaporate in the innocence of the world.

"Still waiting for your father to invite me to eat another plate of bittersweet duck."

"If you'd seen what he cooked yesterday," she began as she struggled to fit her hips between the sides of the armchair. Then she crossed her long-distance runner's legs, and the Count saw Manolo's eyes were about to flee behind his nostrils. "He prepared quails stuffed with vegetables and cooked them in basil juice . . ."

"Hey, wait a minute, give us the full story! What did he stuff them with?"

"First, he crushed the basil leaves in a little coconut oil and boiled them. Then added the quail which was already bread-crumbed, basted in pork-fat and stuffed with almonds, sesame and five kinds of uncooked herbs: Chinese bean, spring onion, cabbage, parsley and a little something else, and finished it off with a sprinkling of cinnamon and nutmeg."

"And was it ready to eat?" asked the Count, his morning enthusiasm peaking.

"But it must have tasted foul, I bet?" interjected

Manolo, and the Count gave him a withering look. He wanted to say something cutting but first tried to imagine the impossible mixture of those strong, primary flavours that could only be blended by a man with old Juan Wong's culture, and decided Manolo might be right, but he didn't give up.

"Ignore the boy, China, his lack of culture will be the death of him. But you stopped inviting me long ago."

"And you never ring me, Mayo. You even sent Manolo to bring me in on this job."

"Forget it, forget it, it won't happen again." He stared at the sergeant, who'd just lit a cigarette at that hour of the morning. "And what's up with this guy?"

Manolo clicked his tongue, meaning, "Leave me alone", but he needed to talk.

"Oh, only a terrible row with Vilma last night. Do you know what she said? She reckons I invented an excuse about work in order to go out and lay someone else." And he looked at Patricia. "And it's all his fault."

"Manolo, give me a break, please?" the Count pleaded, looking at the dossier open on the table. "You're in a really bad state if you're telling people I force you to do things . . . Did you explain to Patricia what we're after?"

Manolo nodded reluctantly.

"Yes, he told me, Mayo," Patricia intervened. "You know, I don't hold much hope we'll dig anything important out of the paperwork. If Rafael Morín is in some scam and as efficient as they say, he'll have hidden his clothes before taking a dip. We can but try, I suppose."

"You've got a team together?"

"Yes, two specialists. And you two as well?"

The Count looked at Patricia and then at Manolo.

He realized his headache had disappeared but tapped his forehead and said:

"Look, China, just take Manolo along. I've got a number of things to see to here . . . I've got to read the reports which have come in . . ."

"There are none," the sergeant informed him.

"You looked at everything?"

"Nothing from the coastguards or the provinces, the Zoilita business will gradually sort itself, and we've arranged to see Maciques at the enterprise."

"All right, that's fine," the Count tried to wriggle out. He'd not seen eye to eye with statistics for some time and took pains to avoid that kind of routine research. "I won't be much use to you there, will I? And I want to see the Boss. I'll come and see you around ten o'clock, all right?"

"All right, all right," parroted Manolo, shrugging his shoulders. Patricia smiled, and her slanted eyes vanished into her face. Could she see anything when she laughed?

"See you soon," said Patricia, grabbing Manolo by the arm and dragging him out of the cubicle.

"Hey, China, wait a minute," the Count asked, and he whispered in her ear. "What did the quail taste like yesterday?"

"What the kid said," she whispered back. "Foul. But Dad scoffed the lot."

"Just as well." And he smiled at Manolo as he waved goodbye.

"Business deals involving lots of money are like jealous women: you can give them no reason to complain," said René Maciques, and the Count looked at Manolo; the lesson was for free and he'd got it quite wrong.

René Maciques was barely forty and not the fifty he'd imagined; and was no librarian but a television presenter persuasively using his voice and hands and constantly trying to tidy his bushy eyebrows with index finger and thumb. He was wearing a guayabera that seemed enamelled, it was so white, with a white embroidered pattern down the sides that was even brighter, and he flashed a glib gleaming smile. Three gold pens poked out from one pocket, and the Count thought only an asshole would try to show off his status with a display of pens. "If one is involved in that kind of business, one has to look trustworthy, appear relaxed as if the deal were already signed and exude quiet conviction. As I said, like a jealous woman: because at the same time, one must hint, quite matter-of-factly, that signing is no life or death matter, that one is aware of more attractive options, although one knows this couldn't be bettered. Big business is a jungle where every animal is dangerous and one needs more than a rifle over one's shoulder." And the Count thought, the king of the metaphor, this one! "And I know no comrade more adept than Rafael at doing deals. I had the opportunity to work a lot with him here in Cuba and in negotiations abroad, on really challenging contracts, and he behaved like an artist, sold at the top and always bought at below market price; and buyers and sellers were very satisfied, although they knew in the end that Rafael had hoodwinked them. And best of all: he never lost a customer."

"And why did he spend *his* time sealing these deals if he had experts in the different areas?" asked Mario Conde at the cue for applause for the speech from an unexpectedly silver-tongued Maciques.

"Because he felt fulfilled doing it and knew he was the best. Each commercial area within the enterprise

175

has its own expertise, whether according to line or geographical area, do you see? However, if the deal were very important or threatened to get stymied in some way, Rafael would advise the experts, draw on the business contacts he'd established over the years and enter the ring."

So he was a torero as well? the Count wanted to ask because he guessed Maciques might be a hard nut to crack as his obsolete if irrefutable verbiage spewed out. He looked down at his notebook, where he'd written BIG MONEY BUSINESS, and allowed himself a moment for thought: was Rafael Morín everything he was cracked up to be? Although from a considerable distance, he'd seen the social and professional rise of a man now declared missing. He leaped like a clever, well trained acrobat, one who jumps fearlessly into the void because they've put in place a safety net that assures them, up you go, just do it and you'll triumph, I'm here to protect you. Marriage into a wealthy family was half the battle: Tamara, her father, and her father's friends, must have smoothed the path for him, but for justice's sake he must accept the rest was down to him, no doubt about that. When Rafael Morín spoke from a microphone at high school twenty years earlier, his mind was already dead set on the idea of making it, of climbing all the way to the top, and was getting in training. At the time people's ambitions were usually abstract and vague, but Rafael's were already well formed, and that's why he got on the fast track and set out to secure every certificate, every recognition, every award and to be a perfect paragon, self-sacrificing and worthy, cultivating en route friendships that would at some stage be useful, yet he was never out of breath or without a smile. And he showed himself to be extremely able, always ready to make the slightest sacrifice to skip over several steps on the ladder to heaven, conveying good vibrations, trust, forging an image of himself as ever prepared and possessed with the necessary flexibility that made him look useful, malleable and reliable: a man who took on and completed every task he was charged with and quickly bounced back for the next. The Count was familiar with these stories of lives that blow with the wind and imagined the infallible cocky smile he'd put on when speaking to deputy minister Fernández-Lorea about how well things would turn out, Comrade Minister, according to the latest estimates received. Rafael Morín would never have argued with a superior, would only have had exchanges of opinion; he'd never have refused to carry out a ridiculous order, would only have offered constructive criticism and always through the right channels; he'd never have taken a jump without testing the safety net that would welcome him lovingly and maternally, if he had an unexpected fall. So where had he gone wrong?

"So where did he get the money to give the presents he gave?" asked the Count when he finally managed to read the only thing he'd jotted down. And was surprised how quickly René Maciques responded.

"I imagine he saved it from his daily allowances."

"And would that be enough for the hi-fi system he had at home, to buy his mother Chanel N° 5, for the big and small gifts he gave his subordinates and even to say his name was René Maciques and rent a room at the Riviera and take a twenty-three-year-old sparkler to dine at L'Aiglon? Are you sure, Maciques? Did you know he used your name with the women he picked up or did he never tell you, even in confidence as it were?"

René Maciques got up and walked towards the air conditioning unit built into the wall. Fiddled with the controls, straightened the curtain that had got caught up in one corner of his office. Perhaps he felt cold. That same night, while pondering the latest twist in the fate of Rafael Morín, Lieutenant Mario Conde recalled this scene as if he'd lived it ten or fifteen years earlier, or as if he'd never wanted to experience it, because Maciques returned to his chair, glanced at the policemen and no longer looked like a television presenter but the timid librarian the Count had imagined when he said:

"I just refuse to believe that, comrades."

"That's your problem, Maciques. I've no reason to lie to you. Now tell us about those presents."

"I told you: they must have come from what he saved out of his daily expense allowance."

"And could that run to so much?"

"I've no idea, comrades, you'd have to ask Rafael Morín."

"Hey, Maciques," said the Count as he stood up, "would we also have to ask Rafael Morín why you came here at lunchtime on the thirty-first?"

But René Maciques smiled. He was back on camera, stroking his eyebrows, when he said:

"What a coincidence! I came to do just that," and pointed at the air conditioning unit. "I remembered I'd left it switched on and came to turn it off."

Now the Count smiled and put his notebook back in his pocket. He was praying Patricia would find something that would allow him to pulverize René Maciques.

The only time Mario Conde shot at a man, he'd learned how easy it was to kill: you aim at the chest and stop thinking as you pull the trigger; the act of firing almost spares you the moment the bullet hits the man and knocks him to the ground like a hail of stones where writhing, wracked in pain, he does or doesn't die.

The Count was on leave that day, and for months he'd tried, as with everything else in his life, to find the thread to the tangled events that had put him, pistol in hand, in front of a man and forced him to shoot. It was two years after they moved him from the General Information Department to Investigations, and he'd met Haydée while investigating a violent robbery that had taken place in the office where she worked. He chatted to her a couple of times and realized the future of his marriage with Martiza was a thing of the past. Haydeé became the obsession of his life, and the Count thought he'd go mad. The passionate onslaught of their love, expressed daily in rooming houses, borrowed flats and other happy hunting grounds, was violently animal and offered him innumerable unexplored pleasures. The Count fell outrageously in love and performed the most extravagantly satisfying sexual deviations he'd ever experienced. They made love time and again, never endingly. When the Count was exhausted and blissful, Haydée knew how to extract that little bit more: he only had to hear her releasing a powerful yellow jet of pee or feel the magnetic tip of her tongue licking its way up his thighs and curling round his member to want to start all over again. Like no other woman, Haydée made him feel a male object of desire, and in each encounter they played love-games like inventive explorers or pent-up celibates.

If the Count hadn't fallen for that frivolous innocent abroad who was transformed whenever sex was nigh, he'd never have been standing, fretful yet happy, on the corner of calle Infanta, half a block away from the office where Haydée worked until five thirty pm. If that afternoon Haydée, in her rush to their next dose of delirium, hadn't made a mistake adding six and eight and getting twenty-four, as she noted in an impossible tally, she would have left at five thirty-one, and not five forty-two, when the din in the street and blast from the gun got her up from her desk all worried and anxious.

The Count lit his third despairing cigarette and didn't hear the cries. He was thinking about what would happen that afternoon in the flat of a friend of a friend who was on a two-month course in Moscow, which had become the momentary shelter for their still clandestine passion. He imagined a naked sweating Haydée working on the most sacred places of his trembling anatomy and only then saw a man streaming blood and running towards him, his green shirt darkening over his belly, apparently about to fall to the ground and beg forgiveness for all his sins, but he knew forgiveness wasn't in the mind of the other man who, with a limp in his left leg and a shattered mouth, was clutching a knife and running at him. For a long time the Count had thought that if he'd been in uniform, it might have stopped the man in a hurry who nobody else had challenged, but when he dropped his cigarette and shouted "Stop right there, you bastard, stop. I'm a policeman" the man straightened up, lifted his knife above his head and directed his hatred at the intruder in his path who was shouting at him. The strangest thing was that the Count always reran the scene in the third person, as if it were outside the perspective of his own eyes, and he saw the guy who was shouting take two steps backwards, put his hand to his waist and strike silently, and shot the man who was

180

still wielding a knife over his head less than a yard away. He saw him fall backwards, twist round in a way that seemed rehearsed, drop the knife from his grasp and start writhing in pain.

The bullet entered at shoulder level, barely splintering his collarbone. The only time Mario Conde shot someone, it all ended with a minor operation and a court case where he testified against his aggressor, who'd long since been cured and repented his alcohol-induced violence. But the Count endured several months of doubt as to whether he'd aimed at his attacker's shoulder or chest, and swore he'd never again resort to his pistol outside the shooting range, even if it meant engaging in hand-to-hand combat with a man with a knife. Nonetheless, he'd have reneged on that most solemn pledge if it ever came to René Maciques. I swear by my mother he would.

"Don Alfonso, let's be going to headquarters," he said and wound up the car window. The driver looked at him and knew he shouldn't ask any questions.

China Patricia and her team were sailing on a sea of salaries, contracts, service orders, purchases, travel, sales, memoranda, pledges, countersigned cheques and reports of agreements and disagreements all affirming that everything is fine and dandy, astonishingly correct; Zaida was on a different sea, of tears; it was true: the relationship between her and Rafael was really more than that of a boss and his secretary, went beyond the walls of the enterprise, but it was no crime, surely, because Rafael never suggested anything of the sort, never said anything along those lines, never ever, and she swore Rafael drove her home on the thirtieth and she'd not heard from him since. Manolo applied pressure and she cried, my son little Alfredo loved him so much and he got out of his car and went to wish him a Happy New Year; Maciques, of course, there were things he didn't know, he was only in charge of the office, they should question the deputy financial director, he'd be back from Canada on the tenth, and again he didn't think so; and the Boss, looking at the ash on his Davidoff, because he'd have to speak to his son-in-law because he couldn't stand any more from him, he took the boy off and turned up pasted at eleven thirty pm, his blood pressure had shot up with all this bother, but he wanted the case solved now, today, Mario, in three days Japanese buyers are coming who'd begun to negotiate a big deal with Rafael Morín for the purchase of sugar derivatives, a deal worth millions of dollars, Morín had worked several times with them and the minister wanted a reply, and he asked, Mario, do you need help?, two days had gone by and he still hadn't come up with anything.

The Count looked up and saw the cold glare of Monday 5 January and thought how tonight the temperature would be ideal for waiting till midnight to put out three bunches of grass and three bowls of honeyed water, in a corner of his house, for the camels, and a letter addressed to Melchior, Gaspar and Balthazar, but the telephone rang and he reluctantly jettisoned the idea of a letter to the Three Kings.

"Hello?" he said as he half sat down on his desk and stared at the tops of the laurel trees.

"Mario? It's me, Tamara."

"Oh, it's you, and how are you?"

"Last night I stayed up waiting for you to call."

"I know, but things got very difficult and I didn't leave here till late."

"And I called you this morning at around nine thirty."

"Nobody told me."

"I didn't leave a message. Why did they call you yesterday?"

"Just routine. Zoila is a friend of René Maciques and doesn't even know Rafael personally. We're making progress."

"And still no news of Rafael?" And all he really wanted to know was the intention behind that question. He almost preferred to believe Tamara was desperate for news of her husband and also thought how technically she was still suspect number one, as she added: "Uncertainty will be the death of me."

"Mine as well. I'm tired of all this."

"Of all what?"

And he hesitated for a moment, because he didn't want to get it wrong.

"Of being Rafael's private policeman."

"Have you been to the enterprise?"

"I was there just a minute ago. I left the Fraud Squad experts there."

"Fraud Squad? Mario, do you really think Rafael's involved in something like that?"

"What do *you* think, Tamara? Do you really believe he could buy everything he bought you with what he saved from his daily allowances?"

A protracted pregnant silence followed at the end of the line and finally she said:

"I don't know, Mario, I really don't. But I can't see Rafael mixed up in anything of that sort. He," she hesitated, "isn't a bad person."

"So they keep telling me," he muttered and wiped unexpected sweat from his forehead.

"What did you say?"

"That that's what I think as well."

And silence descended again.

"Mario," she said, "I'm not worried by what happened yesterday, that . . ."

"But I am, Tamara . . ."

"Oh, you just don't understand," she protested, feeling she needed to confess and he was making it more difficult for her. "Why do you think I'm calling you? Mario, I want to see you again, really."

"It doesn't make sense, Tamara. We'll see each other, and then what will happen?"

"I don't know. Must you think everything through a thousand times?"

"Yes, I must," he admitted, feeling his headache was on the way back.

"Won't you come?"

Mario Conde shut his eyes and saw her in bed, naked and nervous, open and expectant.

"I think I will. When I've found out what's happened to Rafael," he said as he hung up and felt the pain gather behind his eyes. It was like an oil slick spreading over his forehead and expanding, but the pain brought an idea, when I find out what's happened to Rafael, and Lieutenant Mario Conde reproached himself, you idiot, why didn't you start there?

"You come to die in my arms?" quipped Captain Contreras, and his contented, no-regrets fatso smile reverberated off the walls. He left his chair that gave a sigh of relief at an unlikely rate of knots for such an elephantine mass of humanity and walked over to shake the lieutenant's hand. "My friend the Count. Life's like that, my boy, brickbats today and thanks tomorrow, though some people are disgusted by what we do, you know? Naturally, nobody likes playing with shit, but someone has to and in the end they come

184

knocking on my door, you didn't, because you're a friend, although you've never wanted to work with me, but life is full of surprises." And he started laughing again. His paunch, tits, triple chin and cheeks danced for joy. He laughed so easily, so very easily, that the Count always thought Fatman Contreras laughed too easily. "Let me have a look, then."

The lieutenant handed him the photo. Captain Jesús Contreras scrutinized it for a few minutes, and the Count tried to imagine the constipated archive of his brain at work. What passed once through Fatman Contreras's eyes was forever engraved on his memory together with the most recondite distinguishing features. It was the pride of his life, and he knew he was always useful, if not indispensable, because Fatman was directly responsible for investigating foreign currency fraud and nobody could ever say he was short of work. The aim of his team – the Contreras Tubbies, as they were known – was to be the daily thorn in the side of Havana's speculators and dollar-sellers, and over recent months it had chalked up an enviable record for nailing speculators.

"He's not in the trade," he concluded, still looking at the photo. "What does your computer say on the matter?"

"That he's as clean as a baby's bottom straight out of the bath."

"I knew it. So what do you want from me?

"That you should get your informers and under-cover agents to check him out in case he ever sold dollars. He handled a lot of Cuban money, and I think that's how he got it. I also want you to investigate another guy whose photo I'll send you shortly."

"What are their handles?"

"This guy's Rafael Morín, and the other's René

Maciques, but don't worry about names, work on their faces."

"Hey now, Count, isn't this the fellow who disappeared?"

"Welcome to the party, Fatman."

"You gone mad? Don't go getting me into deep water. The man is a big deal ... A minister keeps calling the Boss and stuff like that. You dead sure he's been messing with greenbacks?" asked Contreras, dropping the photo on the desk as if it were suddenly a red-hot potato.

"I'm sure of fuck all, Fatman. It's a hunch from the heart or rather from a headache. Fatman, he was getting lots of money from somewhere, and it wasn't on the black market."

"Yes, it was, for all you know. But you're stirring shit, Conde and when the shit hits the fan ..." replied Fatman, returning to his bruised chair. "OK, when do you need to know by?"

"As of yesterday. The Boss is in a foul temper because I've been three days on the case. He'll soon want blood, and I suspect it will be mine he'll be after. So give me a helping hand, Fatman."

Then Captain Contreras laughed again. The Count was astonished he should find everything so amusing, because Fatman was in fact the hardest policeman he'd known, no doubt the best in his line of business, although his cheery obese face hid almost three hundred pounds of complexes. The ever-present smell of burnt grease he gave off and the hurried ends to both of his attempts at marriage were too much of a burden for him. But he fought back with laughter, convinced he'd been born to be a policeman and that he was a good one.

"All right, all right, as it's you ... Send me the

other photo and tell me where I can contact you if something turns up."

The Count stretched his hand out over Captain Contreras's desk, ready to suffer in silence the tight grip of a fist that could throttle a horse.

"Thanks, Fatman."

He left the office in the fallout from Fatman's guffaws and walked up to the Boss's office. Maruchi was typing, and the Count wondered at the fact she could talk, even look at him and still type.

"You're late, Marquess. I mean, Count. The major went out a minute ago," the girl told him. "He went to a meeting at Political Headquarters."

"Uh-uh, just as well," replied the lieutenant, who preferred to defer his confrontation with Major Rangel. "Can you tell him to wait till five thirty? I think I'll sort this case today. All right?"

"No problem at all, Lieutenant."

"Hey, wait a minute," he asked, and the secretary stopped typing and looked resigned. "Do you have a couple of aspirins?"

"What's new?" smiled the Count.

Manolo, Patricia and her experts in the Fraud Squad looked at him in a state of shock. He'd only left the enterprise an hour ago saying he'd be back in the afternoon, and now here he was demanding results. The lieutenant cleared a space on the desk in the deputy financial manager's office they'd been lent for the investigation and sat down, giving respite to less than one buttock.

"Nothing as yet, Mayo," said Patricia as she closed the folder labelled SERVICE ORDERS. "I warned you it wouldn't be easy."

"I don't understand why the hell they need so much paper," protested Manolo, opening his arms as if trying to embrace the huge office space occupied by the files that comprised the daily records of the enterprise. "And that's only for 1988. We'll soon have to invent an enterprise to deal with the papers of this enterprise."

"But just imagine, Mayo, despite all the controls, audits and checks, there's more theft, embezzling and siphoning off of funds than anybody could imagine. If there were no paperwork, it would be impossible to control."

"And have you found everything on Rafael's trips abroad and the business he was doing there?" asked the Count, who'd decided not to light up.

"There are the contracts, cheques and expenses records. And, of course, the breakdown for each business deal," replied Patricia Wong, pointing to two mountains of paper. "We had to start at the beginning."

"And how long will you need to make sense of it, China?"

The lieutenant laughed again, with that Chinese laugh of resignation that closed her eyes. No, she can't see, she can't.

"Two days at least, Mayo."

"No, China!" shouted the Count, and he stared at Manolo. The sergeant's eyes were begging "Get me out of here, man" and he seemed skinnier and more helpless than ever.

"I'm not Chan Li Po, that's for sure," protested Patricia, crossing her monumental legs.

"Fine, let's do two things, China. Use any excuse to get Maciques's file because I need a photo of him. And secondly, prioritize, you know, just prioritize, and while you're at it, right, look into all the agreements and payments in relation to allowances for Rafael, Maciques and the deputy financial director who's currently in Canada. Also look out the marketing expenses, in Cuba and abroad, and take a long hard look at the presents declared as the result of good contracts. I'm sure nothing extraordinary will turn up, but I need to know. And in particular, look at two areas, China: what Rafael did in Spain, the country he most visited, and check out all the deals he signed ever since he started to direct the enterprise, with the Japanese firm . . ." and then extracted his notebook from his back trouser pocket and read, ". . . Mitachi, because these Chinamen will be in Cuba in a couple of days and there may be something about them."

"This is all quite feasible, but don't call them Chinamen, if you don't mind," protested the lieutenant, and the Count remembered how Patricia had recently had an attack of nostalgia for Asia and had even joined the Chinese Society of Cuba, given her status as a direct descendent.

"Patricia, it boils down to the same thing more or less."

"Oh, Mayo, don't be so pigheaded. Go and tell my father that and see if he invites you back for dinner."

"Forget it, forget it. It's not that important."

"Hey, you seem very chirpy. You got something on the go?"

"If only, Patricia . . . All I've got is an ancient prejudice and what you can find now. Help me. Look, it's eleven thirty. You could get what I asked for by two . . ."

"By four at the earliest."

"No can do. I'll be here at three. Now let me have my boy back."

Patricia looked at Manolo and could read the torture in his squinting eyes.

"No problem, given his level of knowledge of finance and accounting . . ."

"Thanks for the compliment, Lieutenant," replied Manolo, already settling his pistol in his belt and smoothing his shirt so the weapon was less visible.

"OK, see you at three."

"Yes, but go now, Mayo, because if you stay around I won't be finished by five. Rebecca," she gave an order to one of her team of experts, "get that photo for the lieutenant. Enjoy, Manolo."

After ten years on duty Mario Conde had learned that routine doesn't exist just because of a lack of imagination. But Manolo was still too young and preferred to solve everything through a couple of interrogations, a lead pursued to the end of the trail and, if really necessary, a pause for thought before forcing through a resolution. He'd met success too often in his short career, and the Count, without sharing many of his theories, respected the thin gangling lad. But the lieutenant often insisted on police routine to try to track down the inevitable sore thumb. Lots of routine and ideas that unexpectedly surged out of his deep subconscious were his two favourite tools. The third was always understanding the people involved: if you know what someone is like, you know what he might do and what he'd never do, he'd tell Manolo, because sometimes that's exactly what people do, namely what they could never do, and he'd add for good measure: "while I'm a policeman I'll never stop smoking or stop thinking that one day I'll write a very romantic, very sweet, very squalid novel, but I'll also plug away at routine enquiries. When I'm no longer a policeman and write my novel, I'd like to work with lunatics because I love lunatics."

Out of pure routine and to see whether he still had something new to learn about Rafael Morín's character, the Count decided to interview Salvador González, the secretary of the party cell, a professional cadre in the organization sent to the enterprise by the municipality barely three months ago.

"I don't know how useful I can be to you," Salvador confessed as he spurned the cigarette the lieutenant offered. He opted to fill his pipe and accept a lit match. He was a man well into his fifties and seemed both straightforward and out of his depth. "I hardly knew Comrade Morín, and I've only got impressions of him as a party member and an individual and I don't like to be impressionistic."

"Describe one of those impressions," asked the lieutenant.

"All right, at the General Accounts Meeting, he was really very good. His report was one of the best I've ever heard. I think he's a man who's understood the spirit of the times. He called for quality and high standards at work, because this is a very important enterprise for the nation's development. And he subjected himself to self-criticism because his style of leadership was to centralize, and he asked comrades to help him in a necessary redistribution of tasks and responsibilities."

"And now let's have another impression."

The general secretary smiled.

"Even though it's only an impression?"

"Uh-huh."

"All right, if you must. But remember, it *is* only an impression . . . You know what travel means for anyone, not only in this enterprise but in the country as a whole. A person who travels feels different, chosen, as if he'd broken the sound barrier . . . My impression is that comrade Morín liked to get people's good will by offering them opportunities to travel. It's an impression I picked up from what I saw and from our conversations."

"What did you talk about? What did you see?"

"Nothing very exciting. When we were preparing the Final Accounts Meeting he asked me if I liked travelling."

"Then what happened?"

"I told him that, when I was a kid, I read a Donald Duck comic where the duck goes to Alaska with three nephews prospecting for gold, and for a long time I was dead envious of the ducklings whose uncle took them to Alaska. Then I grew up and never went to Alaska or anywhere else and, excuse my French, but I decided that Alaska could go frig itself."

"Don't you have any other impressions?"

"I'd prefer to keep quiet about them."

"Why?"

"Because I'm no longer an ordinary worker or even an ordinary party member. I'm general secretary in this enterprise, and my impressions could be seen as arising from my present post and not from me as an individual."

"What if I turn a blind eye? What if you forget your post for a moment?"

"That's very difficult for either of us, Lieutenant, but as you're so insistent, I will tell you something and hope I'm not making a mistake," he declared, and he initiated a pause that he prolonged as he knocked his pipe against the ashtray. He's not going to tell me anything, thought the Count, but he didn't despair. "They say a cautious man is worth two, and I'd always thought Rafael Morín a cautious man *par excellence*. But of the two men who surface from such caution, there's always one who's less so: he's the one who's gone missing."

"Why do you think that?"

"Because I'm almost certain your colleague, the slant-eyed mulatta, will find something. You can feel it in the air. Naturally, it's only an impression. I could be wrong, right? I've got it wrong with other comrades. I hope I'm wrong in this case, because if I'm not, I won't just have made a mistake as an individual, if you follow me?"

"Just a bit of routine, OK?"

"Get fucking lost, Conde," said Manolo, sprawling over the car boot. It was just gone twelve, a feisty mid-day sun was trying to chase the cold off, and its warmth was pleasant, you could even take your jacket off, put your sunglasses on and feel like saying: "Let's have another go at Maciques, but at headquarters, not here. Let's go."

The Count rubbed his specs on the hem of his shirt, looked at them against the light and returned them to his pocket. Unbuttoned his shirt cuffs and rolled his sleeves twice and thrice in uneven bulges up to his elbows.

"We'll wait, it's only just twelve, and China said three o'clock, and Fatman will only have just got going. I reckon we deserve lunch . . . don't you? Who knows when we'll get finished today?"

Manolo stroked his stomach and rubbed his hands together. The sun's efforts weren't enough: a persistent perfumed breeze blew in from the sea and chased off the timid warmth.

"Do you reckon I've got time to go to see Vilma?" he asked, not looking at his colleague.

193

"So did she or did she not kick you out?"

"No, she's just a jealous bitch."

"Like a business with lots of money."

"More or less."

"But you like her, don't you?"

Manolo tried to kick a car-flattened bottle top and then rubbed his hands together again.

"I think so, comrade. She wears me out in bed."

"Take care, kid," replied the Count, smiling. "I once had one like that, and she almost killed me. The worst of it is that afterwards none can compete. But he who dies from pleasure . . . Come on, hit the road, drop me off at Skinny's and pick me up at two, two fifteen. Does that give you enough time?"

"Why do you think I'm faster than Fangio?" he asked and was already opening the car door.

The Count preferred not to talk to him on the road. He thought driving at fifty miles an hour in Havana was slightly barmy and decided it was best to let Manolo concentrate on his driving and Vilma's frenzied love, and that way they'd perhaps arrive intact. The worst thing about the speeding was that he couldn't think, although he was happy enough: he didn't have much to think about, he could wait and perhaps start exercising his brain later.

"Two o'clock here," he repeated to Manolo as he got out in front of Skinny's house and went to cross himself as he saw him career round the corner. Two tits always have more pull than a carthorse, he reflected as he crossed the very minimal garden that Josefina kept as pretty as she could with what her hands could get hold of. Roses, sunflowers, red *mantos, picuala* and an old set of chopsticks blended colours and scents on a clean dark earth where it was a mortal sin to throw a cigarette end, even if Skinny Carlos were the culprit.

The door to the house was open as usual, and as he went in he was hit by the smell of a strong sauce: juices from bitter oranges, peeled garlic, onion, pepper and olive oil were bubbling in the pan, juices to bathe the victuals that Josefina would present to her son whose scant pleasures she cultivated more lovingly than her garden. Ever since Skinny had returned, maimed for life, that woman who retained the freshness of her smile had devoted herself to living for her son with a cheerful, nunnish resignation now in its ninth year, and the daily act of feeding him was perhaps the ritual that most expressed the pain of her love. Skinny had refused to abide by the advice of his doctor who warned him of the dangers of his obesity, as he assumed that death had been deferred only briefly and he wanted to live with his usual gusto. If we're going to drink, let's drink; if we're going to eat, let's eat, he'd say, and Josefina satisfied him well beyond her means.

"Set another place," the Count told her as he entered the kitchen, kissed the woman's sweaty brow and prepared his own to receive a return kiss which in the event never came, because the lieutenant suffered an attack of love and melancholy that forced him to hug her as tightly as a strangler and say "I love you so much, Jose" before he let her go and walked over to the side-table where the thermos of coffee stood and thus he fought off the tears he felt were imminent.

"What you doing here, Condesito? You finished work early?"

"If only, Jose," he replied as he drank his coffee. "I came to eat yucca in that sauce."

"Hey, kid," she replied and left off preparing food for a moment. "What's the mess you sorting now?"

"You can't imagine, love, one of my usual piles of shit."

"With that girl who was at school with you?"

"Hey, what's your beast of a boy been telling you?"

"Don't be silly. You could hear your carryings on yesterday half a block away."

The Count shrugged his shoulders and smiled. What could he have said?

"Hey, and why are you looking so elegant?" he asked as he looked her up and down.

"Me elegant? Forget it, you can't imagine how elegant I can be when I put my mind to it . . . No, I've just come from the doctor's and not had time to change."

"What's wrong, Jose?" he asked as he bent down to see her face, that was looking over the stove.

"I don't know, love. It's a pain that goes back a long time and it's getting unbearable. It starts burning here under my belly, and sometimes I feel a knife's been buried down there."

"And what did the doctor say?"

"He didn't really say anything. He sent me off for tests, an X-ray and that thing when you have to swallow a hosepipe."

"But didn't he say anything else?"

"What else do you expect him to say, Condesito?"

"I don't know. But you never told me. I'd have spoken to Andrés, the one who studied with us. He's a fantastic doctor."

"Don't you worry, this doctor is good too."

"What do you mean 'don't worry', dear? You never do say anything. Tomorrow I'll talk to Andrés about the tests, and Skinny should ring . . ."

Josefina put the saucepan down and looked at her son's friend.

"Should ring no one. Not a word to him, please?"

Then the Count decided to pour out another dose

of coffee and light another cigarette, but not to hug Josefina and tell her he was really scared.

"Don't worry. I'll call. The stew smells good, doesn't it?" And he walked out of her kitchen.

Mario Conde's strolls down memory lane always ended in melancholy. When he crossed the watershed of his thirtieth year and his relationship with Haydée petered out in the last whimpers of unbridled sexual combat, he found he liked remembering in the hope that he would improve his life and treated his destiny like a guilty party he could bury under reproaches and recriminations or moans and groans. His own work suffered from such an attitude, and though he knew he wasn't a hard or particularly wise man, or even exemplary in his behaviour, although some of his colleagues considered him a good policeman, he thought he might have been more useful in another profession, but he then transmuted his gripes into punctilious efficiency that earned him a reputation he considered fraudulent and quite inexplicable. And now Tamara had come back to disturb the considerable calm he'd reached after his fallout with Haydée by dint of nights at baseball games, drinking, nostalgia-provoking music and overflowing plates, while he chatted to Skinny, all the time wanting it not to be true, for Skinny to be skinny again, for him never to die and not look like a giant greasy meatball, shirtless and trying to soak up the midday sun in his backyard. The Count saw the rolls of fat gather over his belly and the small red spots covering his back, neck and chest, like bites from voracious insects.

"What you thinking about, you wild man?" he asked as he ruffled his hair.

"Nothing, you savage. I was thinking about the whole Rafael business, and my mind suddenly went a complete blank," his friend responded, looking at the clock. "What time they coming to pick you up?"

"I'm off now. Manolo will be here in two ticks. If I can't come tonight, I'll ring you and tell you where it's at."

"But don't think too much. You'll get indigestion."

"Do I have any choice, Skinny?"

"No, my friend. Just clear some of the shit out that head of yours because what's fucked won't get unfucked by you spending your whole day thinking. You know, it's just like baseball: if you're going to win, you need a good set of bongos. And ours rumble away, even when we're awake. That's why you and I almost beat the lanky coal-merchants from the high school in Havana, you remember that?"

"Like it was yesterday," he replied and stood up ready to hit and then took a swing. They both watched the ball fly off and hit the fence right under the scoreboard in the loneliest reaches of centerfield.

"Surprise, surprise!" exclaimed Lieutenant Patricia Wong in English, her eyes vanishing with her laughter as her right hand brandished the stapled papers which seemed to be the source of her cheerfulness. China's outburst of excitement went through the Count like a transfusion: went straight into his body and began to course through his veins at a startling rate, making his heart beat fast.

"Have we got him?" he asked as he searched his jacket pocket for a cigarette and almost shouted when he saw his comrade's eyeless face sway affirmatively.

"Fuck, we've finally got something," snorted Manolo,

intercepting in midair the cigarette the Count was lifting to his lips. The lieutenant, who hated his colleague's sporadic but often repeated jape, forgot his usual insults and pulled up a chair next to Lieutenant Patricia Wong.

"Come on, China, how's it looking?"

"Like you said, Mayo, like you said, but more complicated. Look, this is what must be behind it all and we still have to review a stack of paper, one hell of a stack," she emphasized and started looking for something among the forms. "But it's red hot, Mayo, just listen. In the last half of 1988, which is all we've looked at, Rafael Morín went on two trips to Spain and one to Japan. He's got more flying hours than Gagarin . . . Look, he went to Japan to do business with Mitachi, but more of that later."

"Go on, go on," insisted the Count.

"Listen, he went to Spain for sixteen and eighteen days respectively and to Japan for nine, and in each case had to wrap up four contracts, except on his first visit to Spain when there were only three. He had a heap of dollars for marketing expenses – I'd never imagined people got so much – I'll tell you exactly how much later. There's a sheet that lists them by the business contacts to be made, but cop this, he'd always double his numbers, as if he were going to work or be away more time. That's bad enough, but the daily expenses beggar belief, Mayo. The pro-formas he must have filled in for the three trips I mentioned aren't here, but what's more incredible is that he filed a claim for expenses for a trip to Panama that was cancelled and didn't reimburse them. I can't explain that. Any auditor would spot it."

"Yes, it's odd, but is there more?" the lieutenant asked as Patricia put the sheets on top of the desk. His glee began to wane; such hamfistedness didn't bear the stamp of Morín.

"Hey, wait a minute, Mayo. Let me finish."

"On your way, China, show us you're better than Chan Li Po."

"I will. Look, this is the fuse to a real time bomb: the import and export enterprise holds an account in the Bank of Bilbao and Vizcaya in the name of a limited company registered at a post box number in Panama and which has a branch in Cuba. It's a kind of corporation and is called Rose Tree and was apparently set up to sidestep the American embargo. The Rose Tree account can be accessed via three signatures: those of Deputy Minister Fernández-Lorea, our friend Maciques and, naturally, Rafael Morín, but there always had to be two signatures . . . You with me?"

"I'm giving it my best, my most heartfelt shot."

"Well, hold on to your chair now, *macho*: if I've not been misled by the papers here, because there are others that aren't where they should be and I don't want to slander anyone, but if I'm not mistaken, a big amount was taken out in December and isn't tied to any big deal signed around then."

"And who was responsible?"

"Don't be naïve, Mayo, only the bank knows that."

"OK, so I'm naïve . . . Now shock me: how big is 'big', Patricia?" he asked, getting ready to hear the figure.

"A good few thousand. More than a hundred, more than two hundred, more than . . ."

"Fuck me," exclaimed Manolo, who started searching for another cigarette. "And why did he need all that?"

"Wait a minute, Manolo, if I were an oracle I wouldn't be chewing dust and paper here."

"Forget it, China, just carry on . . ." the Count begged

her, mentally reviewing an image of Tamara, Rafael's speech on his first day at school, the head of the camp ringing that bell, their playing field on October Tenth, the cocky unfailing laugh of the man who'd gone missing, and he laughed and laughed.

"I think it's all about Mitachi. Mayo, the Japanese weren't coming till February, and Rafael had first to go to Barcelona to make a purchase from a Spanish limited company I've still not checked out, but I bet you anything that Japanese capital is involved. And if that's so, I'll take a second bet, that it's Mitachi capital."

"Hold on, China, hold on, explain yourself."

"Hell, Mayo, you going brain dead?" protested Patricia, as her smile engulfed her eyes. "It's as clear as water: Rafael Morín must be doing business with Mitachi as an individual and was playing with money belonging to the enterprise or, rather, the Rose Tree. You on my wavelength now?"

"And how!" said Manolo, taken aback and trying to smile.

"And you reckon papers have gone missing, China?"

"That's right."

"Could they be in other filing cabinets?"

"Could be, Mayo, but I don't think so. If it were just one . . ."

"So they've been removed?"

"Could be, but what's odd is that they didn't take everything, including the ones for the daily allowances that Morín himself could doctor."

"So too many of some and not enough of others?"

"More or less, Mayo."

"China, I know why there are too many of some, and I think I know where to find the missing ones."

When Major Rangel told me, You don't have to wear your uniform here, you shouldn't work in uniform, and I saw him there in his olive-green jacket, his rank embroidered on his epaulettes and round his collar, and looking so impressive, I thought it was a joke, that I should resign there and then because it was almost like giving up being a policeman when you'd only just made it. The first time I went into the street in uniform, after I'd passed out the Police Academy, I felt half embarrassed, and half that I was really somebody, the gear fitted me like a glove and gave me something extra, made me stand out, and I thought people were always going to be looking at me, even if I didn't want them to, because I wasn't like everybody else. I did and didn't like that; it was really peculiar. As a kid I'd spent my life in disguise; as I was so skinny, I wasn't like other kids who wanted to be policemen, generals or astronauts. I dressed up for a while as Zorro, then as Robin Hood and then as a pirate with a patch over my eye and should probably have gone into acting and not the force. But I did become a policeman, and the fact is from the start was thrilled to be in uniform and really thought I was seriously playing at being a policeman until the day I drove up to a shack in El Moro in an academy patrol car. When we got out of the car, we were immediately surrounded by lots of people, I reckon the whole barrio was there, and everybody looking at us, I straightened my cap: it wasn't mine and wasn't new. I pulled up my trousers and put on my dark glasses, I had an audience. I was important, right? The woman who'd suffered the attack had already been taken to hospital. There was a god-awful silence, because we'd arrived, you know, and a grey-haired black man, who was really old, the chair of the committee for the block, said "This way,

202

comrades" and we went into a small house – it had a zinc roof and its walls were part un-plastered brick, part cardboard and part zinc – and when you went in you felt like an uncooked loaf on the tip of the spatula entering the oven, and you don't understand why there are still people who live like that, and there she was on the small bed, and I almost fainted. I don't even like telling people, because I remember and see it as if it were yesterday, and can feel the heat from the oven: the sheet was splattered in blood; there was blood on the ground, on the wall, and she was curled up and motionless, because she was dead; her father-in-law had killed her while attempting rape, and later I discovered she was only seven years old, and I cursed the day I became a policeman, because I really thought these things didn't happen. When you're a policeman, you find out they do, and worse, and that's your job, and you begin to doubt whether you should do every-thing by the book or whether you should just get your pistol out and put six bullets into the guy who'd done it. I almost asked to leave, but I stayed in there, and was sent to headquarters and the major told me: you mustn't come in uniform and you'll work with the Count, and I think you'll get to like being in the force. You don't understand me, do you? Although I no longer walk the streets in uniform and people don't know who I am, I couldn't care less, and you've helped me not to care less, but people like Rafael Morín have helped me more. What a specimen! Whoever gave him the right to gamble with what's mine and yours and the old man's who's selling news-papers and the woman's who's about to cross the road and who'll probably die of old age without know-ing what it is to own a car, a nice house, to stroll around Barcelona or wear perfume worth a hundred dollars, and is probably off right now to queue for three hours to get a bag of potatoes, huh Count? Whoever?

"Oh, it's you? How are you, Mario? Do come in, Sergeant," she greeted them with an embarrassed smile, and the Count kissed her on the cheek like in the old days and Manolo shook her hand; they exchanged pleasantries and walked towards the living room. "Anything new, Mario?" she asked finally.

"There's always something new, Tamara. Papers have gone missing at the enterprise, and it could be evidence against Rafael."

She forgot her irrepressible lock of hair and rubbed her hands. She suddenly shrank, seemed defenceless and embarrassed.

"Of what?"

"Of thieving, Tamara. That's why we're back."

"But what did he steal, Mario?"

"Money, loads of money."

"Oh, for heaven's sake," she exclaimed, eyes glistening; and the Count thought she might cry now. He is her husband, after all? He is the father of her child, isn't he? Her boyfriend from their school days, right?

"I want to inspect the safe that's in the library, Tamara."

"The safe?" That was another surprise and came as a relief. She wasn't going to cry.

"You know the combination, I suppose?"

"But it's been empty for a long time. I mean there's not been any money or anything like that. As far as I recall, there are just the title deeds to the house and papers relating to the family pantheon."

"But you know the combination, don't you?" Now it was Manolo who was insisting. He'd become a lean, rubbery, edgy cat once more.

"Yes, it's in Rafael's telephone book as just another number."

"Can you open it now, comrade?" the sergeant repeated, and she looked at the Count.

"Please, Tamara," he asked as he stood up.

"What's this all about, Mario?" she asked, although she was really wondering herself as she led them into the library.

She kneeled in front of the fake fireplace, removed the safety grille, and the Count remembered how it was the eve of the day of the Three Kings who always preferred to bring their presents down the chimney. Perhaps his had arrived, amazingly early. Tamara read out the six numbers and started to turn the handle to the safe, and the Count tried to glance over the shoulder of Manolo, who was in the front row. She moved the wheel a sixth time to the left and finally pulled open the metal door and stood up.

"I hope you're mistaken, Mario."

"Hope on," came the reply, and when she moved away, he went over to the fireplace, kneeled down and extracted a white envelope from the cold iron belly. He stood up and looked at her. He couldn't stop himself: he felt palpably sorry for that woman who'd stripped him to the bone and frustrated him and whom, he now realized more than ever, he'd preferred not to have seen again. But he opened the envelope, took out a few sheets of paper and read while Manolo rocked impatiently on his heels. "Better than we'd imagined," he said, stuffing the papers back in the envelope. Tamara was still rubbing her hands, and Manolo couldn't keep still. "Maciques has got an account in the Hispano-American Bank and owns a car in Spain. The photocopies are here."

Major Rangel contemplated the sweet-scented death agony of his Rey del Mundo as if he were watching the death of a dog that had been his best friend. Momentarily, as he placed the butt in the ashtray, he regretted he'd not treated it more lovingly. He'd had an awful smoke listening to Lieutenant Mario Conde's explanation.

"Seeing is believing," he pronounced and tried to avoid seeing his cigar go out, perhaps so he didn't need to believe it. "And how was he able to perpetrate so many dreadful things?"

"Dreadful things are all the rage, Boss . . . Wasn't he a totally trustworthy cadre? Wasn't he a man eternally on the up? Wasn't he purer and saintlier than holy water?"

"Don't be sarcastic, because that won't explain anything . . ."

"Boss, I don't know why you're shocked at the lack of controls in an enterprise. Whenever and wherever they do a really surprise audit, they find dreadful things that beggar belief, that nobody can explain, but which are for real. You've already forgotten the millionaire manager of the Ward ice-cream parlour and Cheep Cheep fried chicken chain, and in . . ."

"OK, OK, Mario, but let me feel shocked, if you don't mind? One always prefers to think people aren't that corrupt, and, as you say, Rafael Morín was a completely trustworthy cadre, and look what he got up to . . . But let's leave that for later, now I want to know where that fellow is holed up. I want to know so I can hand the case to the industry minister neatly sorted."

206

The Count scrutinized his dry listless cigarette, the ink from the *Popular* brand that had run, the tobacco flaking out at both ends and the packet that was falling apart, but it was his last one, and when he lit up he enjoyed the strength hidden in that smoke.

"Do you need more people?"

"No, just let me finish what I'm saying. Look, everything points to the fact that Rafael Morín was going to show his true colours on a trip to Barcelona in January. He intended vanishing there with all the money of which part was already safely invested, and as he knew for the moment nobody would be checking the paperwork, he may have overstretched himself and started cooking his allowances and marketing expenses, to have money on account, you know? One of Fatman Contreras's informants, I mean Captain Contreras, Yayo el Yuma, says his photo reminds him of someone, but he'd have to see him personally to be sure. So it's also possible he changed dollars into Cuban pesos he could spend here, for, according to Zoilita, he did like to throw it around."

"And still no news from the coastguards?"

"Nothing as yet, and I don't think there will be, although it's beginning to make more sense that his problems were here and he has been sent to a better place ... But I'm sure Maciques is behind whatever has happened ... Because if not, why on earth would Rafael keep those papers belonging to Maciques at home? In any case it all went awry when Rafael found out a delegation from Mitachi was coming to Cuba earlier than expected. Look, here's the telex. It arrived the morning of the thirtieth. It seems they were very interested in doing a deal, and when there's a good deal to be done, the Chinese don't worry about Christmas trees and New Year. And Rafael knew that the deputy

207

minister, perhaps the minister and other people from other enterprises, would join in the bargaining. As I was saying, he realized he was caught and went into hiding or was put out of harm's way. So it's more than likely he left the country illegally, but he hasn't, otherwise the shout would have gone up over there. Just imagine, Boss, he was a big wheel in the Cuban economy. And if I'm sure of one thing, it's that Rafael wouldn't risk his skin trying to make his escape on a raft made from two truck inner tubes. He'd find the safest route and then get to Miami . . . Rafael Morín is in Cuba."

"And what if he avoided creating a fuss so his account in Spain wasn't frozen?" Major Rangel rubbed his eyes, and the Count noted he was reacting anxiously, which wasn't his style.

"I reckon that even if he didn't want a fuss, the people in Miami would have made one. What's more, time was on his side. And he was a trustworthy cadre, was he not?"

"So you keep telling me."

"Well, he knew nobody would ever imagine anything of this sort, and he'd only have to go into the first Miami bank he found to have money on tap. He reckoned nobody would suspect a thing for a few days and that nobody would ever imagine a guy who made a regular eight or ten trips abroad every year skiving off in a motorboat."

"Yes, you're probably right . . . But he didn't take the paperwork to do with travel allowances. China found them."

"That's where two and two don't make four. I thought Maciques had put them there at midday on the thirty-first, but by midday on the thirty-first Rafael already had his hands on those papers."

"So, what an earth is Maciques's role in all this?"

"This is what I'd like to find out; I'm sure he's up to his neck in shit. He knows the whole story, or at least the main plot, because on the third, when Manolo questioned him, he was very on edge and kept going back and forth, as if trying to wriggle out of the conversation. And today he was quite different. He was very self-confident, as if there was no mess, and he was quite convinced he wouldn't have any problems even if Rafael's fiddle over allowances, marketing expenses and the like were rumbled, which he knew we would do eventually: if not today, tomorrow or the day after . . . The time that has passed since his boss disappeared apparently gave him peace of mind, because he never imagined Rafael was keeping those documents in that safe."

"So he was in partnership with Rafael Morín?"

"No, he was just an accomplice. He had some four thousand dollars in the bank and Rafael had hundreds of thousands. There's something not quite right there. But Manolo and I will question him again to see if we can extract something new."

The major stood up and walked over to his office's picture window. It was barely six pm and already getting dark in Havana. From up there you could see the laurel trees from a perspective that was of no interest to the Count. He preferred the view from his small window and stayed seated.

"You've got to find that bastard even if he's six feet under," the Boss grated in his most terrible visceral tone. He hated such situations, felt cheated and annoyed that they only reached him after such dastardly things had been perpetrated. "I'll call the industry minister. He can sort the business of the money in Spain and give it some thought, because it's more his problem than ours. But tell me, Mario, why would a man like Rafael Morín do something like that?"

"So visiting time again. I think we should go back to the beginning."

"But what do you hope I will tell you, Sergeant?" René Maciques responded, looking at the Count as he walked in and sat in a chair by the window. The lieutenant lit a cigarette and exchanged glances with the sergeant. Go on, put the boot in.

"What did you and Morín discuss on the thirty-first?"

"I told you, the usual work-related things, our good financial year-end and the reports we had to file."

"And you didn't see him again?"

"No, I left the party shortly before he did."

"And did you know anything about this fraud?"

"Sergeant, I've already told you I didn't, and could never have imagined anything of the sort. And still can hardly believe it. I don't know why he would do such a thing."

"What's your level of involvement in the matter?"

"Mine? Mine? None whatsoever, Sergeant, I'm a mere office manager who makes no decisions."

The Count extinguished his cigarette and stood up. He walked over to his desk.

"Your innocence is most moving, Maciques."

"But the fact is . . ."

"Don't strain yourself. Does this remind you of anything?"

The Count took two photocopies from the envelope and put them on his desk, in front of Maciques. The office manager looked at the two policemen, leaned forward and stayed like that for what seemed an eternity: as if he'd suddenly forgotten how to read.

210

"The lieutenant asked you a question," said Manolo as he picked up the photocopies. "Does this remind you of anything?"

"Where did you find these papers?"

"As usual, you make it necessary for me to remind you that we are the ones asking the questions . . . But I'll give you an answer. They were quite safe and sound in a strongbox in Rafael Morín's house. What do these documents mean, Maciques?" Manolo repeated, placing himself between the man and the desk.

René Maciques looked up at his interrogator. He was now a perplexed, gloomy old librarian. Sergeant Manuel Palacios took his time. He knew he'd reached a decisive point in the interrogation, when the man under arrest must decide to tell the truth or put his hope in deception. But Maciques didn't have options.

"It's one of Rafael's ruses," he said nevertheless. "I know nothing about these papers. I've never set my eyes on them. You said he did things using my name. Well, here's another example."

"So Rafael Morín wanted to put you in a spot of bother?"

"So it seems."

"Maciques, what might we find in *your* house if we did a search?"

"In my house . . . Nothing. The usual. One travels abroad and makes purchases."

"With what money? Entertainment expenses?"

"I already explained how one can save from the daily allowances."

"And when you wrap up a big deal, don't you get a bonus in kind? A car, for example?"

"But I never wrapped up any big deals."

"Maciques, do you have it in you to kill a man?"

211

The office manager looked up again, the glint gone from his eyes.

"What are you inferring?"

"Do you or don't you?"

"Of course I don't."

And he kept shaking his head: no, no.

"Why did you go to the enterprise on the thirty-first? And don't say to switch off the air conditioning."

"What would you like me to say?"

Then the Count walked back to his desk and stopped next to Maciques.

"Look, Maciques, I'm not as patient as the sergeant. I'm going to tell you straight what I think of you, and I know that one way or the other you'll end up confessing today, tomorrow or the day after . . . You're a piece of shit, as much a thief as your boss, more careful though less powerful. Right now the validity of these papers is being checked in Spain, and perhaps the bank will give us some information, but the car's a clue that's much simpler than you think. For some reason I've still to fathom, Rafael kept these papers under lock and key, perhaps to protect himself from you, because he knew you were quite capable of putting on his file the allowances he didn't spend and the expenses he doubled. And Rafael will turn up, I don't know whether dead or alive, in Spain or Greenland, but he will turn up, and you'll talk, but even if you don't, you're covered in shit, Maciques. Don't forget it. And to help you think more clearly, you're going to spend some time on your own. From today you will start a new life at police headquarters . . . Sergeant, get the papers ready and ask the public prosecutor for an order for the temporary arrest of citizen René. One that can be extended. Be seeing you, Maciques."

Mario Conde looked at the other laurel trees, the ones very close to the sea that heralded the Paseo del Prado, and repeated his question. A bitter wind blew in from the mouth of the bay forcing him to keep his hands in his pockets, but he needed to think and walk, lose himself in the crowd and hide his Pyrrhic glee and the frustrations of a policeman pleased to strip bare the evil wrought by others. What had led Rafael Morín to do something like that? Why did he want more, still more and more besides? The Count contemplated the Palace of Matrimony and the shiny black '57 Chrysler decked out in balloons and flowers waiting for the nuptial descent of the over-forties who still had it in them and still smiled for the inevitable photo at the top of the steps. He observed the ones with staying power defying the cold in the queue at the pizzeria on Prado and saw the notices, stapled to the trunk of a laurel tree, of those who needed to move. They made honest and dishonest proposals but just needed a few square feet of ceiling where they could live. He watched two dead-set, unconnected homosexuals walk by shivering with cold; their well-intentioned, ingenuous eyes looked him up and down. He spotted a peaceful mulatto, leaning against a streetlamp, looking like a lethargic Rastafarian, his perfect dreadlocks tucked under his black beret, perhaps waiting for the first foreigner to step up so he could suggest five pesos for one dollar, Mister, seven for one, bro', and I've got grass, anything to get through the doors to the forbidden world of abundance armed with a passport. He switched to the lamppost on the pavement opposite: a blonde in incredibly lascivious make-up was dying of cold, though she promised to be hot, even if it snowed, with a mouth made for a blowjob; the blonde for whom a nationally produced mortal like Mario Conde was worth less than a drunk's spittle and who wanted dollars like her friend the Rasta mulatto and would suggest thirty for one: her youthful sex, perfumed, well-trained and guaranteed against rabies and other sickness, in exchange for the dollars she yearned after; the blowjob came extra, natch. He watched a kid skating jump onto a wooden box and skate off into the dark. He reached the Parque Central and almost decided to get entangled in the eternal arguments over baseball that raged there daily, whatever the temperature, to find a reason for yet another defeat for those bastard Industriales; balls, balls is what they're lacking, he'd have shouted in honour of Skinny, who was neither skinny nor nimble enough to be shouting on his own behalf. He contemplated the lights in the Hotel Inglaterra, the shadows surrounding the Teatro García Lorca, the queue in front of the Payret cinema, the dismal drab entrance to the Asturian Centre and the aggressive dilapidated ugliness of the Gómez edifice. He felt the irrepressible beat of a city that he tried to make a better place and thought of Tamara: she was expecting him and he was on his way, perhaps to ask her the same question, and nothing else.

Several months later, when the Rafael Morín case had been truly laid to rest, and René Maciques was rotting in jail and Tamara was as beautiful as ever and looked at him with eyes that were always glistening, he'd still ask the same question and imagine a sad Rafael Morín, a petty potentate in Miami with his five-hundred-thousand-dollar fortune that was a mere lottery prize that would never buy him the things he acquired with his power as a trustworthy brilliant cadre, always on the up. But that night he just stopped next to a group of fans and lit a cigarette. They all thought and shouted out loud in an act of group therapy: the team manager was an idiot, the star pitcher a dud and the guys from way back really good, if only Chávez and Urbano, La Guagua and Lazo would come back, they fantasized, and then he stuck the shoulder of his imagination between two enormous frightening blacks who eyed him suspiciously, where does this asshole come from, and shouted into the centre of the group: "They don't have balls," and he'd leave the professional gripers to their gripes, as he crossed the street and entered the haze of fumes, dry piss and pre-Colombian vomit in the doorway to the Asturian Centre, where a couple were trying to consummate their ardour behind a pillar, and finally ran into the barred doors to the Floridita, SHUT FOR REPAIRS, and abandoned there all hope of a double shot of neat vintage rum, sitting in the corner that was Hemingway's exclusive property, leaning on the bar where Papa and Ava Gardner kissed scandalously and where he'd set his store, many years ago, on writing a novel about squalor and where he'd have asked himself the same question and supplied the only answer that allowed him to live in peace: because he always was a bastard. What else?

"Can I put some music on?"

"No, not now," she said as she leaned her head on the back of the plush sofa, looked up at the ceiling and felt freezing again and folded her arms after she'd pulled down her jersey sleeves. He lit a cigarette and dropped the match in the Murano ashtray.

"What are you thinking?" he asked, also sinking back on the sofa. "A ceiling is a ceiling."

"About what's happening, everything you've told me, what else do you expect?"

"You really had no idea? None whatsoever?"

"What can I say, Mario?"

"But you might have seen or suspected something."

"What was there to suspect? The fact he bought that hi-fi system or brought us whisky or a bicycle for our son? Is a dress worth a hundred and fifty dollars cause for suspicion?"

He thought: it's all so normal. All that has always been normal for her: she was born in this house and lived that normality that makes you see life differently; and he wondered whether it wasn't Tamara's world that had driven Rafael mad. But knew it wasn't so.

"What will happen now, Mario?" she now asked the question, had had enough of ceilings and silence and leaned her shoulder on the back of the sofa, tucked a foot under a thigh and chased her imperturbable wavy lock away. She wanted to gaze at him.

"Two things still need to happen. First, Rafael has to show up, dead or alive, in Cuba, or wherever. And second, Maciques must tell us what he knows. Perhaps that might help us find Rafael's whereabouts."

"It's like an earthquake."

"Yes, it is," he agreed, "everything that's not secure is collapsing, and I imagine you feel the same way. But I think we've seen the best. Can you imagine Rafael arriving in Barcelona, accessing all that money and defecting?"

"There's an idea. We'd go to live in Geneva, in a house on a hill with a slate roof."

She said that, got up and disappeared into the dining room. He could never not: he looked at her as he always had, only he'd already observed that rump, traced the shape of her body, one ill-equipped to pirouette; his hands and mouth had travelled its length and breadth, but the memory hurt like a sharp thorn left to fester. A house in Geneva, why Geneva? And he ran his fingertips through his hair and thought how

216

he'd started to go bald. I'd forgotten my bald patch, and he too abandoned the sofa, the house in Geneva and Tamara's rump, and looked for a record with which to cheer himself up. Got it, he told himself when he spotted the Sarah Vaughan LP, *Walkman Jazz*, put it on the turntable and turned the volume down low, and the wonderful black woman sang "Cheek to Cheek" for him. She came back to Sarah Vaughan's warm dark voice, carrying two glasses.

"Let's finish off our stocks: the whisky in Rafael Morín's cellar is on its last legs," she said, offering him a glass. She went back to the sofa and swigged her first mouthful like a hard-boiled matelot.

"I know how you must feel. This isn't easy for you or anyone, but you're not to blame and I even less so. If only it hadn't happened and Rafael had been what everybody imagined him to be and I wasn't mixed up in all this."

"You regretting something?" she rasped. She'd regained normal temperature and rolled her sleeves back to her elbows. Took another swig.

"No, I regret nothing, I was referring to you."

"Better not speak on my behalf. If Rafael stole that money, let him pay for it. Nobody ordered him to. I never asked him for anything, and you know that only too well, Mario Conde. I thought you knew me better. I don't feel guilty on any count, and what I enjoyed I enjoyed like anyone else would have. Don't expect me to confess and do penance."

"I see I know you less well than I thought."

Sarah Vaughan was singing "Lullaby of Birdland", the best song he knew for escaping into the magical world of Oz, but it seemed as if she couldn't shut up and he knew it was best if she just talked, and talked and talked . . .

217

"Yeah, and you think I'm ungrateful, and I don't know what else, and that I should say it's supposition, that my husband is incapable of such things and then burst into tears, don't you? It's what one does in such situations, isn't it? But I don't have a tragic vocation, and I'm not a long-suffering egotist like you . . . I'd have preferred none of this to happen, it's true, but do you know what it is to have a clear conscience?"

"I really don't remember anymore."

"Well I do, in case you didn't know or were imagining something else. I told you the other day: Rafael had what they let him have or what was his due or whatever, and everyone knew that when he was travelling he would bring things back and it was all quite normal and he was an excellent comrade. Everyone knew and . . . Ah, I won't say anymore on the subject unless you want to question me and, if that's the case, I won't say another word, least of all to you."

He smiled and returned to the sofa. He sat down very close to her, touched her knee with his, thought for a moment, then dared: slowly put his hand on her thigh, afraid it might run away, but her thigh stayed under his hand, and he gripped her live firm flesh and met a slight tremor, well hidden under the skin. Looked into her eyes and saw the shiny dampness transform into a tear that welled up, hung on an eyelash and rolled down Tamara's nose, and he knew he was ready for anything, except to see her cry. She rested her head on the Count's shoulder, and he knew she was still crying: a tired silent lament. She then said quite matter-of-factly:

"The fact is I saw this coming. This or something similar. He was never satisfied. He was always dreaming of more and liked to play the powerful executive. I think he imagined he was the first Cuban yuppie or something of the sort . . . But I also got used to the easy life, to having everything all the time, to him speaking to a friend so I didn't have to do community service in Las Tunas and for us to have holidays in Varadero and so on. In the end I was afraid of changing my style of life, although I think I'd not loved him for a long time. When he went on his travels I liked being by myself at home with my son, not having to worry he'd be back late, that he'd say he was tired and would get into bed and go to sleep or shut himself up in the library to write reports or tell me how difficult it was all getting. I'd also known for some time he'd been going with other women. He couldn't deceive me on that front, but as I said, I was afraid to lose a tranquillity I really enjoyed. And what I did with you I'd not done with anyone else, please do believe me."

He couldn't see her eyes, hidden as they were behind her impertinent lock, but he knew she'd stopped crying. He watched her gulp down her whisky and followed suit. She got up, said, for God's sake, went back into the kitchen, and the palm of his hand felt the warmth he'd stolen from Tamara. He now knew he could go to bed with that woman who'd been driving him crazy for the last seventeen years, and he put his tumbler down on the glass table, forgot the cigarette burning in the Murano and abandoned his pistol on the sofa cushion. He felt ready for it and walked into the kitchen behind her. Began to caress her hips – hips of a would-be rumba dancer – her belly he was already familiar with, and reached for the most discussed breasts in La Víbora High School, and she let him caress her until she couldn't stand it anymore and turned round and offered him her lips, her tongue, her teeth and saliva smelling of single malt scotch, and he pulled at her jersey zip – she no longer wore bras – and lowered his head to nibble her dark nipples until she gave a start from the pain, then pulled down his trousers, fumbled taking her knickers off and kneeled like a repentant sinner to breathe in Tamara's femininity, to kiss and consume her, ravaged by an ancient, never satisfied hunger.

And with a strength he'd forgotten he possessed, he lifted her up, took her over to the table, sat her down and felt her as he'd never felt another woman. They made love again on the living-room sofa. And a third time in her bedroom before finally calling it a day.

He lifted the lid of the coffee pot and saw the dark black coffee bubbling up from its red-hot entrails. The light was beginning to break over the trees and filter through to the kitchen windows, and he added four spoonfuls of sugar to his jug of breakfast beverage. It looked as if it would be a sunny morning, and he anticipated it wouldn't be so cold. He stirred the first coffee in the jug till the sugar melted, then returned it to the coffee pot, where a thick yellow foam formed. Then he poured himself his half-cup so he could start to think. She was asleep upstairs, ten minutes to seven o'clock and to when she gets up, he calculated as he lit his first cigarette. It was a necessary ritual without which he couldn't start life each day, and he thought about Rufino and about what would happen if he fell in love with Tamara. He couldn't imagine it happening, he told himself, and even shook his head to confirm that this was so, I still don't believe it, he muttered and he saw his and Tamara's clothes on the chair where he'd placed them before making coffee. His vanity as a man satisfied by a memorable sexual performance hardly left room for thought. He knew he had defeated Rafael Morín and regretted he'd not yet shared the second part to the story with Skinny, the successful feats of conquest and colonization. He knew he shouldn't, but, as soon as possible, I've got to tell him.

"Good morning, Lieutenant," she said, and he

almost jumped out of his chair as he realized at that precise moment that if he didn't flee, he would fall in love.

He liked to hear a woman's voice at the start of the day and found Tamara was more beautiful then, with her dressing gown mostly unbuttoned, her lips unadorned and one side of her face marked by the fold in the pillow, her hair relentlessly impertinent, irrepressibly covering her forehead, and her eyes reddened by lack of sleep. He could see she was very happy with her state as a woman who's well-served and better serviced, so well that she would sing while cleaning a grimy pan, and she came over, kissed him on the mouth and then, only then, asked for her coffee: it was all quite conclusive: he fled or was lost.

"It's a pity one has to work in this world, isn't it?" she said, hiding her smile behind her cup.

"What would happen if your husband came in through that door?" asked the Count, expecting to hear another confession.

"I'd offer him a cup of the coffee, and he'd have no choice but to say it's really good, you know?"

He travelled in a crowded bus and never stopped smiling; he walked six blocks and kept smiling; he walked into headquarters, and everyone saw him smiling and still laughing when he climbed the stairs and went into his office, where Sergeant Manuel Palacios was waiting for him, feet on his desk and face stuck behind a newspaper.

"What's got into you?" Manolo asked, also laughing, reckoning good news was on its way.

"Nothing really, today's the sixth of January, and I'm waiting for my present . . . What's new, then?"

222

"Oh, I thought you'd something to tell me. Nothing you could call new . . . What are we going to do with Maciques?"

"Start all over again. Till he's exhausted. He's the only one who's allowed to get exhausted. Did you see Patricia?"

"No, but she left a message with the duty officer saying she was going straight to the enterprise. She left at eight last night, and I think she was back welcoming the dawn there."

"Have you seen the reports?"

"No, not yet. I just got here and started to read all the stuff about AIDS in the newspaper. Fucking hell, comrade, soon you won't even be able to get laid in this world."

The Count smiled, was still smiling as he said:

"Uh-huh, take good note, then. I'm going to have a look at the reports so we can start on Maciques."

"Thanks, Boss. May you always wake up smiling," retorted the sergeant, weaving his way back to the desk.

He preferred to go down the stairs and, while he did so, he thought how he was in a mood to write. He'd write a very squalid tale about an amorous triangle, in which the characters would live, in different roles, situations they'd lived previously. It would be a nostalgic love story, with no violence or hatred, about ordinary people and ordinary experiences, as in the lives of the people he knew, because you must write about what you know, he told himself, remembering how Hemingway wrote about things he knew and Miki wrote about things he knew he ought to write about.

When he was in the hallway he walked round the corner towards the Information Department, which Captain Jorrín was just leaving, and he seemed tired and groggy, as if getting over an illness.

"Hello, Maestro. What's the matter?" He shook his hand.

"We've caught one of the culprits, Conde."

"That's good."

"Not so good. We questioned him last night, and he says he did it by himself. I wish you could see him, a stubborn hulking bastard who reacts as if he couldn't care less about anything. And you know how old he is? Sixteen, Conde, sixteen. I've been a policeman for thirty, and I'm still surprised by such things. The fact is I'm past caring . . . You know, he admits he did it, that he pulverized the kid to steal his bike, and tells it as if he were talking about a baseball game and just as nonchalantly when he says it was all his own work."

"But he's no kid, Captain. How did you catch him?"

Jorrín smiled, shook his head and wiped a hand over his face, as if trying to iron out the wrinkles lining his face.

"From a statement given by a witness and because he was riding the bike belonging to the kid they killed, without a care in the world. Did you know people exist who do this kind of thing just to assert their egos?"

"So I've read."

"But forget your books. If you want to check it out come and take a look at this boy. He's a case . . . I don't know, Conde, but I really think I've got to say goodbye to all this. It gets more and more painful . . ."

Jorrín barely managed a farewell and walked towards the lifts. The Count watched him leave and thought the old sea-wolf might be right. Thirty years are a lot of years in this profession, he muttered, and pushed open the door to the Information Department. He smiled, greeted all the young women and sat down in front of Sergeant Dalia Acosta's desk: she was the departmental duty officer, and he always wondered how one woman's head could gather so much hair.

"Anything from the coastguards?"

"Not much. Not many people try it when this north wind is blowing, but, look, this has just come in from East Havana. Take a look . . ."

The Count took the computer printout the sergeant was flourishing in his direction and read the first remarks after the heading:

Unidentified corpse. Evidence of murder. Signs of struggle. Case opened. Forensics' preliminary report: 72 to 96 hours since death. Found in an empty residential house, Brisas del Mar. January 5/89, 11.00pm.

And he turned the sheet over on her desk.

"When did this come in, Dalita?"

"Ten minutes ago, Lieutenant."

"And why didn't you call me?"

"I called you as soon as it arrived and Manolo told me you were on your way."

"Any more information?"

"This other sheet from Forensics."

"Let me have it. I'll return it later. Thanks."

I was still in uniform, always carried a briefcase and spent hours in the archives with Felicia, that old computer that seemed a mysterious, over-efficient window on the world. My pistol was in my belt, but my cap had no such luck; I tried never to wear it after reading in a magazine that caps are the number one cause of baldness; it was almost nine pm and all I wanted to do was collapse on my bed, and I was thinking about bed as I walked to the bus-stop when I heard a klaxon hooting, I cursed as I always curse people who blow their klaxons like that, and looked up to see what kind of guy it was, he'd have two horns and perhaps a trident in his hand, and I saw an arm waving at me from above the car roof. At me? Yes, at you. I couldn't see clearly because the windscreen was glinting and it was dark, and I went over hoping to hitch a lift. I hadn't seen him for almost five years, but I'd have recognized him even if it hadn't been for a hundred.

"Hell, buddy, my hand almost dropped off hooting at you," he said, smiling his usual smile, and heaven knows why I was smiling as well.

"How're things, Rafael?" I asked, putting my hand through the window. "It's been ages. How's Tamara?"

"You going home?"

"Yes, I just finished and was . . ."

"In you get, I'll drive you to Víbora." And I got into his Lada, that smelled brand new, of leather and liniment, and Rafael drove off, the last time we spoke.

"What you up to now?" I asked, as I always ask anyone I know.

"The same as usual, in the Ministry for Industry, waiting to see what turns up," he informed me casually, talking in that affable persuasive tone he adopted with friends, very different to the hard, even more persuasive tone he'd employ from a platform.

"So they've given you your own car?"

"No, not yet, this one's assigned to me and, you know, it's as good as mine, because I've just come from a meeting at the Chamber of Commerce, and that's how I spend my life. I work hard . . ."

"How's Tamara?" I repeated, and he barely managed to say she was all right, that she'd done her social service here in Bejucal, and was now at a new clinic they'd opened in Lawton. No, we still don't have children, but we'll order one any day now," he added.

"And how are you getting on?"

I tried to see what film they were showing at the Florida when we drove through Agua Dulce and I thought I'd tell him not so good, that I was just a bureaucrat processing information, that last month Skinny had been operated on again, that I didn't know why I'd married Martiza, but I didn't feel like it.

"Good, pal, good."

"Hey, drop by one day and let's have a drink," he suggested as we reached October Tenth and Dolores, and I thought how it was the first time Rafael had ever said anything like that to me, or to Skinny or Rabbit or Andrés or any of us, and when he pulled in at the traffic lights in Santa Catalina so I could get out, I responded in kind: "Yes, be seeing you. Give my regards to Tamara."

And we shook hands again, and I watched him turn into Santa Catalina, his red indicator blinking; he gave two farewell toots and drove off in the car that smelled brand new. Then I thought: you bastard, you're only interested in being my friend because I'm in the police. And I had to laugh, that last time I saw Rafael Morín.

His eyes no longer shone; his voice no longer boomed at the masses. His freshly-shaven, washed and wide-awake face no longer bore that squeaky clean sheen. He no longer smiled automatically and confidently spread light and good vibrations. It seemed he'd put on weight, a sickly purplish fat, and his brown hair urgently required a comb.

"Look who it is," said the Count, and the forensic doctor pulled the sheet back over him again, like a curtain falling on the last act of a play that lacked emotion or charm.

"Well, if it isn't my friend the Count," he said, and the Count thought: He's blacker than the tar the roads could do with.

Lieutenant Raúl Booz smiled, and his white young colt's teeth brought a shaft of light to the jet-black expanse of his face. Nobody would guarantee he was more than seven feet tall or weighed in at three hundred pounds, but the Count turned into a bag of nerves just looking at him. "How can he be that big and black?" he asked himself as he got up and shook Detective Lieutenant Raúl Booz's hand.

"You already know Sergeant Manuel Palacios, I believe?"

"Yes, of course," replied Booz, who also smiled at Manolo and settled down on the sofa that filled the space next to a wall in his office. "So you were the one looking for this guy?"

The Count nodded and explained the story behind the disappearance of Rafael Morín Rodríguez.

"Well, I'm going to hand him over to you all sewn up, my friend. It will be the easiest case you've ever had. Take a look at this." And he handed the Count a file that was on the sofa. "There was a hair with capillary tissue under one fingernail. Naturally, it must belong to his killer."

"And what are the results of the autopsy, Lieutenant?"

"As clear as daylight. He died on the night of the first or early in the morning of the second. Forensics can't be sure because the cold helped preserve the body, and that's why nobody knew a corpse was there. He had a fractured second and third cervical vertebra, which pressed down on his spinal cord, and that was what killed him, and his brain was severely banged about, but that wasn't lethal."

"But what happened, Lieutenant, what do you reckon?" Manolo interjected, ignoring the file the Count was handing him.

Lieutenant Raúl Booz, head of the criminal investigation squad in East Havana, looked at his own fingernails before answering.

"The station in Guanabo got a call last night at about ten saying a strange smell was coming from an empty house in Brisas del Mar and that the back-door lock had been forced. It's a block of only two houses, one that's empty in winter, and the one belonging to the woman who called that's about twenty yards away. The people in Guanabo went to look and found a dead body in the bathroom. All the signs pointed to the man dying when he fell against the bath, but the blow was so hard he can't just have slipped, Palacios. He was pushed and before that there was a skirmish during which the dead man scratched his murderer and took out the hair we analysed. He's a white man, in his forties, between five foot four and five foot eight tall and, naturally, black haired . . . That's just for starters."

"And enough to finish on, Lieutenant," replied the Count.

"But there is a complicating factor. Although the murder was probably not premeditated, something very strange happened afterwards. The murderer stripped his victim and took his clothes away, and there's no sign of the briefcase or leather bag the dead man must have been carrying before the fight, given

229

the traces of leather on his hands, and it must have weighed a fair amount because he kept passing it from one hand to the other."

"And any traces of cars or anything like that?"

"Nothing of the sort. The fresh fingerprints belong to the dead man, and are on the broken door, in the kitchen, on an armchair in the living room and in the bathroom. It looks as if he was waiting for someone, almost definitely the murderer. And we combed the surrounding area round about but no sign of the dead man's clothes or briefcase. But this case is a doddle, don't you think?"

"And, Booz, how about if we ring you in two hours to confirm that the murderer goes by the name of René Maciques?" the Count asked as he stood up and straightened the pistol threatening to leap from his belt.

The Count thought about lighting a cigarette but stopped himself. He preferred to get out his pen and fiddle with its catch. The monotonous sound echoed aggressively in the silence of the cubicle.

"Well, then, Maciques?" Manolo finally asked, and Maciques looked up.

What a chameleon, thought the Count. He was no longer the lively conversationalist of their first encounter or the punctilious librarian they had recorded. A mere day without a shave had been enough to transform the head of office into a potential model tramp, and his shaking hands brought to mind a dire devastating winter.

"He was to blame," said Maciques, trying to sit straight in his chair. "He was the one behind all this mess when he realized they were going to finger him. I don't know how everything else happened."

"I think you do, Maciques," Manolo insisted.

"It was just a manner of words. I meant I can't really explain it . . . He came to see me on the night of the thirtieth and told me the Mitachi people had brought forward their visit and this was going to put him really in it. I never found out what *it* was, although I can imagine, it must have been to do with money, and he told me he had to leave the country. I told him that was madness, it wasn't so easy, and he told me it was really easy, that he had ten thousand Cuban pesos and a pile of dollars to pay for a motor launch and I should find him one. That was when he blackmailed me with the bank account and ownership of the car. I still don't know how he managed to photocopy those papers, but the fact was he had them. Well, no, he'd already planned the car bit: he got it as a present and gave it to me, and naturally I sold it, it was red-hot and I sold it . . . Then I repeated it was madness and told him he wasn't playing straight with me, and he replied by telling me to get a launch and forget everything else. And the truth is I didn't even make a start, for I thought there must be a way to get those papers back."

"By killing him, Maciques?"

The man shook his head. It was a mechanical reaction but as intense as the way his hands were shaking.

"No, Sergeant, some other way . . . But to gain time I told him I'd contracted a launch for daybreak on the first, after the party on the thirty-first, I told him, it's the best time to leave, the skipper's got permission to go fishing, and we should be in Guanabo at four, and I wish you could have seen him at the party. He was already imagining himself out of Cuba and was more petulant and arrogant than ever, the lousy shit, I tell you, be glad you never met him . . . I think I should

231

have stopped it all at the start. But you know what fear is? Fear you might lose everything, probably go to prison, never be anybody again? That's why I did what I did and picked him up at his place after we left the party and drove to Guanabo. Then I parked some-where by the Veneciana, next to the river, and told him I was going to see the guy, and what I did was to walk to the beach and stay there a while. When I went back and told him it would have to be that night he went mad. I'd never seen him like it before; he called me an asshole and a number of other things, and said I should be grateful he was going, because if he wasn't, he would put me in it, and a few more choice expres-sions. Then I drove him to the house. I knew it was always empty in winter, because a friend of mine rented it from the owners in September, and we went in and I told him to wait there till nightfall, that the skipper had told me they'd leave very early, and then I drove back to Havana."

"And what were you thinking, Maciques?"

"I wasn't thinking anything. About what I did that night. About going to see him and telling him that everything was ready. It was then I had the idea about taking the briefcase with all the papers and telling him to find his own launch. And do you know what the first thing was he said to me when I arrived? That he'd write to me from Miami and tell me where he'd hidden the photocopies; they were in a safe place and nobody would ever find them. Then I was the one who went crazy. I told him what I'd been thinking about him for quite some time, and he threw a punch at me, really a big slap, his hand open, like that, and hit me here just above my ear and that was when I pushed him and he fell against the side of the bath . . . And that was all," said Maciques as his head sunk between his shoulders.

"And it was you who put his Panama allowances and the other things in with the papers at the enterprise?"

"I had to protect myself, didn't I? Because I suspected he was going to do the dirty on me, and I had to protect myself. The fucking bastard," he concluded, expending his last drop of vital energy.

"And did you really think you were going to wriggle out of this one, Maciques?" asked the Count as he stood up. For a moment he'd thought that aged defeated man was worthy of pity but only for a very fleeting moment. The spectacle of defeat couldn't erase the feeling of repulsion the whole affair had prompted. "Well, you got it wrong, and you got it wrong because you are just like your defunct boss. The same shit from the same latrine. And don't lose the fear you had, Maciques, hold on in there, for this story is only just beginning," he said as he looked at Sergeant Manuel Palacios and walked out of the office. The headache had started behind the eyes, and evil intent was spreading across his forehead.

Where's that sparrow? he thought. The previous day he'd seen it in its nest, and all that was left were feathers and dry plaited straw in the fork of the laurel tree. It can't still be flying, if it fell it would have had no hope of escape, no escape from the kitchen cats, and he hoped the sparrow could fly.

"How many days does it take a baby sparrow to fly, Manolo?"

The sergeant put down the folder where he was filing the latest reports and the statements signed by Maciques and looked at the lieutenant.

"What's got into you today, Conde? How the hell should I know? It's not as if I were a sparrow."

"Hey, kid." He pointed his index finger at him. "Go easy. You also come up with some darned silly questions. Go on, get this ready for the Boss."

"And speaking of Roman Emperors, do you reckon he'll give us the leave he owes us?"

The Count sat down in the chair behind his desk and rubbed his eyes. The headache was now a distant memory, but he was sleepy and beginning to feel hungry. He wanted to get this Rafael Morín affair over and done with. He was annoyed he hadn't laid bare the real depths of a character who went breathlessly from being a leader to a private entrepreneur, from saint to sinner, and died from a single blow, leaving unanswered so many questions he'd loved to have asked.

"We have to wait for Chinese Patricia to finish at the enterprise. She told me she'd have everything else ready tomorrow morning, and then we can both give the Boss the complete report, and I think he'll give us a couple of days. I need them. And I think you do too. How's it going with Vilma?"

"OK, she's got over her tantrum."

"Just as well, because putting up with you when a woman's on your back isn't easy. But in any case, this business is almost over and I probably won't see your face for the next month . . . Hey, in the end, who told Rafael's mother and Tamara?"

"The major called the industry minister."

"I'm sorry for his mother."

"But not for his wife? Won't you try to console her?"

"Go to hell, Manolo," he replied, smiling.

"Hey, Conde, what does it feel like when you close a case like this?"

The lieutenant placed his hands on his desk. They were open, palms upwards.

"Like this, Manolo, empty-handed. The evil had already been done."

The Count and Manolo looked at each other, and then the lieutenant offered his colleague a cigarette, as the cubicle door opened and in walked a cigar followed by a man.

"Very good work with Maciques, Sergeant," said Major Rangel, leaning his back against the door. "You excelled yourself as you always do, Mario ... What manner of man was Rafael Morín?"

The Count looked back at Manolo. He didn't know if Major Rangel wanted a reply or was just musing aloud. It was very unusual to see the Boss outside his office and speaking so disconcertingly, and they preferred to stay silent.

"When will I have the full dossier?"

"At ten o'clock?"

"At nine. Patricia's finishing this afternoon and will leave the enterprise to the Fraud Squad. They might dig up something likely. So nine am. Then you two can disappear and not show your faces till Friday, if I don't call you before. And tomorrow I'm going to stir things up around this Rafael Morín affair. You just watch me. It's all very well this 'take it easy that's enough on corruption' and then we're the ones who have to pull the chestnuts out of the fire." And his voice sounded like a much bigger, younger man's, a voice accustomed to demanding and protesting. He looked at the unbroken ash of his cigar and then at his two subordinates. "And they rattle on about delinquents. They're babes on the tit compared to fellows like him or Maciques, and who knows what goes on up and down the greasy pole, but I'll be calling for blood ... A respectable director of enterprise handling thousands and thousands of dollars. I really don't understand a thing, damned if I do," and he opened the door and started to follow his cigar out the room. "But tomorrow at nine am I'll leave here with the report under my arm . . ."

"No, don't start fantasizing. And look, it's not cold now, and we've got to be here early in the morning to write the report, so the case isn't closed," Manolo begged as he switched on the car engine, and the Count whispered: "Consort with kids and . . ."

"What's this woman done to you, Manolo? You know, you're shit-scared of her."

The car left the headquarters parking lot, and Manolo was still shaking his head.

"Forget it, you won't screw me up. It's not worth two shots. I'm off to Vilma's, and you can do whatever the hell you want. I'll pick you up at six. Where should I drop you off? Besides, if I have a couple, I can't get it up, and we start squabbling . . ."

The Count smiled and thought "he's beyond redemption" and lowered his car window. It was undoubtedly getting less cold and the night was off to a peaceful start, ripe for whatever. He wanted a couple of shots, and Manolo wanted Vilma. Two reasonable options. After all, the Rafael Morín case was over, at least as far as the police was concerned, and the Count was beginning to feel empty inside. He'd got two days off which he never knew how best to spend. It had been some time since he'd dared sit opposite a typewriter, perhaps he never would again, to begin one of those novels he'd been promising himself for so long, and the solitude in his house was a hostile calm that made him felt desperate. He anticipated his fling with Tamara would probably be short-lived and would soon conflict with the everyday detail in two lives that were miles apart, two worlds that might coexist but could merge only with difficulty. Should I write my novel about old Valdemira's library?

"We'll pass by the undertakers in Santa Catalina. Rafael Morín's corpse must have arrived there by now."

"What's the point, Conde?" rasped Manolo who'd always hated wakes and could see no reason to attend another.

"I don't know what the point is. Everything doesn't always have to have a point, right? I just want to poke my head into the wake for a moment."

"That's fine," the sergeant accepted. "But it's not work, right? I'll leave you there and go on. See you at six in the morning."

The car drove along Santa Catalina, and the Count saw people queuing to buy cold drinks; the love motel had recently been reinstated, and a neon sign erected of two red hearts transfixed by a green arrow of hope, and a couple of youngsters were going inside and looking for reception; he saw the stop with a bus packed with stressed people in a hurry, film posters and the driver shouting bastard at him as he passed him on the right, and he thought how nobody had death on their mind, and that was why they could still live, love, run, work, insult, eat, and even kill and think, and then he saw the twin's house, shadowy between its hedges and sculptures, its big gleaming windows and a fate that had changed for the moment. Rafael Morín had departed that place to play for all or nothing, and had lost his confident dazzling smile once and for all.

"See you at six," he said when he saw the undertakers. The lobby was empty, and he thought perhaps the morgue hadn't yet released the corpse of his fellow school student. "And take care you don't get her pregnant."

"Don't play that tune. I don't want any such complications in my life." Manolo smiled, shaking his boss's hand.

"Come on, don't play hard to get, Vilma's got you well taped."

"OK, my friend, so what?" Sergeant Manuel Palacios laughed again and accelerated away, and the Count thought "He'll kill himself one of these days."

He went up the few steps to the undertakers and read just one name on the board: Rafael Morín Rodríguez, Room D. It wasn't a good day to be dying, and undertakers weren't in great demand. He headed to Room D but didn't dare go in. The sweetish scent of flowers for the dead that impregnated the walls of the building hit him in the pit of his stomach, and he decided to sit on one of the big chairs in the corridor, next to the ashtray on a stand and the public telephone. He lit a cigarette that tasted of wet grass. Inside lay Rafael Morín, dead and ready for oblivion, and it would be a very sad funeral: none of his New Year's Eve, management-board and trips-abroad friends would come. The man was plagued in more than one sense, and perhaps not even his wife would want to be there. His old friends from high school had fallen by the wayside long ago, would only find out months later, perhaps have their doubts, and wouldn't believe it was true. He imagined what the wake could have been like in other circumstances, the wreaths of flowers piled up all over the floor in that room, the laments at the loss of such an outstanding cadre, at such an early young age, the funeral oration, so moving and so packed with generous heartfelt adjectives. He dropped his cigarette in the ashtray and walked over to the door to

238

Room D. Like an intruder he gingerly put his face to the glass door and observed the almost empty room just as he'd imagined: Rafael's mother, holding a handkerchief to her nose, sobbing amid a group of neighbours: the two women who had been doing their washing on Sunday morning; one held the old lady's hand between hers and was speaking into her ear: for all of them Rafael's failure was in some way their own failure and the finale to a tragic destiny the man had tried to elude. Tamara was in front of her mother-in-law, and the Count could just make out her shoulders and artificial indomitable curls. She was still; perhaps she'd cried a couple of silent tears. Two chairs from her, also with her back to the door, was another woman the Count tried to identify. She seemed young, her hair style showing off the nape of her neck and straight shoulders, the taut skin on the arm that was visible, and then the woman looked at Tamara and revealed her profile: he recognized Zaida and acknowledged she was being loyal to the end. Seven women; a single female colleague from work. And, at the back, the sealed coffin, wrapped in grey cloth, shockingly bare as it awaited the flowers that always arrived late for a common wake. It would be a sad funeral, he thought yet again and went into the street.

He looked for a cigarette in his jacket pocket. He was really dry, and noticed Baby-Face Miki on the pavement opposite, as he waited for a gap in the traffic and wondered why he was coming to the wake. But he felt he could take no more, quickened his step and walked up the street that ran parallel, spontaneously bursting into song: "Strawberry Fields forever, tum, tum, tum . . ."

Skinny Carlos looked at his glass as if he couldn't

understand why it was empty. He felt like that after the fourth or fifth shot, and the Count smiled. They'd already seen off half a bottle of rum and hadn't seen off their sadness. Skinny had wanted to go to the wake, and the Count refused to take him, why do you want to go, don't be morbid, he said accusingly, and his friend ordered him not put any music on. Skinny felt the respect for death of those who know they will soon die and have decided to drown their bad memories, fatal thoughts and gloomy ideas in rum. But those fucking bastards always come up for air, thought the Count.

"So what do you intend to do with Tamara?" asked Skinny when his glass regained its rightful weight.

"I don't know, you beast, I don't know. It won't work, and I'm afraid of falling in love."

"Why on earth?"

"Because of what might come later. I don't like suffering for the sake of it and so prefer to suffer in advance, right?"

"I always said you liked punishing yourself."

"It's not easy. You know, it really isn't," he said, gulping his rum down. He put his glass on the small table in the centre of the room. "I must go. I've got to write a report in the morning."

"You going to leave me almost a pint? You're not eating? Do you want old Josefina flying into a tantrum? No, wild animal, no, for I'm the one who will have to listen to her saying you don't eat properly, that you're really skinny and that I'm the bad boy for starting you on the rum, that you've got to look after yourself more and asking when are you going to marry the nice girl, get this, and have a kid. And I'm not up for it today, you know. It's been fucking awful enough as it is."

The Count smiled but wanted to cry. He looked over his friend's head and saw on the wall the faded Rolling

Stones poster and Mick Jagger's buckteeth; the photo taken at the coming of age party for Rabbit's sister, Pancho smiling, Rabbit trying not to laugh and Skinny in his special party hairdo, the fringe he hid at school over his eyebrows and almost closed eyes, putting an arm round Mario Conde's shoulders, looking as if he'd had a fright, soul brothers from time immemorial; the tatty medals under false colours Skinny had won when he was a very skinny baseball player; the now almost invisible Havana Club label that someone had stuck to the mirror years ago during one hell of a drinking binge and that Skinny had decided to preserve for eternity in that same spot. It was a sad wall.

"Skinny, have you ever thought why you and I are mates . . .?"

"Because one day I lent you a knife at high school. Come on, don't harp on about life. It just comes as it comes, fucking hell."

"But it could be different."

"Lies, you brute, lies. That's just one tall, tall story. Hell, don't get me on that tack, but I *will* tell you one thing for nothing: the guy who's born to get honey from heaven, gets it in jarfuls and if that bullet's meant for you, it does your life in. Don't try to change what can't be changed. Don't whinge. That's right, pour me another."

"One day I'll write about this, I swear I will," said the Count, pouring two generous shots into his friend's glass.

"Right, just do that, get writing and don't just keep thinking about doing it. The next time you want to bring the subject up, please put it in writing, OK?"

"One of these days I'll tell you where to get off, Skinny."

"Hey, what's the point of all this chitchat?"

Mario Conde looked at his glass and looked like Skinny looked when it was empty but didn't dare say a word.

"Nothing, just forget it," he replied because he thought one day he wouldn't be able to converse with Skinny or call him my brother, wild animal, pal or tell him life was the most difficult profession going.

"Hey, and in the end where did he put the suitcase full of money?"

"He copped out and threw it into the sea."

"With all those notes?"

"That's what the man said."

"What a fucking shit."

"Right, a fucking shit. I feel very odd. I wanted to find Rafael and really didn't mind whether he was dead or alive, and now he's appeared it's as if I'd like to disappear him again. I'd rather not think about him but can't get him out of my head, and I'm afraid this might last a long time. Whatever can Tamara be feeling, do you reckon?"

"Hey, put some music on if you want," Skinny suggested, "Whatever."

"What do you fancy?"

"The Beatles?"

"Chicago?"

"Formula V?"

"Los Pasos?"

"Credence?"

"Uh-huh, Credence," they concurred, and listened to Tom Foggerty's rich voice and the guitars of Credence Clearwater Revival.

"It's still the best version of 'Proud Mary'."

"By a long chalk."

"He sings like a black. Just listen."

"You're kidding. He sings like God."

242

"Up on your feet, lads. Man doesn't live on music alone. Time to eat," said Josefina from the doorway where she was taking her apron off, and the Count wondered how many more times he'd hear that call from the wild that summoned the three of them to the incredible feast Josefina struggled daily to create. It would be a difficult world without her, he told himself.

"Let's have the menu, *Señora*," the Count demanded, already in place behind the wheelchair.

"Cod Basque-style, boiled rice, a Polish mushroom soup I've improved with cabbage, chicken giblets, tomato sauce, fried ripe plantain, and a radish, lettuce and watercress salad."

"Where do you find all this, Jose?"

"Better not to ask, Condesito. Hey, let me have a drop of that rum. Today I feel happy for some reason or other."

"This is all for you," the Count offered her a shot and thought: "Hell, I really love her."

What you call an empty room, he muttered, breathing in a deep consistent smell of solitude. There's an empty bed, he thought, scrutinizing the mysterious shapes in the screwed up sheets that nobody bothered to smooth out. He switched the light on, and solitude hit him between the eyes. Rufino was hurtling round his goldfish bowl. Don't exhaust me, Rufino, he told him and started to undress. Put his jacket on the chair, threw his shirt in the direction of his bed, placed his pistol on his jacket and, after he'd prised off his shoes with his feet, dropped his jeans on the floor.

He walked into the kitchen and poured the last remains of coffee powder he'd found in an envelope into his coffee pot. He washed out his thermos once he'd got rid of the white fetid coffee he'd left there the morning of the previous day that now seemed distant, very distant. The reflection of his face in the pane of glass confirmed his impending baldness yet again, and he opened the window onto the nocturnal peace and quiet in his barrio and thought how this might also be a perfect night to sit under a lamp on the street corner playing a few rounds of dominos, soothed by healthy intakes of gut-rot. Only it was a long time since people had gathered there, on such a night, to play dominos and down cheap liquor. Now we're not even a shadow of our former selves and will never be the same again, he muttered, wondering when he should call Tamara. Solitude will be the death of me; he sweetened his coffee and poured himself a huge cup of early-morning coffee while lighting up the inevitable cigarette.

He went back to his bedroom and looked at Rufino from his bed. The fighting fish had ground to a halt and also seemed to be looking at him.

"I'll get you some food tomorrow," he told him.

He abandoned his empty cup on a night table stained by other abandoned cups and went over to the mountain of books waiting their turn. He slid his finger down their spines, looked for a title or author that attracted him but gave up halfway. He stretched out a hand towards his bookcase and picked out the only book that had never accumulated dust. "May it be very squalid and moving," he repeated loudly and read the story of the man who knew all the secrets of the banana fish, which is maybe why he killed himself, and fell asleep thinking the story was pure squalor if only because of the quiet brilliance of the suicide.

Mantilla, July 1990–January 1991